NATIVE

A FIRST CONTACT NOVEL

I0553349

L.G. CONAWAY

ARBORVALE
BOOKS

Copyright © 2024 by L.G. Conaway
ISBN - Paperback: 979-8-9905533-0-9
Second Edition: November 2025

All rights reserved. No part of this book may be used or reproduced in any form whatsoever without written permission except in the case of brief quotations in critical articles or reviews.
This book is a work of fiction. Names, characters, businesses, organizations, places, events and incidents either are the product of the author's imagination or are used fictitiously. Any resemblance to actual persons, living or dead, events, or locales is entirely coincidental.

Printed in the United States of America.
Cover design by Sid@sk_ebookcovers

For special discounts available for bulk purchases, fundraising, and sales promotions, contact Arborvale Books or admin@arborvalebooks.com.

ARBORVALE BOOKS
960 Peace Lane, No.9
Prescott, Arizona 86305
www.arborvalebooks.com
admin@arborvalebooks.com

1

REDACTED INTERVIEW TRANSCRIPT

All interviewer questions, crew interruptions, and duplications have been deleted. All AI transcripts from the investigation's Forensic File have been integrated in appropriate date/time order.

Go to the toilet. Help yourselves to some snacks. Settle in. This is a l-o-o-n-g story. This was all so long ago... I have my old phone records here. Is that okay? Good. Let's begin...

* * *

I was my mother's heartbreak and my father's disappointment. Mom said, "A tragic waste of potential." Dad said, "Oceans of talent, all of it less than five centimeters deep." Mom never came around, but Dad changed his mind before the end.

I was twenty-fi..., no, I was only twenty-four, ... and collaborating with Zhang on a new rugged performance clothing line. I wrapped up modelling the clothes at a photoshoot in New Caledonia on the southern continent. I was headed back across the equator and halfway around New Philadelphia to Novy Samara. New Caledonia was only about fifty thousand people at that time. Spectacular scenery, but still a frontier town. Zhang did not provide transport. I only had two days to make it to Lord Dennison's yacht party after the photoshoot. So, rather than pay for a private cab all the way home, I bought a grav sled ticket.

I was on my way to catch the sled when I spotted a heavy-worlder on the boarding platform. He was easy to spot. He was tall at around 195 centimeters, which is hardly out of the ordinary. But he was double the width of a normal gravity man. He hovered above the crowd with that odd floating stride of heavy worlders experiencing normal gravity.

Turned out we were both headed to the next sled. It was a shabby old eight-man shuttle with bright new blue paint, which only made the interior seem shabbier. We were the only passengers. Even with his bulk taking up space we were rattling around in an area designed for four times more people. I didn't even bother to put my backpack in the overhead compartment. I tossed it on the seat next to me. I swiveled my seat to face the heavy-worlder across the central aisle. Naturally, since we were alone, we introduced ourselves once we had settled in.

"Welcome to New Philadelphia. How long have you been planet-side?" I asked.

"That obvious, huh?"

I nodded.

"Only about 18 hours since I got off the interstellar. Just enough time to catch a nap and get fed. You okay without any other company all the way to Novy Samara?" he said with a charming smile.

"It's fine," I said, feeling the weight of my trusty stunner in its holster. "More snacks for us. I'm Li Carroll."

"Ge Oates," he said and extended his hand for a shake.

I shook his hand. "Well, we can never date. Li and Ge, we rhyme." I evaluated him as we spoke. He was a handsome man – dark hair, perfect teeth, regular features. All on an enormous scale. His shoulders had to be 150 centimeters wide. Legs like tree trunks. Massive slabs of muscle. Unmistakably born and bred on a Jovian world.

"Ah. All my hopes crushed," he grinned, obviously not meaning a word of it.

"Why not go straight to Novy Samara? Why land here?" I asked.

"Cheaper destination even with the added cost of a public sled ticket. Limited research funding." He tossed his large, professionally equipped camping backpack onto the seat next to his.

"Where are you from?" I asked him.

"Ganesh; you know, the jubilee planet. Ganesh makes one hundred chartered colonies. You?"

"Third generation native of New Philadelphia," I answered. "Descendant of the Star Dancer, our first colony ship, scion of the Founding Families, etc." I wondered how extensive his genetic mods were. Ganesh wasn't that much heavier than Earth, as I recalled.

We both paused as the sled lifted off with only a minor chorus of creaks and pops and we ascended above the clouds.

"Where you headed?" He asked.

4

So, I told him about Lord Dennison's ten-day annual extravaganza. I happened to mention – oh-so-casually – that I was the featured celebrity gracing the cover of World magazine. I showed him the magazine. He was eyeballing me, too. I was quite easy on the eyes, back in those days.

"That's what got me the invite," I said. "At least, I'm pretty sure that's what did the trick."

"So, you're a model?" Ge asked, looking genuinely surprised.

I snickered. "Hardly. I am the influencer's influencer, an arbiter of taste, I don't *follow* fashion trends, I *create* them. In fact, I'm collaborating on a fashion line with Zhang."

"Ah. A *high-powered* model." Ge condescended.

Offended, I snapped, "I went into fashion when I was fourteen years old. I studied the history of fashion and textiles. I learned how to sew, and more importantly, how to create patterns. I worked my ass off to get the money I needed for my genetic modifications. You know a lot of fourteen-year-olds who maintain a 4.0 GPA *and* run profitable online businesses?"

Ge looked surprised, as though the hard work of fashion was completely unknown to him. "Uh, no."

"I don't stand around at photo shoots and hire people to do my thinking for me!"

"Huh." Ge eyed me speculatively. "I had you pegged as a student."

"Yes, that too."

"Major?"

"Do you want them chronologically or alphabetically?"

He donned a look of insincere sympathy. "Tough time with the exams?"

I thought, *Why does this wad think that a fashion career makes me an idiot?* and snorted. "I will have you know that I placed in the top 5% world-wide in the entrance exams. I never had a grade below 90% in anything, even my languages."

He looked mystified. "Then why all the majors?"

"Couldn't find anything that held my attention long enough to actually make it through." I shrugged. "Your major?"

"I'm doing my post-doc in xenoecology. Oddly, New Philadelphia has a lot of partial surveys since being colonized, but no complete survey. Even on frontier planets, complete surveys are routine. It's a perfect opportunity for me to make it through my post-doc, though. So, what's the big deal with Lord whatsit's party?"

5

"Lord Dennison. It is the social event of the year. Perfect dating opportunity."

"But if you're already successful?" He questioned.

"Oh, right." I couldn't restrain myself. "Because it is incomprehensible why anyone would want to attract an intelligent high-status man and live in the lap of luxury doing precisely what they please. Yeah. Nothing appealing about that."

I abruptly realized Ge was getting to me. I was *way* too irritated. I decided to take control of the situation, excused myself to go to the ladies' room. I didn't need to go, but it was the only other compartment on the sled. I took deep controlled breaths and triggered relaxation points.

Ge showed every sign of the academic snobbery that my mother indulged in. According to Mom, only the life of the mind was valuable; a body was merely a convenient transportation device for getting the mind to research facilities, classes, and symposia. Since I couldn't muster up enough interest in any academic field to earn an advanced degree, I was an insignificant person. Ge was obviously a like-minded ivory tower academic. I felt completely justified dismissing him.

With that thought, I went back to my seat.

Ge asked, "So why are you interested in fashion?" But he said it like, "Why are you interested in a career *as trivial* as fashion?" I got defensive, like I did every time I talked to my mother. I pasted on a professional smile and treated our conversation like a hostile interview with a tabloid reporter.

"My lost dancing career," I answered.

"Dancing?"

"Yup." I smiled and launched into the well-rehearsed story, "I loved ballet. Had ever since I saw my first performance at the age of six. My dad took my mother and me to see the incomparable Albina Mikhailov in a revival of Swan Lake. Mom expected me to be bored and brought toys to keep me quiet. Surprise! I was transfixed.

"I spent the next few weeks humming snatches of the music and dancing around the house. Calculating that dance was an excellent way to tire me out, Mom gave me lessons. When I was thirteen, I won a prestigious competition. The best ballet academy on New Philadelphia offered me a scholarship for choreography.

"They explained that I would never be a dancer. But I could be a choreographer; 'cause you can be butt-ugly and still be a choreographer. It turns out that at 180 centimeters and 70 kilos, I am too tall, too muscular, and too curvy. Just too bulky to dance."

6

"Bulky!" Ge exclaimed, "You're a tiny, delicate thing!"

"Compared to the ladies on your home planet, no doubt. But, for here, too big to grace the stage. So anyway, with the full force of crushed thirteen-year-old feelings, I turned down the scholarship. I flailed around for most of that year. Tried science. But my brother, Mark, one-upped me with a first prize regional win for his science fair entry on number clouds. So, I tried gymnastics. But my brother one upped me with that one too, by winning more prestigious track awards. Then, I happened to be at the mall when Dabney Willard waltzed in."

He watched me with a blank face.

"Dabney – since you are an off-worlder and don't know – is *quite* the celebrity. Us normal mortals were ushered out of her way. She got a lot of fawning attention and expensive gifts from merchants in exchange for footage of her gracing their shops. Bingo! A career path that offered high income, prestige, and the added benefit of being impossible for my brother. I was hooked," I concluded.

"So, your career was born out of sibling rivalry?" Ge asked.

It took everything I had not to roll my eyes in exasperation. "That's how it started. Oddly, Mom, who had never shown any interest in my other activities, was supportive. She wouldn't pay for my genetic mods but did offer to match whatever I came up with. Hence, my obsession with making money. By the time I was fifteen, I got a child performer exemption and a modified school schedule. By the time I was sixteen, all the genetic mods were done."

The grav sled rose above some towering clouds and Ge and I stopped to admire them in all their black, gray, and purple majesty.

He said, "Glad to be above that storm. You were saying?"

"Eleven years after I started, I got my picture on the cover of *World*. Now ordinary mortals are ushered out of *my* way when I go shopping."

"So, all of this," he gestured to me, "is gen mods?"

"Nope. The black hair, light skin, and green eyes are all original equipment. Dad's Irish; Mom's Chinese. They lengthened my nose, so it's less pug than it started out. They straightened my teeth, fixed my acne, added a couple of centimeters to my bust, and corrected my knock-knees. Everything else is original equipment."

"You went through all that for changes that are subtle at best, just to launch a fashion career?" Ge asked.

"Aiyee! Somebody's a little foggy on the concept of small talk!"

Ge shrugged. "I prefer big talk. Small talk is a waste of life span."

"Hmph. I have a different view. Conversation is an art that is essential for life in the public eye. I got coaching."

Ge looked dumbstruck. "You can get coaching in *small talk*!?"

"Mastery of social skills is hardly a small matter." I took a deep breath and decided to head the conversation in another direction. "So, what drew you to xenoecology?"

"Camping." Ge responded. "My family camped a lot when I was a kid. Cheapest vacation for a family of nine. Then, I got into the University of Queensland Australia on Earth for pre-med. Saw a completely new ecology. Visited most of the major terrestrial biomes. Switched to xenoecology. Broke my mother's heart. She was set on having a doctor in the family."

"What have you noticed about the ecology of New Philadelphia?"

"So far, kinda frustrating," he answered. "So many imported terran species that I only saw remnants of the original temperate forests." He shrugged. "At least I know local conditions support terran species."

"Come on, you can't stop there." I smiled. The distraction was working. Ge wasn't nearly as condescending when I was asking him questions. "Fork over with the bio; where from, extent of genetic mods, the whole nine yards."

"Minimal genetic mods. Mom and Dad were just naturally big, sturdy types. Basically, it boils down to denser bones, enhanced collagen and muscle synthesis, and enhanced circulatory valves. We have simple ventricles pumping lymph, for instance. Ganesh is only 11% above Earth normal, after all. They emigrated to Ganesh as newlyweds. Dad started out in mining. Got trapped for three days in a mine collapse. When they dug him out, he bought some land and took up farming. Raised seven kids. Kept buying land. They have a nice spread. A dozen tenant farmers. Mostly retired now."

I was condescending right back. "How sweet. A Ganeshan farm boy."

It worked, much to my amusement. Ge said, "A farm boy who made it into a Terran university and traveled the known galaxy!"

I smiled sweetly. "So, what does a xenoecologist actually do? Is life just one continuous camping trip in various biomes?"

"Nah. More like college professors. Field trips interspersed with data analysis, computer biome modeling, and teaching classes."

* * *

#Forensic Investigation File:

AI: EMERGENCY ALERT – IMMEDIATE C-LEVEL AUTHORIZATION REQUIRED. INTRUSION DETECTED. An eco-survey of New Philadelphia is underway. Surveyor's authorizations and registered itinerary, attached.

CSO: Another attempt? Tiresome.

AI: They persist precisely because no one returned; they want to find out what happened.

CSO: Yeah. Recommendation?

AI: The eco-surveyor is traveling from New Caledonia to Novy Samara over the Jutoma wilderness. I suggest immediate, discrete, permanent intervention. Grav Sled Maneuver (reference Security Manual CLVL 10.3451.0a-d) is appropriate. There will be little collateral damage, and the sled will be unrecoverable, thus hampering forensic investigation. I also recommend tracking the target's energy signature online to confirm a successful intervention. Do you wish to authorize the Grav Sled Maneuver with attendant tracking?

CSO: God, this is annoying. **AUTHORIZED.** Code: hd88*HT-837105jdf.3psnjqx57.

AI: AUTHORIZATION VERIFIED. Grav Sled Transport Maneuver underway.

2

LANDING

"Hey! Why have my ears popped? We shouldn't be descending yet." I fumbled for my phone and barked, "Ask the sled why we're descending."

The phone piped up with, "The sled says you have arrived at your destination.

"Uh – NO!" I looked at Ge, worried. "Oh God. We're over the Jutoma, thousands of kilometers from the destination!"

My phone said, "The sled is non-responsive. All navigation data shows we have arrived at our destination."

"I'm getting the same story from my phone," Ge said. Then he took a look out the window. "Jesus! It's muddy water and floating vegetation as far as I can see."

"How long to touch-down?" I asked, my voice shaking.

The phone replied, "Seven minutes 38 seconds."

"No. *No.* NO! Grav sleds don't fail. They do not fail. Somebody did this!"

"Yeah." Ge looked worried. "But, on to more important things. We've gotta find the escape boat," Ge said.

"Grav sleds never go down. I don't think they *have* escape boats."

"Yeah, they do. Legal requirement." He turned to his phone. "Where is the escape boat?"

His phone responded, "Behind the service hatch in the forward bulkhead, to the starboard side."

"Which — which side is starboard?" The words came out stupid and thin. My heart was jackhammering, hands shaking so hard I couldn't feel my fingers, rational thought was a distant memory.

Ge opened up a previously invisible compartment in the front bulkhead. He grunted, "Useful." Ge hauled out a big bundle. "You better change. That dress is not practical for vehicle escape."

I glared at him, even though I knew he was right. I grabbed my backpack. Slipped into the bathroom, and in a breathless panic hastily changed. I dropped the boots twice. Tried to jam my pants on before

I'd even peeled off the dress. My breath hitched, hands shaking so hard my fingers wouldn't obey. *Dammit, Li — you're going to get yourself killed. Move.*

I dragged in two sharp breaths. Out of silk. Into gear. *Hurry. Move. Now.*

I filled the hole left in my backpack with all the little traveler pillows and blankets stashed around the passenger compartment.

I cast a longing glance at the food vending machine, "I wish we could take all that. I think it will be a while before we find food."

Ge looked at me oddly. He walked over to the machine, struck the transparent cover with his open palm. The cover rebounded and popped out of its frame. I snatched up a pillowcase and started filling it with every item of vending machine food I could grab. My vision was greying out around the edges, and I did some deep breathing to keep from passing out.

Meanwhile, he methodically searched every nook and cranny of the sled. He unearthed thermal blankets, a miniature first aid robot, some batteries, and a case of energy bars. He sat down with his phone and started calculating. He was concentrating hard, ignoring me. I started hauling the deflated escape boat to the door.

Ge looked up; his face twisted in disgust. "In a brilliant piece of engineering design, once expanded to full size it's too big to fit through the passenger hatch. This sled doesn't have a cargo hatch, so we have to land to shove it outside and open it up."

"Oh." I wasn't contributing anything at that point; apparently panic drops my IQ by about a hundred points.

"I've calculated we'll have at least two minutes after landing before this compartment floods. As heavy as this sled is, it's also airtight and will float for a bit before getting sucked under. If we're ready, that's enough time to escape. If we shove the boat out too soon, it'll be a kilometer away before the sled comes to a halt."

He's still talking, numbers...two minutes...my ears are ringing... can't breathe trying to focus...

"Oh," I repeated. I was not responding well to the emergency. I should have admired Ge's cool reasoning and quick action, but no, I was too panicked to notice.

"When we land, I'll open the hatch, shove the boat out, and hop in. I'm strong enough to hang on to the hatch and keep up with the sled while it sheds momentum. You throw in your luggage and hop in after. Then I'll let go. We'll need to move fast to avoid being sucked down by the undertow when the sled sinks."

11

"Wait," I frowned with concentration, my brain finally kicking into action, "Do you have any rope? We can tether the boat to an anchor in the cabin then cut it once we're in the boat. You're strong, but this will be a very bumpy ride, so…" I shrugged.

Ge looked at me with newfound respect. "Good idea."

He didn't need to sound so surprised; I thought resentfully.

He rummaged around in his kit, got out a rope and secured it to the back leg of the passenger seat closest to the hatch. He pulled out the other end from the center of a neat coil and carefully anchored that to a cleat at the nose of the limp deflated body of the eight-passenger boat. He let out about three meters of slack and draped the rest of the rope coil on his shoulder.

Ge turned to his phone. "Audible count-down to landing."

His phone piped up with the count, we had less than a minute left. In some ways that was a blessing, because I didn't have much time to freak out. The shabby sled, with eight lumpy seats on either side of a central aisle with its scratched-up windows and run-down gray plascrete paneling, suddenly seemed like a paradise in comparison to the Jutoma.

Ge grinned, the first sign of his spiking adrenaline level. "Brace for impact."

As the countdown approached zero, I stood with my knees slightly bent and clutched the back of the passenger seat across the aisle from Ge.

The sled slammed into the water as though into a stone wall — a cannon-crack and a sheet of filthy spray exploding across the windows. Even braced, my arms wrenched, teeth slammed, a hot white bolt lit my spine, and the impact blasted every scrap of air out of my chest. For one suspended heartbeat I hung there gagging, unable to inhale, body screaming for air with nowhere for the pain to go.

The sled made a sickening lurch accompanied by the screams of warping metals and snapping plastics. It took a steep nose-dive, so the floor was suddenly at a disorienting 20-degree angle and listing sharply.

Ge had the hatch open before my brain caught up. He shoved the folded mass out toward the swamp, did something fast at the nose, and the thing exploded into shape, a blinding turquoise flash against the black-green below. Too bright. Too cheerful. Wrong.

Ge dropped it into the swamp. I was glad of that rope because the boat promptly pulled backwards, as the sled was still diving forward. Ge let out some lengths of the rope coil on his shoulder and leapt into the boat wearing his backpack and carrying the pillowcase of junk food with the extra coils of rope slung over one shoulder.

12

The sled bucked and shuddered like a panicked animal. I half-crawled, half-slid down the tilted aisle, vision strobing, ears filled with the roar of breaking plastic and crushing metal. I flung my backpack; wild, high, stupid, certain it would vanish into the swamp. He caught it like it weighed nothing.

Then I was at the hatch clutching both sides, convinced I was about to die. The steamy heat and fetid stench of rotting vegetation and filthy water engulfed me. My throat slammed shut. My hands locked on the frame. My whole body went rigid. My limbs locked and were completely unresponsive.

Ge shouted, "Just jump! This isn't gonna get any better, doll."

Him calling me 'doll' pissed me off so much that it broke the freeze. I aimed straight for his chest in proper ballerina-trained fashion. I was also off-target, high and to the right again. Ge caught all 70 kilos of me seemingly with no effort and set me in the craft. I sat down rather abruptly, weak in the knees. He cut the rope as far up as he could reach and flicked the tiny boat motor into life.

Seized by inspiration born of desperation and clueless as to where the paddles were stowed, I grabbed one of the service trays I had lifted from the grav sled and began paddling. Ge promptly caught on and did the same. Between the two of us and the motor we finally made progress. As we slowly crept away from the grav sled's undertow, the sled continued to plow through the swamp. It lurched and listed to one side, taking on the syrupy algae-packed swamp water. Then it disappeared with a sickening slurp and a rising cluster of large noisome bubbles popping and splattering on the surface.

I stopped paddling. Ge flicked off the motor. "Made it out alive. On the bright side, I've trained for exactly zero minutes for this; and we're still alive. So far, I'm setting personal records."

"Yup. I would congratulate you but I'm still processing all this." My terror and relief gave way to fury. Angry tears stung my eyes. "I was *so close!* So close to getting my mother off my back. So *damned close* to finally making it! This is monumentally unfair!"

"Hey, any landing you can walk away from – or, uh, paddle away from – is a good landing!

"I know that!" I snapped. Then I continued more moderately, "I should be grateful that I'm not at the bottom of the Jutoma. You handled this emergency a *lot* better than I did. But it's impossible to feel grateful right now, when all my hopes and a decade's worth of effort and sacrifice just died in a swamp."

13

"As soon as we can find solid ground for landing, we can call a cab and have you home in no time," Ge suggested. "Professional crisis averted."

"Are you *out of your mind?!*" I gaped at him. "We have no idea who did this or why, and you want to give them another shot at killing us!? No, thank you. Until we figure this out, I vote we continue to play dead. Which reminds me, we should set up emergency squeals and let 'em run down."

"Paranoid much?"

"*Yes!* In the wake of narrowly escaping death, I am *very* paranoid. We want them to think they succeeded so they won't keep trying. Emergency squeals that die out naturally from drained batteries is what would happen to our phones if they were successful," I explained. "We can recharge them later."

"Oh, okay, if it'll make you happier," he said. I set my phone to broadcast an emergency squeal. Then I popped it into my luggage to darken the solar cell so that the phone would run down in a natural way. I did the same for Ge's phone.

I said, "Where there's life there's hope. But I'm not feeling real hopeful right now. Couldn't have picked a worse spot to land. It's gotta be 5,000 kilometers to the nearest human habitation."

"Are you suggesting that we *walk* to the nearest settlement?"

I sighed gloomily, "As much as I hate it, that's our best option."

"Fear not, fair maiden. Ge good hunter. Bring much game. Superb camping skills. Witty banter as needed. Besides, it's only about 4,800 kilometers to Novy Samara."

I couldn't help myself. I grinned. "Oh, I feel *so* much better!"

Ge started to reach toward the water.

I lunged for his arm and grabbed it to stop him. "Nemes!"

He looked startled.

"Tiny 1- to 2-millimeter aquatic worms that burrow into your flesh, inhabit your blood and lymphatic stream. Reproduce at an alarming rate, eat you from the inside out."

"Jesus! I had forgotten that from the reports."

"Yeah. We have them in stagnant water up north, too. Especially in summer. Every school child on New Philadelphia is warned away from standing water. I reiterate; couldn't have picked a worse place to land."

"So, if the crash didn't kill us, the swamp will?"

I nodded in agreement.

Ge continued, "Relax. I routinely hurl myself into death-swamps before breakfast. Hanging out in a seven-meter lifeboat for the rest of our days is not an option, though. So, where's the nearest settlement?"

"A few hundred kilometers south of Novy Samara. There are scattered settlements along the New Irtysh. If we head north, we'll run into the New Himalayans. Once we're past the mountains, it will be the steppe country. Eventually we will run into the New Irtysh or one of its tributaries. The rivers will take us to the capital."

"Walk in the park!"

"Yeah. And the swamp, and the jungle, and a temperate rain forest, and the mountains, and the dry steppes, and the plains, and more temperate forest…"

"Hey! We're drifting," Ge interrupted me.

3

UPRIVER

"And this is exciting news because?" I asked.

"Drifting means a current, a current means a river estuary. A river means an easy way north. All we have to do is paddle against the current until we spot the river. Get out of this stinking steam bath and into some shade," he explained.

"Deal!" I promptly agreed. "How can you be sure the river goes north?"

He smiled, enjoying his role as expert wilderness guide. "You said the mountains are to the north. All rivers draining into this swamp arise in or near the mountains. It may wander around, but any large river will eventually take us north. And it's a lot easier to navigate a river than it is to hack your way through a jungle."

"Oh," I replied. "How can you tell the direction of the current?" I asked.

"Streamers in the scum on the water."

"Oh. And eww."

"Yeah. Roughly thatta way," Ge gestured to the northeast. He retrieved paddles from the onboard supply locker. I began paddling but made very little progress compared to Ge. I quickly learned to use my paddle as a rudder to keep the boat from pulling too far to one side or the other as Ge paddled.

The scent of decay gradually faded to the background as our noses grew numb, but the hum of insect life never slowed down. Other than the bugs, the Jutoma was completely silent. The oily opaque water was dark, except when I looked ahead it reflected a headache-inducing brilliant white light like a mirror. The only thing breaking the monotony of the unbroken slimy water were tufts of tough weeds in clumps floating by or clinging to floating vegetation. All of the floating branches that had been washed into the swamp had a two-centimeter ring of slime at the water line. I could hardly wait to escape it.

16

Pretty soon the current became stronger. There were lots of scum streamers and a definite push against our little lifeboat. More and fresher flotsam floated by. Ge flicked the tiny assist motor back on. Soon, it became obvious we were moving against a flow of water.

I was in pretty good shape at the time, but I was not trained for paddling. My shoulders and back were killing me, but I remained grimly silent, unwilling to be the slightest bit vulnerable in front of Ge.

Ge, on the other hand, was doing his level best to show off for me. He paddled one-handed. "Look at me, inventing new survival techniques in real time. If we survive this, I'm putting 'amphibious extraction specialist' on my résumé. Under hobbies."

I spotted the jungle line first. "Land ho!"

"Looks like we'll make it in time to camp on land. Excellent." Ge seemed satisfied. I was less certain. Now that I was stranded alone with Ge, intrusive thoughts of my first sexual encounter arose. After a decade of therapy and practice, I was able to trigger my relaxation response and firmly tucked those memories away.

Ge asked, "What's *that* face all about?"

I gave him a long look. "I'm contemplating the joys of bunking in a one-man tent with somebody your size."

"No worries," said Ge. "I'm equipped for an extended survey. It's an eight-man tent."

The estuary was so huge that we couldn't be sure when we actually entered it. We paddled with the little motor assisting us for a couple of hours before we could be sure we were on the river. When we could see jungle on the banks east and west of us, we were certain.

We were both dripping sweat. But the Jutoma was so humid that sweating didn't help much. I was in pretty good shape, but paddling was grueling, and my shoulders were screaming.

"I suggest we use up the refrigerated stuff before their coolpaks give out. You want "Berry Ice Kefir" or "Pineapple Banana Yoghurt? Oh, wait, we have some hotpacks, too. You have stuffed cheese biscuits or…stuffed cheese biscuits."

"Stuffed cheese biscuits are my new favorite. Let's start with that, and I'll move on to the kefir for dessert."

I thumbed the packs to heat and gave Ge two to my one. He shipped his paddle and grabbed his snack. We only stopped paddling for a second and promptly started drifting southwest even with the assist motor on. Well, that was no good. So, Ge paddled, and I steered, and we snacked on junk food one-handed so we wouldn't lose momentum.

17

"Hey, that looks pretty open over there." I motioned to the eastern bank; a low sandbank clothed with dark squat trees with huge buttress roots like Earth mango trees.

"Yeah. Suspiciously open. Lemme see." Ge grabbed a large protruding branch on a floating tree limb, carefully avoiding the water. He casually broke off a branch that was the thickness of my wrist, creating a meter long baton. He hurled it at the clear section of jungle on the east bank.

A God-awful screech arose from small animals inhabiting the canopy. The screech was soon followed by a rain of excrement from the trees. Within a few seconds the smell hit us. Suddenly the fetid swamp seemed like a breath of perfume by comparison. I have never smelled anything *that* bad before or since. Both of us were gagging and our eyes were streaming.

"Openness explained," Ge forced out. "Nothing stands a chance against feces that toxic!"

I nodded my agreement. It was still too foul to open my mouth to speak.

"Keep going?" he asked.

I nodded vigorously and finally managed, "Keep going!"

In spite of tired muscles, we paddled with all our might and put that foul stench behind us as fast as we could. As the stench faded, Ge noticed an island in the river. It was large with lots of trees and bushes.

"Looks promising," Ge said.

We circled it. It did not have anything resembling a sandy or muddy beach. Oh, no. It had very perilous rock cliffs and marginally less terrifying perilous rock beaches. Although I was reluctant to admit it, considering what a pill he'd been in the grav sled, Ge looked damned good paddling an emergency boat.

On the second circuit, Ge paddled furiously. He drove the lifeboat onto the shallowest of the rock beaches. As soon as the hull scraped rock, he did one of his giant 'your gravity is too puny for me' leaps and cleared the water.

Ge said, "Toss me the rope."

I did and he hauled the boat onto the beach. I hopped out and began stretching out my shoulders to ward off the inevitable soreness. "I need a toilet."

Ge rummaged in his backpack and whipped out a folding camp toilet complete with a sanitary disposal bag.

"You know you're in a bad way when the sight of a camp poop bag sparks joy. If you will excuse me." I turned to step into the bushes, but Ge leaned over me and shook the bushes.

"Better to startle anything in the bush *before* you step in," Ge grinned.

"Ah. Good point," I answered.

I realized how vulnerable we were in the wild. I suppressed visions of venomous snakes slithering up on me in my helpless state by imagining that I was in my safe clean bathroom back home. Job done; I stepped out to give him a chance. Ge disposed of our waste and the dissolvable sanitary bag by tossing it in the river. We used my hand sanitizer and started looking for a camp site. We found a gnarled old giant of a tree, with branches that very nearly swept the ground.

"The second whorl of branches will make a decent camp," he announced.

I stared at the tree, thinking very dubious thoughts.

Ge laughed. "Don't do much camping, I take it. Just watch."

So, I did. He uprooted young trees, some as big as my leg, and crisscrossed them in a 'v' pattern between the two widespread but uneven branches. By using the thicker base of the trunks on the lower side, he built a wooden sling that was pretty level.

Ge returned to the beach, grabbed the boat, and flipped it over.

"What are you doing?" I asked.

"Checking for hitchhikers," he replied.

Once he checked the bottom, he shoved it into the tree, stern to the trunk, bow pointing outward. Ge tweaked and fiddled and shoved in branches under the boat, hopping in and out of the boat frequently to check his work. He tied the boat into its temporary sling and re-tied a few knots. It held his weight just fine.

"Try not to look so impressed. I'm only *slightly* superhuman." He grinned as he worked. I rolled my eyes, but he'd hit the nail on the head. I *was* relieved to be stuck in the jungle with a professional-level wilderness guide. He set up his tent inside the boat, collapsing the sides to fit within the lifeboat and put our luggage inside.

"Your hotel room awaits, Miss Carroll." Ge grinned, poking his head out of the tent.

"Thank you." I climbed in. It was dead level and quite secure. I started to line the bottom of the boat with passenger pillows; Ge unrolled a comfy-looking camp mattress.

"I have a complete cooking set-up. We could cook a proper dinner," Ge offered.

"Nah. I'm too tired," I replied. "Just give me an energy bar. This is all in a day's work for you, but I'm exhausted."

I didn't even take off my boots. I just lay down on my improvised bed. According to Ge, I didn't go to sleep so much as I passed out.

* * *

I don't know what woke me up. The smell? A small noise? But I was instantly alert and completely aware of danger. Ain't instinct a wonderful thing? Wolverats were swarming the tent. It was bowing inward with their weight.

I screamed, "WOLVERATS !"

4

WOLVERATS

Ge woke up muzzy headed. I grabbed one of the service trays and began beating them off through the tent fabric. Now Ge didn't know about wolverats except by report, but he knew panic when he heard it and was alert in seconds.

I could see their needle-sharp little claws penetrating the sturdy tent fabric. "Poisonous! Don't let them get a claw into you."

I flipped onto my back and kicked at them with my boots and frantically beat at them with the tray.

"They're solo hunters," Whack! "only swarm…" smack "when mating." I grabbed my paddle and wailed on the tent with both hands. "Thank God," thud, thud, "they're only…" I kicked at the tent, "…a kilo each!" I grunted while beating them back.

Ge grabbed his paddle and a skillet from his kit and joined me. I snatched my stunner and began spraying the menaces through the tent walls. Soon there were enough wounded and stunned wolverats on the ground that the wolverats stopped swarming the tent. They took to the ground and ripped their wounded and stunned companions limb from limb and devoured them. The screams and stench were terrible.

We sat in the boat panting, letting the adrenaline bleed off.

Ge said, "I read about wolverats, but nothing in the report prepared me for this!"

"Ghastly creatures. They look like innocuous terran rodents. But they have longer needle-fanged snouts and prehensile tails. Nasty solo, but they're the most dangerous animal on this planet when they swarm," I explained.

I noticed a few drops of bright blood seeping from a shallow scratch on Ge's forearm. I gasped. "One of them got you!"

Ge seemed startled. "It's only a scratch, not even two centimeters long. I'm a large animal, Li, a scratch that small couldn't have introduced much poison."

"It's enough." I grabbed the tiny medical bot from my luggage and put it on his arm. It fussed and whirred and bandaged him up.

21

"See. It's nothing," Ge reassured me. I nodded agreement, but my stomach was in knots because I knew better.

In the three generations that humans had lived on New Philadelphia, no one had ever survived even a minor wolverat wound. The neurotoxin took a week to manifest, but it was a cruel death when it came. I started worrying about how to escape such a powerful man when the poison began to work on him, and he lost his mind.

* * *

#Forensic Investigation File:

AI: DOWNGRADE EMERGENCY ALERT Gravity Sled Transport Maneuver was successful. eco-surveyor's phone energy signature can no longer be detected.

CSO: Let's hope that's the last of 'em. We only have to make it to the vote.

AI: I recommend continuing to track target's phone energy signature to confirm a successful intervention. Do you wish to downgrade Emergency Alert to background monitoring?

CSO: You go on monitoring. **AUTHORIZED**. Code: KVG.735637.

AI: AUTHORIZATION VERIFIED. EMERGENCY ALERT downgraded to background monitoring status.

* * *

The next morning was misty. It did nothing to cool us or the jungle. It only made sweating completely ineffective and the heat even more unbearable. It did however both muffle and amplify all the insects and bird sounds. Even though I was becoming acclimatized, the earthy smell of the leaf mold was particularly sharp in the mist.

"Aaargh! Monsoon season has begun," Ge squinted into the foggy mist. "It would be pretty if it wasn't life-threatening."

"Life-threatening? More like inconvenient," I disagreed.

"Life threatening," he repeated stubbornly. "Huge walls of water from upstream rain events sweep down the river. It can easily swamp the boat. Life. Threatening."

"Oh," I said, and didn't share how much worse it would be when the wolverat poison started to work on him.

Ge depowered the central tent supports and spread the tent out over the frame of the boat. He zipped the tent opening around me and a window around himself so that we stuck out of the tent like a couple of kayakers. Had to admit, it stopped most of the rain infiltration.

We were loaded up and on our way within thirty minutes of sunrise. Ge figured it was eight in the morning at that latitude. Once again, Ge was so much more powerful than me, that my paddle served more as a rudder than as a paddle.

We only spoke in brief bursts, too concerned with paddling. Ge said, "Even though the current is strongest in the center of the river, that's where we should aim to stay."

"Huh?" I answered. "Why? If it's easier at the edges…"

"Local fauna dropping from the trees. Poisonous plants dropping toxic sap or fruit or thorns on us. Nope. It's a lot safer in the middle of the river in a tropical biome."

"Oh." Once again, I found myself relieved to be in Ge's company, with all his survival skills.

My guts twisted as I thought about his fate. I wasn't smitten or anything, but I was beginning to like him. On top of that, Ge was my best chance of surviving this misadventure. He certainly didn't deserve a wolverat poison death. From what I had read, it started with memory loss accompanied by increasing psychotic delusion and violent outbursts until the more basic brain functions withered and the person died of massive organ failure. It wasn't a fate I would wish on my worst enemy.

The rain varied from misting with the sun struggling to peek through, to steady drizzle. I questioned Ge about every wilderness survival topic I could think of. He answered my questions, displaying a breathtaking depth of knowledge all while admiring the local flora.

It was mostly shady, even in the center of the river. The jungle trees were towering giants stretching 75 or 100 meters into the sky. Each trunk was draped with creeping vines, and the undergrowth was dense. There were occasional flashes of bright color from birds, fruit or flowers deep in the trees. The variety was so overwhelming that I stopped trying to sort it all out.

The hum of insects was as pervasive as the swamp; but here, the jungle was alive with other sounds. Bird songs, barks, cries, warbles, and hoots from unseen animals surrounded us. It still smelled like compost, but fresher and less rank than the open swamp. It would have been lovely if it wasn't so brutally hot and clammy.

I spent a lot of time worrying about how to escape Ge once the wolverat poison manifested and he started to lose his mind. And worse, survive after I lost him. But further gloomy speculation halted because, suddenly, it got dark. Like, solar eclipse dark.

"Li, we need to get off the river," Ge said.

"Huh? It's not raining that hard." I was annoyed. "Isn't the idea to get as far north on the river as fast as we can?"

"We've been on the river for nearly six hours. The river rises in the afternoon after heavier rain squalls. It's only drizzling here, but the heart of the storm is further upstream, too far for us to see."

"Oh. So, we need high ground?"

"Yeah. I'm looking." Ge spotted a promising spot in the gloom.

He ran the boat against the muddy river's edge and repeated his performance from the island. I never even got out of the boat. He hauled me in the boat to a likely knoll about a football pitch away from the riverbank. The heavy undergrowth faded abruptly a few meters from the river. He secured the lifeboat to a giant tropical tree that had a meter-wide trunk. He tied it up as high as he could reach and left a few meters slack in the line.

"We have some play when the waters rise. Don't want to anchor so far down that we get pulled under," he explained with a smile.

We pitched the tent in the boat, making sure that every square centimeter of the boat was closely covered by the tent tightly secured to the sides.

Dripping wet, Ge and I toweled off with passenger blankets. I mopped up the boat and rolled the wet blankets into a bundle in the prow to deal with later. I laid out my cushions. Ge set up a little lantern and unrolled his mattress.

We had settled in to have a cozy chat when we heard it. It seemed distant, but it was there. Sort of like a waterfall. A thrumming or a rushing sound which grew louder.

"I hope we're far enough away from the river," I worried.

"We are." Ge smiled as he settled down cross-legged. "I went a few meters beyond where the vegetation changed from riparian new growth to more mature dry land growth. I also tied us off to an old-growth tree. We'll be fine."

A tremendous lightning flash penetrated the tent – even under the dense jungle canopy! – immediately followed by a huge thunderclap. Both of us jumped. It was getting noisier, sounding like a cross between a howling wind and the deeper thrum of a waterfall. Rain was coming down in sheets, loudly slapping the sides of the tent. We had to raise our voices to be heard.

In a few seconds we gave up speaking. The flood was upon us, and the roar was accompanied by the sound of cracking wood as the waters broke young trees and swept large debris from upstream into the mature trees.

We sat out the worst of the flood in silence. I must have looked pretty scared. My knee had begun bouncing without my permission, the small rhythmic thud of it against the floor lost under the roar outside. I unzipped my pocket, fumbled out my phone, and typed in the glow cupped against my chest:

Is the boat holding?

I held the screen toward Ge. He frowned, tilted his head, then nodded once; firm, confident, and tapped out a reply on his own screen so I could read it:

Yes. Ropes good. Tree good. Don't move around.

Another crack: a large log smashing somewhere upstream, made me flinch so violently that my teeth clicked together. My fingers moved again:

Could we get ripped loose?

Ge's answer came slower this time. **Unlikely. I left slack. We will rise with water.**

The water was already climbing – I could feel it in the shift of buoyancy beneath us, that imperceptible lift, like a floor inhaling underfoot. My throat tightened. I typed:

Should we check the lashings now?

He gave the tiniest shake of his head. Then a new message appeared on his screen: **Door stays closed. Too dangerous.**

The boat lurched hard as the current seized it, yanking us to the very end of the slack. The whole hull juddered against the rope, vibrating under us like a plucked string. My breath came sharp through my nose. My fingers were shaking so badly I made three typos before I got the next line out:

Can the boat survive this? Really?

He read it twice before answering. **Yes. Built for worse.** Then he added a second line, deliberate. **Trust the design.**

I tried. I really did. But my knee was a piston now, bouncing, bouncing, bouncing. I typed again:

What if big debris hits us?

He answered without hesitation this time: **Tree shields us. Do not unlash. Do not look outside.**

I swallowed hard. Another impact. The tent flicked with lightning again; white, blinding, surgical, and thunder cracked so close it felt like something physically struck the air around us. My hands came up over my ears in reflex.

When I dropped them, Ge gently took my hand to reassure me. I could feel his strength which only sharpened my grief. I was crying; and folks, I am an ugly crier. Ge thought it was fear. It wasn't. It was mourning.

5

DISCOVERY

Well, once the roar of the flood receded, I had to explain the waterworks somehow. "I was supposed to be on a yacht eating strawberries and sipping champagne. I worked for over *ten years* to land that cover, and influence has a very short shelf life. I'm going to miss Lord Dennison's party. So, I can kiss my career goodbye!"

Ge looked surprised.

I said, "You *chose* this. You *like* roughing it and being in the middle of nowhere. You're enjoying the up-close-and-personal tour of a new ecosystem. I didn't choose this! This little adventure has deprived me of my reward for over a decade of hard work."

Ge looked abashed. "Oh. Never thought of it like that."

"Uh-huh," I crossed my arms. "You are in your element out here. I only see the isolation, filth, and inconvenience. What do you see in it?"

"I am the master of my fate: I am the captain…"

"…of my soul," I finished for him. "Yeah, I've read Henley. Thoreau, too. It just never occurred to me to reenact their primitive idealism."

So, we got to talking. He told me, "I was the middle of seven siblings – always too old or too young to do anything. I was the kid in my family that got lost in the shuffle. I've been determined to strike out on my own since Eagle Scouts."

"Scouting, huh? I sense a love of wilderness theme emerging, here." I smiled. "How do you go from Eagle scout to post-doc?"

"I was a scholarship kid; got lucky since my advisor, Professor Flemming, knew about my family situation. If I didn't get a scholarship for grad school, I wasn't going. Simple as that. I don't know what strings she pulled, but I got a free ride for her entire graduate program and landed fellowships for my PhD and post-doc."

"Impressive. Scholarships for undergrad are pretty common, but a free ride to graduate school is damned rare. I have now raised my estimation of you," I said. The least I could do is be decent to him in the time he had left.

27

The conversation wasn't entirely one-sided, Ge was getting to know me, too. I told him about my constant internal monologue, where I gauged my every action by my mother's exacting standards. Then the conversation naturally turned to the crash.

I said, "As a popular public figure with a well-to-do father, kidnapping me for ransom makes sense. Killing me does not. No offense, but you're an obscure post-doc student. Not typically the kind of person who attracts criminal attention. Nothing about this makes sense."

Ge agreed, "Yet it was clearly an attack with lethal intent."

I nodded agreement. "That is one terrifyingly competent and unprincipled AI."

"Yeah. Had to be to override the entire suite of sled safety protocols. Plus, even more layers of security through the central dispatch and navigation. This is gonna stir up one hell of an investigation." Ge cocked his head to one side and asked, "Could it be it a case of mistaken identity?"

"That hardly seems likely. My face is recognized planet-wide, and you, my friend, are unmistakable."

We couldn't make heads nor tails of it and moved on to other subjects. We talked well into the night, but still got an early start in the morning, now that we had the 'breaking camp routine' sorted. Same as before, mist alternating with drizzle.

I continued to question Ge about wilderness survival, expanding my inquiries to biomes other than the jungle.

After a couple of hours on the river, Ge suddenly announced, "Mystery explained."

"What?"

Ge pointed into the canopy on the western bank. "That is agriculture. Trees don't fashion netting to support fruiting vines."

I looked where he was pointing. Once seen, it couldn't be unseen.

"Oh. My. God. This is like, *so* illegal! No one is supposed to steal a planet from an intelligent indigenous species! Settlers shouldn't even *be* on New Philadelphia."

"Could this be a rebel human settlement? I mean, it's been three generations," Ge asked.

"Highly unlikely. There's not enough population pressure to force people past the mountains, yet."

"Who holds the colonization grant for New Philadelphia?"

"Megacore. You know, the mining company," I said.

"Yeah. They sponsored the colonization of Ganesh, too. Looks like Megacore knows about the indigenous intelligent species and is determined to keep me from finding them."

I frowned with concentration. "Megacore would be desperate to avoid discovery. Especially now because the vote for full planetary charter is coming up next year. If they can keep this under wraps until after the vote, they stand to make billions."

"Seems like ample motivation for attempted murder," he said.

"Oh, God! What do we do when we encounter them; the natives, I mean? What if they killed all the previous surveyors?" I dove for my luggage. "I'm powering up my phone. I want to find out what happened to the last eco-survey teams. I suspect it was pretty bad."

"Yeah. Me, too," Ge answered.

I found my phone, plugged it into my jump battery and said, "Since they're after you, they're undoubtedly scanning for your phone."

Ge nodded hesitantly. "Still? You think after the sled went down the bad guys would put effort into scanning for my phone?"

"Yes, indeed. This is realpolitik at its worst. I don't think they have my phone signature, though," I pointed out. "And I paid through the nose for top-notch security. If I go incognito, use a disposable avatar, run a blurt search and download the results, I can hop on and off in a few nanoseconds. It would be hard to trace me in that time. Especially if I log on now, during peak traffic."

Ge thought I was being overly paranoid, but he agreed, and I conducted my quick, surreptitious internet search. Once we accessed the download, we discovered that all other eco-surveyors disappeared under mysterious circumstances and were presumed dead. Eleven different teams. Twenty-one individuals when you count us.

Ge said, "Well, that explains the partial surveys."

"Well, *shiny!* Now that I've seen it, they'll be coming for me, too! I have you to blame for my predicament."

"Hey!" Ge protested. "I'm not to blame for Megacore's actions! Although now that we've discovered these fields, I'm quite pleased that their plan backfired."

"You can say that again."

Ge grinned. "Now that we've discovered these fields, I'm pleased that their plan backfired."

I rolled my eyes, grinning. For the next hour as we made our way north, we saw more and more signs of civilization. Boats pulled up on shore. Storage containers nestled in trees. Different stands of fruiting bushes and vines in orderly and obviously unnatural swaths.

The current was stronger and prone to crosscurrents with choppy water. We had to work harder to paddle. Then, at the confluence of another wide fast-moving river, we spotted the docks.

They were huge for river docks. Equal to the size of small ocean port docks. And there were a lot of 'em. There was a swarm of boat traffic. There were tiny slow-moving support crafts, colorful recreational boats, and utilitarian catamarans loaded with goods. The docks had many mechanical counter-weighted cranes and animal-drawn carts for off-loading. There were crowds of the indigenous aliens.

At first glance, they were eerily like us. Bipedal, upright. But weirdly not like us. Their legs were shorter, their torsos wider, and their arms longer.

"Nearly the same proportions as tropical great apes on Earth," Ge said.

Instead of hair, they all sported an array of quills. Not as long or as sharp as a porcupine's quills, they were thicker and arranged in a tidy mohawk. They were dark skinned. Or I should say, dark-furred. As we got closer, we could see they were covered with short shiny flat fur, like the fur on a cat's nose. Most were clothed in very practical-looking colorful coveralls. Although plenty of individuals wore colorful flowing robes.

It was noisy, with dock workers calling to one another and various bells and whistles going off at odd moments. Once they caught sight of us, an eerie silence fell. They were whispering to each other, pointing, and crowding the side of the dock where we were approaching.

"Well, it's too late to sneak away and pretend we're not here." Ge grinned, excited by the prospect. "I propose we approach the natives and hope to God they play nice."

"Doesn't seem like we have much choice," I agreed, chewing on my lip nervously. "I am definitely more afraid of Megacore's AI than I am of the natives. Also, I have my stunner at the ready," I patted its familiar reassuring shape in my front pocket. "Let's go."

We pulled up to a jetty designed for small craft with a handy ladder for ascending to the dock. Ge tied off the boat. He got one foot on the bottom rung and nimbly sprang up to the top of the dock in a single leap. The show-off.

I forgave him for showboating when he turned and politely held out a helping hand to me. I climbed up and joined him on the dock. The crowd around us pulled back, stiff and frozen with shock. They stared at us, their dark eyes wide, both curious and frightened. Their quills all stood upright and quivering, as expressive as a cat's ears.

"Ge, you're intimidating as all hell! Even the tallest ones only come up to my shoulder; we tower over them. Sit down and make nice," I hissed.

I promptly sat down cross legged and opened my hands, palms up and spread my arms in front of me, aiming to be as unintimidating as possible. Ge followed suit.

We stared at the indigenous people, and they stared right back. They averaged about 140 to 150 centimeters tall – the height of a human fourth grader, with that same narrow-boned, pre-adolescent lightness of build.

They had long slender fingers and toes with opposable thumbs on their feet. Their faces were very nearly human, but narrower with more vertical round foreheads. Their noses were not as flat as Terran apes, but not as prominent as humans. Their eyes ranged from yellowy amber through every shade of brown to nearly black. It was obvious that they aged in many of the same ways we do. We saw many of them in various stages of greying.

An older native, frosted with gray, approached and motioned for us to follow him. We scrambled up. He led the way in an awkward swaying gait. Once we got to the end of the dock, we spotted some females. They were slightly smaller than the males and had longer quills. Two females had babies with them, peeking out of their mothers' pouches through clever slits in the front of mom's clothing.

Ge was grinning from ear to ear. "They're marsupial," he breathed.

He'd fulfilled every xenoecologist's dream. He'd get the credit for discovering a new species. Not just any new species, the first intelligent new species. I could feel the happiness radiating from him and thanked God that he had this moment before the end.

We were walking through the jungle, dodging herbivore droppings no doubt left by the draft animals we had seen harnessed to wagons at the dock. I realized belatedly that the 'trees' around us were buildings. Many with commercial intent. The giant trunks sported large doorways for cargo, display windows, and equipment yards. There were many smaller apartments, higher up on the trunks jutting out like strange carbuncles on the bark of the tree.

"Ge, they didn't build their city, they *grew* it!"

We paused while Ge whirled around, checking out the cityscape. "Amazing. Explains why they've flown under the radar this long. Low power signature."

Everything was shaded by the mature canopy above. But our eyes adjusted, and I began to make out differences in the trees around us.

31

Some had smooth bark, some were deeply fissured. The leaves were as varied as the bark of the trees, a confusing mélange of shapes and colors. Even here, the scent of a jungle primeval permeated the air.

We arrived at a small clearing with a fountain in the center. It was a wonderful fantasy sculpture of flowers and local foliage. It was oddly reassuring to know that they decorate their public spaces in much the same way we did.

The street was paved with colorful low-growing mossy plants. There was a network of crisscrossing branches only a little over Ge's head. We soon saw why. The older native who had volunteered to be our guide gabbled at a younger native. The younger native hopped up to the branches and swung down the street at high speed.

"Wait a second," Ge said, "If they're brachiating..." He scanned the heights of the trees nearest us. "Yep. This is the lowest level of a series of roads at different elevations in the trees."

"Brachiating?" I asked.

Ge explained, "They can walk, but are happier and faster swinging through the trees, like terran great apes. Brachiating."

Ge grabbed two likely branches and pulled himself up, stuck his head through the road to have a look. He called down, "I count five levels here. That indicates one helluva population density."

"And a complex economy," I volunteered. "Think about the logistics of providing food for everybody. This fountain isn't a utilitarian water distribution feature. Nope, this is public sculpture."

I suddenly awoke to the fact that we were being rude. I turned to our guide, put my hands on my chest and said, "Li." Then I touched Ge's chest and said "Ge." Then I turned to our guide and gestured toward him, but without touching him, not sure of their etiquette rules. Our guide cocked his head to one side, rippling his quills.

Ge caught on and repeated my performance. "Ge, Li." Then gestured towards our guide.

The guide's quills flicked. He grinned, touched his chest, and said, "Bran Ling."

I was relieved to discover that his expressions and body language were so like our own. I repeated, "Bran Ling." He smiled and nodded enthusiastically. No way to know at that moment how accurate I was, but I felt that I understood his expressions and that he understood ours.

We were rapidly attracting a crowd. I could see and hear the murmuring excited throng around and above us. Thousands of bright inquisitive eyes turned our way from the roads overhead, the windows of the tree-homes, the ground street around us.

Ge glanced around. "We didn't arrive with fanfare, but it seems we didn't need to."

"Yeah." I agreed. "So, it looks like they have a decent communication network, as well."

There was a ripple in the crowd. An older, more elaborately dressed indigenous male approached us. He was wearing multi-layered swirling blue-green robes. His robes were embellished at the shoulders and chest with elaborate metal work. He sported an intricate headpiece woven through his quills. Obviously ceremonial garb, not practical work clothes.

"I am BanTik, governor of this province. Welcome to Ifka'a Kifma'a, home of the Philosophers' Tree."

I felt my knees go watery and sat down quite abruptly on the edge of the fountain. Not only did Megacore's eco-team know about the natives, but they also hung around long enough for the locals to pick up Standard. Really excellent Standard.

Ge recovered before I did. He extended his hand for a handshake, "Ge Oates." BanTik shook his hand, so he had picked up that human custom, too. "My companion is Li Carroll."

"Hi," I said somewhat faintly.

"I offer you the hospitality of my Grove." BanTik grabbed his left fist in his right hand and nodded.

"Thank you, we accept," Ge said, wreathed with smiles. BanTik turned down a different street than he had arrived from. Noticing my distress, Ge picked up my backpack along with his own and turned to follow BanTik. I got up and we walked down the street together.

"Wouldn't you be more comfortable swinging?" I asked.

BanTik smiled. "Yes, but I suspect that you would be less comfortable."

Ge grinned and decided to show off. "We can swing. We're just better at walking." He hopped up and grabbed likely overhead branches. He began swinging down the street with the backpacks casually draped one over each shoulder. Ge turned and swung back to us, "See?"

"Speak for yourself, Ge." I turned to BanTik. "Ge is unusually large and athletic even among our kind."

"Ah." BanTik smiled. "Very impressive. Can you swing?"

"Not as well as Ge can. Besides, we've been paddling for days, and my shoulders are very tired and sore now."

33

We were passing a very large tree with deeply fissured bark. The outside of the bark was a dark gray shading to black, but the fissures were brilliant shades of scarlet, yellow, orange and fuchsia.

"Wow," I observed. "Handsome tree."

"Don't let our Matriarch hear you say that." BanTik smiled. "The Flame Tree matriarch and our own Bay Tree matriarch detest each other. A long-standing grudge over a suitor, I believe."

"Ah. I'll keep that in mind," I replied.

Ge dropped down and was walking by BanTik's side. "How many of you are in this city?"

"At the last census, over 820,000. This is the provincial capital," BanTik announced proudly.

Ge whistled. "Very impressive technologies to keep everybody fed and watered. Is this a pedestrian only city? What form of transportation do you use?"

"This residential section is pedestrian only. We use bree-drawn coaches and wagons for most commercial zones." BanTik's quills flicked in a gesture I interpreted as pride. "Also, we have public basket transport in loops around the city with radiating spokes from the center. You never have to swing very far in Ifka'a Kifma'a."

6

SHELTER

We were in BanTik's home grove before we knew it. The bay trees had smooth, deeply lobed dark leaves that were faintly aromatic. The bark peeled in irregular patches to reveal a soft array of pastel beige, brown, pink, and green blotches. The trees smelled a bit like cinnamon or allspice with some woodsy notes thrown in. It was quite pleasant.

"Each new tree is actually a root-sprout of the original mother bay tree," BanTik explained.

"Ah, grove, indeed," I said. My eyes were adjusted to the shade under the canopy, and I noticed patterns in the ground moss. I also noticed that there were no fallen leaves. They must tidy them up.

"Like aspens on Earth," Ge contributed. "The second-largest single organism on the planet. The trees cover mountainsides."

"So, what's the largest single organism?" I asked.

"A mycelium, the honey mushroom." Ge reached up and ran his fingers along the velvety underside of a leaf. His fingers picked up the scented powder clinging to the leaf. He rubbed the powder between his fingers, examining it closely.

We approached a cleft between two huge buttress roots. It was elaborately carved and colored. Obviously, the front door. Once inside, the spacious foyer was lit evenly with indirect light. The walls were polished light wood. There was a lightweight basket made of woven vines in one corner attached to thick twining tendrils of vines descending through an opening in the ceiling.

"I think we should go up the vine lift separately," BanTik said. "This was not designed for your weight, Ge. I do apologize."

"No offense." Ge grinned. "Most of the furnishings on this planet among my own kind are not quite big enough for me. I'm pretty large, even for a human."

"Genetically modified to thrive on a planet with greater than average gravity," I explained. "Here, Ge, give me the luggage to limit strain on the lift."

35

BanTik's quills flashed. His eyes widened in surprise. "We modify plants, but never people."

"We modify anyone who wants to be modified. We have a lot of laws and procedures in place to make sure nobody is coerced or tricked into asking for modifications." I explained, "The only modifications allowed in young children, for instance, are to cure congenital health problems."

Ge shrugged off the packs, handed them to me, and BanTik and I stepped into the basket. It immediately began to rise with little woody popping and creaking sounds.

"How does this work?" I asked, fascinated.

"The vine senses weight and retracts. When we step off, and the weight is gone, it relaxes again. We have others throughout the tree that do the opposite for descending the tree."

"Clever. I wish that Ge could enjoy all this."

BanTik's quills wavered in what I was beginning to recognize as puzzlement or confusion. "Ge seems to be enjoying this immensely."

"Yes, but he got scratched by a wolverat," I said, eyes welling up with tears, "and there is no cure for that poison."

"Wolverats?" BanTik asked.

"The first night we spent here, wolverats swarmed our tent. They're small, about a kilo each, like so." I gestured with my hands. "Thick prehensile tails. Their short coarse fur is muddy brown. They have sharp muzzles with many narrow needle-like teeth, poisonous claws. They hunt in packs and are the most vicious damned things I've ever known of. They swarmed our tent. We beat them off. Then they attacked and ate their wounded companions on the ground and left us alone. But Ge got scratched during the attack."

BanTik grinned. "Ah, I recognize this animal. We call them waibeeb, and we have the cure. When was he scratched?"

"You have the cure? You're sure this works in my kind? Ge was scratched not last night but the night before," I answered, my mood rising with hope. "We just met; we don't really know each other. But I am *so* glad that I do not have to mourn him!"

We stepped out of the basket into a large richly decorated round room. It appeared to be only slightly smaller than the diameter of the trunk of the tree. BanTik gabbled an urgent command to a member of his household. He turned and explained to me, "I have sent for our doctor. Make yourself comfortable. I must convey the news of your arrival to our Matriarch."

My knees were a bit wobbly from relief, and I had no problem accepting his invitation. I settled into a comfortable plush low couch when Ge arrived.

"BanTik has called for a doctor to see to your arm, Ge."

"Great. It itches like hell."

The couch was resilient, upholstered in soft complexly patterned fabric. The floor was lushly carpeted with a vine pattern figured in greens and blues. A network of beautifully polished light wooden branches crossed the room overhead. There was a gallery surrounding the room above the wooden network. There were low tables against the wall with very elegant pottery and bowls on display. The room was hung with tapestries. After I had been there a few minutes, I realized the swirling motifs of the carpet were mirrored by the wooden ceiling bars. There were no windows, but the lighting was excellent, diffuse with no obvious source.

I did a slow promenade around the room admiring the decorative objects. Exquisite sculptures of plants and animals intermixed with more abstract pieces were displayed. The tapestries were intricate story panels naturalistically colored. Each tapestry depicted an accomplishment by a high-status female. The planting of the original bay tree, the establishment of a new business, and some that I could not interpret without context.

"Never thought I'd be living in a tree house," I said. "But this sure seems like a luxurious tree to live in."

"Agreed," Ge said. "I don't know much about art history or design, but is this art and décor, like, really sophisticated?"

"Yes. It is highly sophisticated. I used to work as a buyer for my dad's art galleries. Some of it is absolutely gorgeous. Their representative art is accurate. The abstract pieces are beautifully proportioned and finished. This is *not* a primitive culture," I answered him.

Ge looked up. "Looks like our reputation precedes us."

He smiled and waved at a group of children. Then he showed off by doing a back flip, his audience murmured and whistled in appreciation. The gallery was rapidly filling up and the household was getting a look at us. I noticed regular patterns. There was one group of natives in solid blue/green coveralls with a swirling logo on the chest. The second larger group of natives wore more varied and colorful clothing. I decided the blue/green coveralls were uniforms and that those were servants. The larger more colorful group was the clan.

A young native waddled into the room. His right hand was shriveled and largely useless. A crippling disability for his species.

37

"Aloo, aloo," he grinned his quills standing tall and quivering with excitement. He clasped his crippled hand in the other in salute. Ge and I returned the gesture. He said, "Iyam TikTik, sonovBanTik. Welcome."

After a brief pause while I translated his accent, I said, "Thank you, TikTik. I am Li Carroll. This is my companion, Ge Oates."

Ge rumbled out, "Delighted to meet you."

Ge and I both sat down, and TikTik scrambled up and squatted on the arm of an adjacent couch, so we were all at comfortable eye-level for conversation.

"Itz bin nearly therdy moonzsince the lazt humanzcame."

Ge asked, "How long is a moon?"

TikTik concentrated hard. He said, "Ah moon iz how long it takes Sister Moon and both of her Daughters to appear in the sky together. About 150 dayz, more or lezz"

It was Ge's turn to concentrate hard. "Ah, that means that it's 300 days for two moons. That's fifteen years minus about 40 days per year, or about 600 days total, or a year and a half. So, that comes to between twelve and thirteen years."

TikTik bobbed up and down. "Yez, yez! We lozt Anna, the lazt human, died of old age about thirdeen yearz ago. Very zad. I waz her student."

"That explains your Standard. How old were you when you lost Anna?"

"Only twelve. Very tender age," TikTik looked woebegone. "She is with her family and her God, but we are without her for many yearz."

"Oh, TikTik, I am so sorry for your loss," I replied. Didn't have a chance to discuss the native's concept of an afterlife though, as the doctor arrived.

She swung in using the overhead wooden network. She had a practical stuffed pouch slung over her shoulder. BanTik followed her. They dropped to the floor simultaneously. BanTik introduced her as AckTik. AckTik sat down and had Ge prop his arm up on the sidearm of a low chair. After puzzling for a few seconds, she figured out the clear biofilm bandage on the scratch and removed it.

The stench of rot was clear, although faint. AckTik took the opportunity to explain the treatment. "These is `mahinia` grubz. They need `waibeeb` poison to pupate. They go in the body eating the poison. They do not go to the brain. Zadly, I must ropen the wound. When they is full, they go out where they go in. Have you had dizzy?" Ge shook his head. "Foul dreams?"

38

"No." Ge said, "Nothing like that."

"Good," AckTik nodded sharply with satisfaction. "No poison in your brain, lah? If it in your brain, we have to do treatment again until the grubz cleared it all."

AckTik took out a tiny scalpel and made a shallow cut along a short segment of Ge's wound. Ge hissed and clenched his other fist but was pretty stoic about it. The stench of rot was immediately stronger. AckTik took a box from her pouch and sprinkled what appeared to be tiny white seeds, smaller than sesame seeds, on the wound. Well, the "seeds" woke up and turned into tiny writhing maggots, burrowing into Ge's flesh.

Ge saw the look on my face and said, "It doesn't hurt. It's itchy and weird but not painful."

"Glad to hear it." I looked away, took several deep cleansing breaths.

"As long as I don't watch 'em, I'm fine," Ge assured me.

I glanced again and saw the buggers writhing under his skin. Relaxation breathing was not doing the trick. My stomach was having none of it.

I dashed to the other side of the room and threw up in a large display bowl. With my luck, I no doubt vomited into a priceless heirloom. I collapsed in one of the chairs, deliberately angling myself to avoid looking at Ge's arm. TikTik gabbled to a servant who cleared my mess away.

"I'm so embarrassed! Sorry, TikTik."

"No zorry," he waved away my apology. "If never zeen before, very upzet." he laid his good hand on my arm, "No worry, lah? You zave Ge's life."

Ge looked startled. "She what?"

"Waibeeb zcratch if not treated always kill, no matter how small the wound, lah," AckTik explained.

"In the three generations that people have inhabited this world no one has ever survived a wolverat wound," I confirmed. My thoughts and emotions were in turmoil. I felt hugely relieved and yet strangely guilty as though I caused Ge's problem.

Ge looked furious. "You *knew* and neglected to say anything!"

"To what purpose, Ge? So that I filled your last few days with increasing dread and grief before the toxin destroyed your mind? I wanted your last days to be filled with discovery and happiness. I spent a lot of time struggling to figure out how to escape you once the neurotoxin took hold and you became violent." And yeah, I was

39

crying when I said it. "Last night during the flood I wasn't crying about missing some damned party."

TikTik closed his fist and touched his chest, "Rezpek, Li. You have great heart." Then TikTik turned to Ge. "She protect your happy, even though she know you dead mean her dead alone in the jungle." He pantomimed with both hands as though to grab Ge by the shoulders and push him down, looking like a scolding grandmother. "You zay zorry."

Ge looked hang-dog guilty, completely cowed by a tiny native who barely topped his waist. "Sorry. And thanks, Li."

"Yeah. Well, I do my best." I had sniveled to a stop and turned to TikTik. "I should tidy up before Matriarch gets here. Where can I do that?"

TikTik waddled over to a hallway, "Please make yourself comfortable. Firzt door on the left."

"Thank you." I grabbed my backpack and made my way towards the bathroom.

I found the toilet, a slit in the floor arrangement, in its own separate room. It was equipped with a bum-cleaning feature. Back in the main bathroom area, the tap was fairly obvious, but I couldn't find anything resembling soap. I fiddled with the carvings on the wall. The flower above the tap released a lightly perfumed squirt of soap. I was unprepared and had to repeat the exercise. Then, I fiddled with the right-hand flower, and the water flowed. Neat. I rinsed out my mouth and did a quick cat-bath. I changed into my dress and sparkly sandals, re-braided the crown of my hair, and brushed out the bulk of it hanging loose behind me.

When I emerged, Ge spoke up, "Wow! you scrub up nice."

"I don't even have any makeup on," I protested.

Ge grinned. "Better and better."

I noticed many more natives filling the couches and chairs. The seating was very orderly, so I concluded that it was assigned. A maid servant swung into the room. Everybody rose from their seat and squatted down with their hands clasped together in front of themselves. I imitated the posture. After a split second, so did Ge.

7

THE BAY TREE GROVE

My first impression of Matriarch was of elegance. Her fur was white-tipped and her face completely white. Her silver fur highlighted her dark brown, almost black, eyes. She wore an elaborate jeweled headpiece with gossamer-fine chains woven in and out of her quills that created a delicate cap dripping with gems. Many swirling layers of the most beautiful colored and patterned fabrics I had ever seen made up her garments. As she moved, the various colors of the underlying translucent layers overlapped in different ways producing a gorgeous iridescent effect. Matriarch stopped and her handmaidens helped her to the floor and onto her throne. Everyone got back into their chairs. Ge and I stood up.

The Matriarch craned her neck to see us in our glorious towering height and gabbled sharply at BanTik.

"Matriarch invites you to sit down," BanTik translated. Although, it sure sounded more like she *ordered* us to sit down. But, whatever.

"The Matriarch asks if you would disrobe for her."

I gulped and squirmed uncomfortably, keenly aware of the need for diplomacy. "Ahem. We have nudity taboos in our culture. Alone, with Matriarch, yes. But never for a crowd and never in front of males," I replied. BanTik translated and Matriarch sniffed.

The Matriarch spoke and BanTik translated. "Matriarch asks, 'Why should we shelter complete strangers not even our own kind?'"

I eyed her and considered briefly before answering, "The prestige of your Grove. You have sheltered our kind before and sponsored the teaching we provide. Also, there will be trade opportunities. Your products are very finely made and would be popular trade goods with my people."

"Also, this will not be permanent," Ge rumbled. "We need to leave fairly soon."

"Matriarch needs to know why," BanTik supplied.

Ge coughed. "Ah, that's where it gets complicated."

BanTik gave him the gimlet eye and Ge sighed.

41

"Under our laws, we should never have settled this planet. We have severe penalties for any company – uh, our version of a Grove – that settles a planet that is already home to a civilized species. I am an ecologist. I came here to survey this world. The people that sponsored the illegal human settlements north of the mountains found out somehow and sabotaged our vehicle. They attempted to kill us to keep me from finding you."

Ge cleared his throat and continued, "Our governing body is meeting to decide whether your planet will be granted full trade privileges. That is scheduled for the end of next year. If we prove you exist before that meeting, they will delay the vote until some political agreement can be reached. All of our people already settled here could be relocated to a new planet, or we could divide up the planet and set up trade with your people, or some other political solution.

"But, if there is no proof that you exist before the vote, under our laws, you will have no political power. It will be very difficult to establish your sovereignty and political rights. Not impossible; but very difficult. It will take many years. It will be equally difficult to establish trade or enforce your own laws, or get rid of us, or whatever you decide to do. It is critical that we prove to our people that you exist prior to the council vote."

That's when I chimed in, "And the meeting of our peoples is inevitable. In our ignorance, we thought this green and beautiful world was empty. Free for the taking. With no constraints, human immigrants will continue to make their way here. Eventually we will come here, to your jungle."

"Matriarch asks, 'If you have severe penalties for settling this world, why would any rational being attempt it?'"

"Profit!" I answered. "The human Grove that established the illegal human colonies will make many times more money than all the wealth of all the people in this large and prosperous city *combined* if the charter is granted."

Ge nodded agreement. "I don't know how it works with you guys, but with us, that's powerful motivation for illegal colonization and attempted murder."

BanTik translated, "Matriarch demands to know why she should harbor so much trouble under her roof; you appear to bring nothing but strife."

"I sympathize with her concerns," I replied. "But I am helpless to answer them. Please apologize to Matriarch for me. If Matriarch does not wish to shelter us, we can seek shelter elsewhere. Tell her that my hair is black with highlights of red. Perhaps that is a sign that we should seek shelter from the Flame Tree Grove?"

BanTik ogled at me but translated. Matriarch flattened her quills and spread them out. I was reminded of a cat folding down their ears in annoyance. Then her eyes narrowed. She shot BanTik a glare strong enough to fell an ox and punched him hard in the shoulder. BanTik winced.

"Sorry, BanTik. Didn't mean to get you in trouble," I said.

BanTik shrugged. "Grandmother will forgive me." He massaged his shoulder ruefully. "Eventually."

Then Matriarch spoke again and TikTik waddled over. He climbed up on her chair and kissed her affectionately on both cheeks, like a young child. TikTik squatted down on the low arm of her throne.

BanTik, glowing with love and pride, (it looks the same on them as it does on us), said, "My son, TikTik, Sees." And yes, the capitals were obvious from the way he said it.

"Ge," I touched his arm briefly and whispered, "I think TikTik is a telepath. I think that's why he's the first of the clan to greet us. BanTik got us off the street so we wouldn't cause a riot and sent in TikTik to vet us."

Ge looked impressed. "Real, reliable telepathy? Wow."

Our whispered conference was cut short. Matriarch began addressing questions to TikTik while BanTik kept up a running translation. "She asks what TikTik has Seen of you. TikTik has Seen that you are a Protector, just like her," the Matriarch's attention sharpened, and she stared at me. I stared right back.

BanTik continued, "He says you and Ge are bright minds, fully the equal of AckTik. He says that Matriarch can trust you. He's telling the story of you and Ge encountering `waibeeb` as evidence supporting his Sight. TikTik believes that you will bring honor and profits to our Grove."

Matriarch slumped in her throne. For a brief moment I sensed her weariness, the weight of responsibility on her shoulders. TikTik patted her arm affectionately, offering silent support. She smiled at TikTik. Obviously, TikTik's support did the trick for us. Matriarch spoke to BanTik. He translated, "She has decided to let you stay. You may guest for a moon but must find ways to support yourselves thereafter."

"I understand." I assumed the respect posture again. "Please thank her properly for us."

Ge copied me and rumbled out, "We are very grateful. I am eager to contribute in any way I can to your Grove.

43

TikTik showed us to our rooms. It was filled with the same diffuse light as in the rest of the house. I asked TikTik, "How do you dim the light for sleep?"

TikTik stroked a section of the molding beside the entry door, the lights dimmed, and then he brought the lights back up. He pointed. The bathroom had a similar carving near the door, as did a section of the wall within reach of the sleeping basket. He showed me how to open and close the window and open and close the cupboard doors.

"How do you get the water in here and what happens to your wastes?" I asked.

"The tree is bred to absorb more water than it needs. Our waste feeds the tree and the tree shares its water with us."

"Brilliant," I said.

Bellhop duties concluded, TikTik escorted Ge to his room. I stood in the doorway and watched to make sure I knew where Ge was. Weird. I had known him less than a week yet felt strangely disquieted at being separated from him.

I unpacked my suitcase and explored the elegant suite. It was stocked with fruit and flowers and a pitcher of water. The bed was a lightweight woven shallow round basket, lusciously padded inside with a lovely silky throw folded neatly in the center. I tested it out. Pretty comfy. I was soon settled in. I mean, it's not like I had an extensive wardrobe to unpack. As soon as I could, I knocked on Ge's door.

I noticed his round basket bed was twice the size of mine. I asked TikTik about it later and he told me they gave Ge a family room. Their habit is for the whole family to climb into bed together.

I said, "I always thought casting a corporation as the bad guy in stories was a clumsy plot device. I'm changing my mind on that."

"Don't rush to judgment," Ge said. "It wasn't Megacore that did this. Some individual is using the complexity and financial power of Megacore for their own purposes. Corporations are usually too concerned with profit to be criminal. No. Historically, when corporations went bad it was the action of one or a few key executives."

Ge's eyes went a little unfocused as he concentrated hard. "I'm gonna write a little search algorithm set it on burst and have it feed your phone everything I can find about Megacore's C-level execs. I should be on and off in a split second. Also heavily disguised; also at peak traffic; also brief enough to prevent a trace."

I volunteered, "I own a real estate company inside a blind trust. I am not listed on any public docs. My own family doesn't even know I own it. I can pull anybody's financials."

Ge said, "Well aren't you a surprise. When I get the search set up, gimme the credentials and I'll throw that in."

"I'm off to see if I can borrow TikTik as a tutor. We only have a few months to learn the local lingo. And I'm dying to know how his telepathy works. God, I feel like I just got photographed bare-ass naked in public."

"Yeah, it's unsettling to think that TikTik knows me better than my own mother. I like your plan. The phones are on the windowsill, but under the shade of the canopy, they won't be charged up for a while. I'm coming."

We stepped out into the corridor and realized we had no way to find TikTik or the dining room or study supplies or anything.

Ge decided for us. "Let's head to the meeting room, there's always staff there."

"Let me get my journal." I turned back to my room.

When I returned with it, Ge asked, "You journal *by hand?*"

"Yup." I smiled. "Invaluable for mastering a lot of vocabulary quickly. The physical act of writing improves memory pretty dramatically for me. I copy out 100 words per day, test myself on them. I forget about two-thirds of them. I copy the ones I've forgotten into the next day's page and add to that until I have 100 again. When I keep it up for a couple of months, I can think in the target language, which accelerates my progress even more."

"Huh," Ge looked thoughtful. "How many languages do you have?"

"Standard, Mandarin, French, English, and Spanish. I'm best in Mandarin, I'm only conversational in French, English and Spanish."

Ge said, "Impressive. I will accept you as my personal language expert. I think the reception room is down this way."

We made our way to the reception room and there were staff there. Not knowing what else to do, I turned to a uniformed male nearest where we entered and asked "TikTik?"

He repeated, "TikTik."

Ge and I nodded enthusiastically. The servant smiled and turned to go down a corridor. We started to follow. The servant flipped up his hand palm up. Their 'stop' gesture is identical to ours. Weirdly unsettling but convenient. Ge and I waited.

TikTik appeared shortly thereafter accompanied by a waist-high blue/black wolverat.

Ge, in that tightly controlled voice guys use when they are terrified and being brave, said, "What is *that?*"

45

TikTik grinned. "That's Buk, my `darlu`. He very friendly. Too lazy to bite anyone. Buk sat down and wrapped his tail neatly around his feet. Ge squatted down and extended his hand nervously. Buk rose and sniffed Ge politely then leaned against Ge's legs. Ge grinned and petted Buk's mane.

"Huh. Buk looks like a giant wolverat – uh, `waibeeb`."

"No, no," TikTik replied. "Zweet temperament, blue fur, big mane, no poison, not `waibeeb`."

Ge straightened up. "Wasn't expecting pets."

"Hey, TikTik." I brought it back to my agenda. "We need immediate language tutoring. Can anybody help us? Can you help us? At first, it's basically a full-time job. I don't want to impose. I don't know what your job is now, so if you can't, I will understand. But it would sure help to have a dedicated teacher."

TikTik grinned. "I See for my Grove. High respeck, low hours. I happy to teach."

Ge held out his hand for a handshake. TikTik shifted uncomfortably, holding his crippled right hand slightly behind his body.

Ge changed to a left-handed shake. "Sorry, TikTik, I forgot."

TikTik smiled gently and shook Ge's left hand.

"First of all," Ge said, "where are we?"

"Ifka'a Kifma'a."

"No, I meant what do you call your world? We call it New Philadelphia, surely you have a name for it."

"Oh, we call our planet `Acora`."

"So, we are on `Acora` and learning to speak `Acoran`?" I asked.

"Yes, but you are learning to speak `Apex Jungle`."

I was taking notes like a fury.

"How do you say 'hello'?" I asked.

"Hello."

"Zoowee?" I tried to repeat.

"No. '`Hello`'" TikTik enunciated clearly and slowly and smiled.

We went through all the basics: hello, goodbye, yes, no, I want, I need, 'How do I...', 'what is the word for...,' 'where is,' 'my name is.' Then, I asked TikTik to write down their alphabet. Ge and I were relieved to discover it is a rational phonetic alphabet, not ideograms and not anything as complicated as Thai. Although they spell top-down, like Mandarin, not left-to-right like Standard.

"Do you have sticky notes?"

"Zticky notez?" TikTik asked.

46

"Small temporary labels so that Ge and I can label our surroundings. It's a good way to memorize words for common objects, like book, wall, light switch, etc."

He spoke to a servant and blank books, pens for Ge and I and sticky notes arrived shortly thereafter. Turns out they are actual leaves. Pens have no ink; they are simple styluses. Pressing on the pages of the leaves scars them and your marks harden to a dark mark. So, all the pages of the blank books are one-sided. The sticky notes are also leaves of various sizes. When placed stem-up on something, then stroked down, they stick. To remove them, stroke up. Simple. Weirdly convergent technology.

Thus equipped, TikTik led us on a tour of the house. I took extensive notes. Ge was sketching. He was zeroed in on light technology, building details, clothing, and implements. I was more concerned with staying oriented and figuring out where all the main rooms were. Soon, we were oriented to the main tree and had set up a study schedule.

"We have big dining hall, and zmaller dining room for core family. I think you zhould eat with core family until more of grove gets to know you. Then you can eat wherever you want."

"How do we know when meals are served?" I asked. My timing was perfect. I heard chimes playing a short simple tune.

TikTik smiled. "Dinner bell."

"Great!" Ge grinned. "I'm starving."

The dining room was as elegant as the main lobby. The table was inlaid with many different colored and grained woods. The chairs were low and wide as they had been in the lobby. There were many courses of food on the table. I tasted many of the dishes, all elegantly presented. Ge and I gorged on fruits and complex vegetable dishes, but there was very little meat on offer. Only two fish dishes.

I realized Ge's problem partway through the meal and looked at Ge with concern, "Ge, how much meat do you normally eat in a day?"

"About two kilos, sometimes more, especially if I'm working hard."

I turned to TikTik on my left. "TikTik, we have a problem."

TikTik looked concerned. "What is that?"

"I'm fine with fish and fruit, but Ge comes from a different planet. He needs a lot more protein and fat than I do. As much as two kilos per day. There is precious little fat or protein in this dinner." I twisted my napkin in my hands nervously. "I feel as though I am a bad guest, particularly in light of your generous hospitality, but poor Ge is going to starve. He's already dropped weight from the thin provisions and hard work of paddling upriver."

"Oh." TikTik's quills flashed. He narrowed his eyes, "How much is a kilo?" After some searching about, Ge located a platter and handed it to TikTik.

"That's about a kilo. I eat two or two-and-a-half times that weight spread out over several meals," Ge shrugged, embarrassed.

TikTik's eyes opened wide. "That's enough for an entire *pack* of darlus!"

"Do your people ever eat meat?" I asked.

"Zometimes. But nothing like thiz!" TikTik responded.

"Yeah, Ge eats more than usual for us, but even I will be much happier with more fat and more protein. Say, a little less than one quarter of what he eats."

BanTik, seated on Ge's right, piped up, "That's half a branch of meat every day!" He turned to TikTik and said, "Don't let Matriarch know. She will object to the expense, even though we can afford it. I will speak with the chef." BanTik turned to Ge, "Will you be alright until tomorrow?"

Ge's stomach gave a huge gurgle, as if on cue.

BanTik's quills quivered, partially raised, which I interpreted as amusement. "This is the sound your stomach makes when it wants more?"

Ge, shamefaced, shrugged and nodded 'yes.'

"I will speak to the chef immediately."

"Ask your chef if I may prepare some of our human delicacies for you all to try."

Ge gave me a look.

"What? I'm not a trained chef, but I can cook."

BanTik left and came back with a two or three-kilo roasted bird that he identified as a brebola. It was larger than a chicken and smaller than a turkey. Ge politely offered me about a 300-gram piece of delicious roasted fowl and devoured the rest with obvious delight. I handed Ge a platter of fish dressed with a delicate somewhat oily tart sauce that I particularly liked. He inhaled that, too. BanTik and TikTik stared, fascinated.

Ge leaned back with a sigh. "First decent meal I've had in over a week. You have my undying gratitude."

The next morning Ge told me he had scanned the C-level Megacore execs and hadn't found anything. I scanned the screen and the hairs on the back of my neck stood up.

"Uh, it's the CSO – Chief Security Officer," I announced.

"Huh? His report is clean," Ge said.

48

"Precisely." I leaned in, "The entire c-suite, even the CFO, has a few little dings, some forgotten snippets that nobody cares about. Grbić, the CSO, has none. He's too good to be true. His background and credit report are fabrications. I would never rent to that guy, knowing how good a liar he is."

"Great," Ge made a sour face. "We found our villain, and it does us no good. Can't do anything about it."

"You're right, *we* can't. But I know an investigator who can. Let me re-configure my phone and sign in under a disposable avatar. I'll get the ball rolling."

I put together a message to my favorite investigator, reassuring her that I survived the crash and planned to "play dead" until the saboteur could be brought to justice. I contacted her from within my blind trust persona and complained that I suspected Grbić of being the saboteur and attached the CSO's resume.

If anybody could break this guy's cover, it would be Elspeth, an impressively competent investigator I had used from time to time. The first time I used her, I asked her for a background report on myself. It was terrifying to find out how much she knew about me. Any time I wanted to find out anything about anyone, I hired Elspeth. Sent everything off to her in a fast blurt with payment through the blind trust and immediately logged off. Only time would tell.

"Wish I could call my Dad and let him know I'm alive," I sighed.

"Why not, Li? You've got decent security on your phone; you could get away with it."

"I doubt it. The CSO has already tried brutal murder, including me, an innocent bystander. If he suspects for a millisecond that either of us survived ... he'll just try again, and maybe succeed."

"I get it. I just think you're over-reacting, Li."

I buried my face in my hands and brushed my hair back. "*Over-reacting?* If I had taken *any* other grav sled, if I'd shared a ride with *anybody* other than you – I would still have a career and my family. My folks think I'm dead. Mom won't be too chuffed, but my Dad and Mark will be devastated."

"Yeah. This sucks. Neither of us deserve this. I think I have an idea. It's been in the back of my mind since I saw the first crops. The best way to make it back in one piece is to show up with Acorans in tow before the vote and make sure there's a lot of press about it. If we're all over the 'net, Megacore's CSO can't touch us. After we gain basic fluency, we've got to mount an expedition to Novy Samara."

"You want to take a group of Acorans 4,800 kilometers to the capital on foot?" I gawked at him.

"Hey, we don't have to make the slog alone. An expedition uses pack animals and boats and guides, and we can go in style. It beats the hell out of our first plan!" Ge grinned, warming up to the idea.

I stared at the floor for a minute. "I was hoping to unmask Grbić and *then* call for a ride home. But that's looking more and more unlikely. I wish I could come up with another better idea, but I can't. I agree with you. An expedition is our best hope."

Ge sighed. "I *still* think you're being overly paranoid; but if you don't wanna risk a call... it's our best option.

"Yeah, even with my security, there's no way to make sure my call isn't traced. We don't know how far the Megacore corruption runs. If we call for help, we might just call our own assassin."

* * *

#Forensic Investigation File:

AI: C-LEVEL HUMAN AUTHORIZATION REQUIRED The energy signature of the collateral passenger accompanying the eco surveyor, previously classified as neutralized, has been detected on the net. The contact was brief, and it was not an exact match. It is most likely to be a data error.

CSO: There was collateral damage? Oh. Yeah, I had forgotten about that. Do you think this represents an ongoing threat?

AI: No. I still classify this as only a potential threat. I recommend further investigation out of an abundance of caution. Do you wish to authorize immediate upgrade from background tracking to active online surveillance activity?

CSO: AUTHORIZED. Code: HEA571!

AI: AUTHORIZATION VERIFIED. Upgraded surveillance underway.

8

EXPLORATION

God, those were good days! Those first few months were golden hours of learning, my friends. Ge and I made a pact to speak Apex Jungle whenever possible.

* * *

One day, as we were holed up in a reading niche studying Acoran textbooks for grade school children (an excellent way of absorbing culture as well as vocabulary) Ge and I got to talking.

"I wasn't my mother's kind of daughter," I said. "She wanted a mind she could quote in journals. Instead, she got me – reliably non-academic. She never knew what to do with me."

Ge waited — the kind of listening that pulls words out of you.

"So, she pivoted," I continued. "If I couldn't be her legacy-brain, then I could at least be her display piece. She dressed me, staged me, rehearsed me for rooms full of people. I wasn't a person; I was a living Barbie doll she posed for credit."

I made a bitter sound. "I don't even think she heard half the words I ever said — she just wanted the silhouette of a daughter she could hold up and say: look at what I made."

Ge was quiet a beat, then said, "I know that shape. Different costume, same script."

I looked at him.

"I was one of seven; five of us boys," he said. "All engineered better than me. Stronger, faster, sharper. There was never room for me to be anything. My value was measured by how little noise I made."

He gave a dry, non-laugh. "You learn to disappear early when excellence fills every cubic meter of air."

I watched his profile in the soft bioluminescence of the reading nook.

"They weren't cruel," he went on. "Just complete. Complete in a way that left no room for me to contribute."

51

He shifted the book on the table with two fingers, almost absently. "Being overshadowed and being used aren't the same injury, but they leave the same scar: you stop expecting to be seen."

The line hit me in the heart.

I exhaled. "So, we were both scenery."

He nodded once. "Exactly."

* * *

I noticed that Ge was getting thinner, in spite of better food. "Ge, you're succumbing to low gravity and losing muscle. Gotta get some workouts in for you."

"Agreed."

We approached AckTik; she was fascinated. The concept of moving with no other purpose than to maintain fitness, was a foreign concept. But pretty soon, the Acorans fashioned a weight vest with weighted wrist and ankle cuffs for Ge. In total, the weights were just about 100 kilos.

We started running together early in the morning. I would run while Ge and AckTik swung overhead. On the way back, Ge and I would both run with some uphill sprints thrown in while AckTik swung alongside us. It wasn't a sophisticated routine, but it did the trick. Ge found some big stones and began lifting them. Ge regained muscle mass, and I kept my girlish figure. AckTik was particularly impressed.

She explained, "I swing zircuitz, want to do the big zircuit."

"What's a 'zircuit'?" Ge asked.

"We swing along marked paths high up, above the houses. Many different paths from easy to hard. The most hard of all is zircuit around all Ifka'a Kifma'a. That'z what I want to do this year."

Ge grinned. "So, to get better at swinging, you have to swing, but with extra weight and on a more difficult course. Then, when you shed the weight and face the actual circuit, you'll fly!"

Pretty soon, they descended into a full-on bro-science training regime discussion.

As long as I kept busy and turned my mind to studying the Acorans, I was fine. But in the small moments of rest, I wasn't fine at all. Ge caught me curled up in a reading nook crying my eyes out.

"Sad story?"

"Yeah," I sniffled to a stop as best I could. "It's about a girl who gets separated from her family and is trying to find her way back. I'm grateful – so *very* grateful – to be here instead of the bottom of the Jutoma; but God, I miss home! I miss my family, my friends, my news feed, coffee. I miss it all!"

Ge sat down on the couch and put his arm around me. "Yeah. Me too."

He comforted me on the couch until I was only sniveling. Then Ge leaned forward, resting his elbows on his legs, clasped his hands together, and spoke while staring straight ahead. The way that men do with difficult conversations.

"This would be so much easier – for both of us – if we were a real couple." He stole a sideways glance, and began to clown around, turned to face me. "I'm handsome," he gestured to his profile and made a muscle. "I'm house-trained... What the hell, Li. Why the friend zone?"

"You only think you like me more than you do because we're isolated together out here."

Ge looked thunderstruck. "You are an acclaimed beauty, in the top 5% of the population for brains, and – a big point in your favor – not a whiner. Yet you think I'm only interested because of a paucity of choice?"

I shrugged. "Not 'only', but a big part of it, yeah. I mean, what self-respecting academic would want anything more than a hook up with a mere fashionista?"

"Gotta admit, my first impression of you wasn't great. But now that I know you, I changed my mind. But there's more going on than that," he said. "What the hell am I doing wrong?"

"Nothing, Ge."

"Then what? I'm not good-looking enough for you? You don't like heavy-worlders? You detest scientists? What?"

"No. Nothing like that. I think you're handsome and a very impressive physical specimen. I have nothing against scientists. In fact, I admire your intelligence, and your birth world doesn't matter."

Frustrated, he cried out, "Then what!?"

I ticked off points on my fingers. "First, you're an academic. My mother is a professor of Chinese literature. I know what that life is like. Academia gets a hard pass from me. I do *not* want to be a tenure groupie! Second, my implant's wearing off. I might have three month's protection or another year; you know how it is. So, I can't get romantic with *anyone*; it's not just you.

"Have you ever thought about making a 4,800-kilometer trek through the wilderness with me either pregnant or nursing a newborn, Ge? What about giving birth in a muddy hollow somewhere with no help and no supplies? Prior to modern obstetrics the primary cause of death in young women was childbirth. How do you think unattended birth would work out for me?"

"Oh."

"Yeah, 'oh.'" I rolled my eyes exasperated. "I will not allow my *wants* to overwhelm my needs. I'm not about to get romantic with you simply because we're isolated together far from human civilization. 'Cause we will make it back. Then we'll go right back to wanting two vastly different and incompatible lifestyles. I don't wanna break my heart – or yours – on a throw-away romance."

"Oh." Ge repeated.

"So, nothin' personal, but..."

"Okay. I get it now. But I'm not giving up on you."

I smiled. "Lovely sentiment. One that I predict you will abandon once we reach civilization and we both have more choice."

"Doubt it. At least, that's not gonna happen for me."

I shrugged, exasperated. "We'll see."

"Yeah, we will," he said.

* * *

I sought out RanLing, the assistant chef. She was plump, vivacious, and wildly excited to learn about our exotic human cuisine. I sniffed, tasted, and eyeballed my way through the kitchen, and I made RanLing breaded brebola cutlets. RanLing worked right alongside me, scaling up my home recipes to catering quantities adequate for the Grove.

Then I tackled cookies. That was *weeks* of failed experiments. But I finally got there in the end. Turns out the Acorans like cookies, too. I was improving my Acoran rapidly. Then Ge got pressure blisters on his palms.

"AckTik," I began one day. "I want to make true-hand clothing for you and Ge in leather." After a few minutes of description, I managed to convey what 'leather' is. We secured some from the Grove's leather workers. I fashioned hand gloves and foot-hand gloves for AckTik and she improved her time once again. By that time, AckTik was convinced that Ge was the Mother's gift for coaching. She enthusiastically espoused his methods to anyone who would listen.

TikTik started giving us tours of Ifka'a Kifma'a. At first, just the Bay Grove. Once we were familiar with the Grove, we branched out to local suburbs. Then, we re-visited the docks. Our little lifeboat was in dry dock with several of the other Grove vessels. Ge fiddled with it to collapse it so it wouldn't run down its batteries. Not a whole lotta light or motion in a boat house.

TikTik was astonished. "Is your boat broken?"

Ge grinned. "No. It stay small for easy carry-with and only open when used."

"This is wonderful! Such a useful thing when porting around obstacles on smaller rivers." TikTik exclaimed.

"For true," I contributed, "it for sudden-bad-thing..."

"Emergency," TikTik supplied.

"Thank you. If emergency happens to boat, you use it for get away. You have emergency with river boat?"

"Yes! We lose people every year to the river!" TikTik's quills were completely vertical and quivering. He was really excited about this new idea. "How does it work?"

Ge scrubbed his face with his hands. "I can't rightly tell you. We call them 'electroactive polymers.' Tiny plants in top of boat change sunlight to electricity. On bottom of boat tiny plants convert movement to electricity. Electricity makes fabric hard and the motor work."

"How does electricity work?" TikTik asked eagerly.

Ge actually groaned. "That's months of explain. Honest, I can't rightly explain it."

I volunteered. "It better to trade silk for electric goods until your scientists learn."

We continued exploring Ifka'a Kifma'a. I found a wonderful little bookshop, the Tree and Branch. I asked TikTik for an allowance so I could buy books. After some back and forth between Matriarch and BanTik, Ge and I were given a small allowance of spending money. As I became more proficient in Apex Jungle, I realized the Acorans had a different starting point for many concepts than humans do.

Their kinship structure and the vocabulary for it was much more elaborate than any human language I knew. They had a unique term for "mother-in-law-on-the-woman's-side-of-the-family;" and a unique term for "daughter-of-my-father's-brother-who is-older-than-I-am." I sketched out the Tik family tree using titles and names to solidify my understanding. I had one hell of a branching diagram when I was done.

Then I found out that kinship charts were routinely printed for the education of children. Oh, well. The extra work helped lock it in my head. Ge was ingratiating himself. Ge was incapable of going for more than five minutes without cracking a joke. All I had to do to find him was stand in a hallway and listen for laughter. If I didn't hear anyone laughing, I checked the reading nooks.

I did a weekly storytelling session with the younger kids telling our fairy tales in Apex Jungle. A great exercise for me and a real boon to the younger mothers. Although I wasn't as popular with the kids as Ge, I found that tales of danger and death were wildly popular. The ancient tales of Pixar and heroes from ancient India, Egypt, Greece and China filled story hour. Kid's stories tell you so much about a culture. My favorite Acoran story – well, everyone's favorite – is the Dawn Mists.

* * *

What? You guys want me to read the whole thing? I don't have a copy handy. Just tell the story? You sure? God, you're as bad as the grandkids! Okay, if you will allow me to paraphrase,

* * *

In the beginning, Acora Mother was covered in thick white mist. From that mist She birthed four Mighty Beasts. Sister Storm who was covered with scales and her quills were tentacles and her eyes were black. Brother Fire was golden like sand and his quills were obsidian, and his eyes were flame red. Sister Wild was covered with plants and her quills were saplings, and her eyes were green. Brother Ice was white as the snow, had ice shards for quills and his eyes were the blue of frozen water.

They each wanted to rule over Acora and were soon locked in combat. It was a mighty war. Their battles carved out rivers and valleys. They hurled boulders so large that they created the mountains. Finally exhausted, they sank back into the mist.

Wild Sister cried out, "I perish. I must have your water, Sister Storm, to nurture life. I must have your warmth Brother Fire to nurture life. I must have your cold air, Brother Ice, to cool the water carried by Brother Fire so that the water falls upon me to nurture life. Can we not agree, my siblings, that each of us have our own domain and save life?

And the Beasts were moved by Sister Wild's plea for help. Sister Storm took the deeps. Brother Fire took the wide plains. Brother Ice took the highest peaks. Sister Wild took the middle ground and clothed it all with life. From that day forth Sister Storm gathers the waters. Brother Fire tickles the water out of Sister Storm. Brother Ice cools the waters and makes it fall upon Sister Wild. That is how we all enjoy the gifts of Acora Mother.

Which shows that you fail when you fight your siblings and succeed when you help them!

* * *

Ge had the sense to ask for any writings left behind by the first group of humans. That unlocked an invaluable treasure trove of guides for manners, customs, economy, and ecology. I understood why TikTik still mourned Anna thirteen years after her death. Her writings were remarkably astute and helpful.

9

SKILLS

At dinner Ge brainstormed with BanTik about mounting an expedition. Ge explained, "If we go our human capital, Novy Samara, with wild tale, most will not believe. If we go with Acorans, with much fanfare, they can't deny the truth."

"Hmm. Our products and books and other evidence won't be enough?" BanTik asked.

"I don't think so," I answered. "Just think about it from the other way around. What if a young couple came to Ifka'a Kifma'a with a human artifact and a wild tale. Some would believe, but the couple would not change public policy, would they?"

"Ah. Point taken." BanTik lowered his quills in concentration. "How many people do you think it will take?"

Ge jumped back in. "We can take river boat as far north as we can go, buy pack animals for crossing the mountain, and take my folding boat. We'll go over the mountains and go by foot and by boat on the other side. I think we'll need a team - mixed male and female. An expert in geography. A doctor. Someone who is skilled in bushcraft..."

"Bushcraft?" BanTik interrupted.

"Oh, yes. As far from city as we will be, we must use primitive skills - build fire, make crude tools and weapons, make primitive shelter, find game. We call such primitive skills 'bushcraft.'"

BanTik nodded his understanding.

"Ge is being modest - he's great at bushcraft," I announced. "We'll need a skilled diplomat," I added.

58

"It bad idea to prove to our people you exist, only to lose trade through bad treaty talks."

BanTik got a gleam in his eye. "You have only forgotten one thing - a Seer. Invaluable to have a Seer during negotiations. Especially if the other party does not know about our ability to See," he chuckled. "One good Seer can eliminate mountains of bree-crap! This sounds like a substantial - and therefore expensive - expedition."

"Yeah," Ge agreed.

I worried, "The problem part is getting your people to agree here before we go. If we get there, prove you exist, and make a brilliant treaty, it will all go to waste without agree from the Groves."

BanTik smiled graciously. "That is straightforward enough. We will pay for the expedition by raising money by subscription from the most influential Groves. It's done all the time to support public works. I can set our lawyers working on it immediately. I mean, once we clear this with Matriarch."

Apparently, Matriarch approved, because BanTik set to work immediately. Unfortunately, the political climate was against him. He worked long and diligently, but the Groves had significant concerns. The Flame Tree Grove worried about being sickened by strange alien diseases. BanTik pointed out that the humans who had visited thus far hadn't communicated any diseases. Frankly, he and AckTik were both of the opinion that humans and Acorans are too dissimilar to transmit disease to one another.

Many Groves were worried about military conquest. Others were concerned about the legal consequences and changing their code of laws. They worried about the complexities of establishing a fair exchange rate with humans. All of them worried about financial exploitation. But mostly, they were deeply concerned about other Groves gaining financial or political advantage from the expedition. It became a delicate balancing act of getting enough Matriarchs on board and willing to put their money where their mouth was.

BanTik began coaching me casually and intermittently, teaching me about government and politics. Told me to memorize the Groves and their matriarchs and presented me with an album of dossiers. I

59

dutifully memorized it all. The First Daughters, Grove insignia and colors, locations, honors and order of precedence. When I returned the album to him a couple of weeks later, BanTik quizzed me on it all. I must have passed, because BanTik gave me reference books about recent history.

BanTik took us to the opera. We were enjoying theater in the round. The largest assortment of tuned percussion instruments I have ever seen were arrayed around the perimeter of the stage. Some were hide topped drums, some wood, and some vertical or horizontal pipe arrays made out of glass or metal. The instruments ranged from tiny hand-held copper bells to huge vertical wooden striker plates operated by two musicians working together. They were each tuned to a different note, so that the drums produced not only rhythm but tune as well. They also used several types of flutes. Acoran voices, solo and in choir, were woven through the music.

They weren't tuned to a classic scale; they seemed to use one closer to the songs from the Middle East on Old Earth. It was a revival performance of the classic Dawn Mists. Bay Tree Grove had excellent box seats. It opened with a thick layer of mist blanketing the stage. I had no idea how they achieved that special effect, but it was impressive. Giant, beautifully crafted puppets of the Great Beasts arose from the mist and acted out the drama.

Dozens of puppeteers on walkways suspended high overhead manipulated the puppets. The puppeteers wore gauzy face masks and blended in with the dark roof of the theater so well and the puppetry was so engaging that I promptly forgot about them and got lost in the story. I thought it was a very moving performance. I was in tears when Wild Sister pleaded for help from her siblings.

I wasn't the only one. The chorus of whistles that greeted the performers at the end was deafening. The musicians and puppeteers took three bows and left. The whistling continued and they came back on stage for a final 'curtain call.' It was one of the most thrilling evenings of theater I have ever experienced.

The best part was that Ge and I understood most of it. The script was laced with archaic `Apex Jungle` which was sometimes confusing. But we were both fluent enough by that time that we made it through.

AckTik obtained special passes for us to the Provincial Library. The library was a grove unto itself with different trees symbolizing different branches of knowledge. Ge was as excited as a kid at Christmas in the barrel tree that held the biology books.

Ge marched up to a librarian, "`How do I check out books?`"

At first, the librarian was confused. Ge explained, "I wish to borrow books and bring them back when I have read them."

"Oh!" The librarian finally comprehended. "You want a *lending* library. I have heard of such a thing in the capital, but we are not a lending library. This is a research resource for the local university. We never let our volumes leave their tree. Hmm. I'll ask the head librarian if we can extend you a special membership. That way, you can read the books here, in the library, like the other students and professors. Our reading nooks are quite comfortable and well-lit."

Ge answered, "Thank you! I am honored to read your books here in the library."

It was quickly arranged, and Ge spent most of his time at the library from then on whenever he could sneak away. That's when Elspeth's report landed in my phone. Ge and I scanned the report on my phone. Elspeth is the best. But, my God, the CSO was a piece of work! Then we made our way to BanTik and TikTik and read it out loud for them.

* * *

Dear Li,

Congratulations on surviving the grav sled accident! Your instincts are on-target. The complete 12,000-word report is attached, but I can give you the gist here.

Born Mateo Dragović (his mother's surname) on the barely habitable rogue mining settlement of Paj during the worst year of the Mining Wars, he was placed for adoption because his father wanted nothing to do with him. Was adopted at age 3 by Vuk and Milica Nikolić. He was the couple's only child.

Dragović was involved in several military actions, and witnessed death dozens of times, including the deaths of other children, before graduating primary school. Uneventful educational history, otherwise; although his teachers noted he seemed withdrawn and "more sensitive" than other students. There was no attempted therapeutic intervention offered to any Paj students due to lack of funding. Scored 132 on an IQ test.

61

Milica died of the complications of untreated alcoholism when Mateo was twelve years old. He suffered head injuries from flying debris during a military action that same year. He received no treatment. His father created a flimsy false identity for them, and they escaped by performing self-surgery to remove their ID chips and stowing away on a large colony ship that had docked for repairs.

Thus, we find Maxim and Drago Petrov arriving on Novy Irkutsk. Maxim found employment as a miner; Drago enrolled in school. Teachers described Drago as a "moody child, can do good work if he wants to, is easily upset." Even then, he was known to bully younger children. Bar Mitzvah at Temple Adath Israel. There were no friends in attendance because neither he nor his father had any friends.

Drago developed an obsessive focus on body building. Became involved in pre-military training and several para-military organizations. Enlisted in the Novy Irkutsk Protective Space Force and a military ID chip was implanted. He quickly rose to the position of instructor in hand-to-hand combat. He was court martialed for "conduct unbecoming an officer" and was demoted. During proceedings received diagnosis of Antisocial Personality Disorder with possible comorbidity of Narcissistic Personality Disorder. Drago left the service shortly after that.

Shortly thereafter, he emerged again as Fenyang Volkov with a slightly modified genetic map and new personal history. He joined and quickly became a captain for the infamous Black Raiders, once again without any ID chip. When Planetary Forces dismantled that piracy operation, Fenyang Volkov was nowhere to be found. Szymon Antonius Grbić emerged with yet another slightly altered genetic map and a proper ID chip.

Grbić founded a marginally legal company of mercenary troops operating on the fringes of raw colony worlds. While masquerading as Grbić, he obtained a master's degree in security management and achieved a PhD in Cyber Security. He rebranded himself as a security consultant.

He was hired as a consultant for Megacore. He leveraged that into a permanent position. One of his managers died under mysterious circumstances, conveniently vacating the position for Grbić. Within a decade he had worked his way up to Chief Security Officer.

I have found four complete false identities, with slightly altered DNA maps, backgrounds, educational credentials, and bank accounts in widely scattered locations all linked to Dragović/ Petrov/ Volkov/ Grbić. He is prepared to act and to avoid the consequences of those actions. He also has control of the best AI on the planet. This man is a smart, ruthlessly ambitious, sociopath.

I agree with you and suspect that "Szymon Antonius Grbić," was the architect of your grav sled accident. I have contacted your parents discreetly through intermediaries and informed them that their personal information has been breached and suggested they undergo a complete security overhaul. Your father acted on that suggestion. Their data and location are now as secure as possible.

My most urgent advice to you is – *stay dead!* Immediately remove and destroy your ID chip. Grbić's AI can easily circumvent the manufacturer's security protocols. Do not return to society without maximum publicity and ironclad security in a very defensible location. Even if you manage to return to society, as long as "Grbić" is free, I further advise replacing every device you have ever used to interact with him and any device that is publicly registered to you on the 'net.

Take very special care, Li,

Elspeth

* * *

"That guy wouldn't hesitate to kill twenty-one people to keep his job," Ge observed.

"A waibeeb on two legs," I agreed.

TikTik looked horrified, quills quivering, and asked, "This is the human that hunts you?"

BanTik's quills settled into deep concern position, and he said, "That certainly changes the risks of the Expedition. If we go, and he finds you, anyone with you will suffer your fate."

I sighed. "I'm afraid so. It's so frustrating! Peaceful prosperous trade and scientific exchange derailed by the greed of a lone sociopath."

Ge rolled his shoulders like a man spoiling for a fight. "Wait. We have the advantage," Ge hunched forward gesturing broadly growing more enthusiastic as he spoke. "He thinks he succeeded. Li and I will remove our ID chips, turn off our phones, let him think he succeeded. He can't find us in the jungle without the phones. I'm pretty sure we can disguise our heat prints and electrocephalic signatures, which drones can use to locate us. If we are disguised and traveling with you, the drones will classify us as a herd of native animals and ignore us."

After a whole rabbit hole of explaining 'heat prints,' 'electrocephalic signatures,' and 'drones,' to TikTik, we continued.

"It might work," I agreed. "I can rig a mesh of copper wire in our clothing so we will appear to the drones as about your size." I gestured to TikTik and grinned. "Of course, with Ge it will take a *lot* of copper. But we have no right to ask any of you to put yourselves in danger in this way. Would anybody still be willing to sign on to the Expedition, knowing that a human predator will be hunting us?"

There was a long thoughtful pause. Then BanTik said, "We must not and cannot allow a lone human criminal to interfere the safety and prosperity of our entire civilization and all of your human colonists. We have to try."

TikTik's quills took on a very determined position. "I will go. I would not be able to live with myself if I did not."

BanTik advised, "We shall continue, but we will make full disclosure to Matriarch and anyone that we recruit. Although, it would be impolitic to share this information too widely."

"Agreed," I said.

Once AckTik understood what we were trying to accomplish, she numbed us up and cut out our ID chips, marveling that they were as tiny as mahinia grubs. You can still see the tiny star-shaped scar behind my ear. Ge crushed them into powder, and I felt much safer.

AckTik arranged for a tour of her alma mater, Ifka'a Kifma'a University, followed by lunch and a question-and-answer session with the scholars that afternoon. I was pleased to note that in spite of being a matriarchal society, men were not discouraged from pursuing knowledge. Both genders were fairly evenly represented in the audience.

We were pumped for information from the concrete, "How many worlds do your people inhabit?" to the technical, "I understand your biological science is quite primitive compared to ours. What technology do you use to replace it?" We were questioned about medical subjects, "How does being mammals affect your society?" The simplest question, from a yellow-robed philosophy professor was profound, "Do you have souls?"

They pumped us dry for nearly five hours. It was very tough sledding. Go ahead, explain the electromagnetic spectrum in a reasonable way in ten or fifteen minutes to a group of highly intelligent people who had no inkling of the fundamental prerequisite concepts. I dare you! We were drooping.

AckTik rescued us by marching onto the platform. She said, "Esteemed colleagues, we must end this session. May I suggest marshalling your questions onto leaves and sending them to our guests at the Bay Tree Grove? I am sure that Li and Ge will be happy to answer any written question they can."

Ge and I both immediately and enthusiastically agreed.

BanTik began to include me in negotiations, rather than simply introduce us to demonstrate our existence. I would show my phone's capabilities. I showed them about every photo I had stored. I looked up many statistics on the phone. The Acorans were particularly fascinated by recorded music. At first, I contributed little and spent my time studying BanTik and his maneuvering and negotiations.

Ge still worked out with me but usually squeezed in separate sessions with AckTik. They took measurements and tested her strength and agility and tracked their progress. With each week, they refined their training regimen.

One night at dinner, Ge suggested river locks to ease trade. The Acorans were fascinated. AckTik arranged for us to spend a week with a team of engineering professors as we explained the concept and built models to demonstrate.

Ge advised them, "Build them bigger than you think you need them. As soon as the limit of portage is removed the boats will grow. It is more profitable to send four cargoes at once with a single crew than it is to send four different boats."

The engineers immediately understood the economics. They began designing locks based on the maximum size boat that the river could support, rather than the sizes currently in use. BanTik arranged a royalty fee for Ge, which was very nice of him. It didn't pay off right away, but it eventually became very profitable for us.

10

FUNDING THE EXPEDITION

One night at dinner, I asked for fashion advice from First Daughter, RinTik. "I only have one pretty clothing. I can't wear it every day. Does the Grove have a maker of clothes? I want to wear your pretty silk not these old things."

First Daughter and BanTik's mother, RinTik, smiled. "Yes, we have excellent seamstresses – makers of clothing. The major problem is that our clothing will not fit you. We do not know how to sew silk for your shape."

"No problem. I know how. I can teach them."

Thus began several enjoyable weeks of working with the seamstresses. In short order, I had a wardrobe of a dozen dresses. I presented myself in my colorful new glory to Ge.

He grinned and said, "Fashion influencer, huh? I get it, now. You'd stop traffic in Brisbane."

The Amber Tree Grove representatives questioned us at length about our human technology. They were especially interested in our weapons and transportation. Then turned that info against us and worried about humans enslaving Acorans.

I think I helped there. I was gaining confidence as I came to understand their negotiation tactics. BanTik began to give me more leash during meetings. I explained, "Which has more wealth; a village with only one or two trade partners? Or capital like Ifka'a Kifma'a, with hundreds of trade partners? Answer is clear.

"Now, make idea bigger. Humans do not have wealth of a single world. We have trade with a hundred worlds. My world is richer than all Acora because human worlds each have the trade of many worlds.

67

"I swear to you on my Mother's eyes, you will grow rich on trade, not suffer abuse. Abuse is danger and expense. Fair trade is more safe and more profits. I can tell you good helper to help with hard human laws."

My little speech did the trick. Amber Tree Grove was the first to pledge financial support. They offered to put the expedition up for several days as we made our way north to the human capitol.

"Thank you, First Daughter LinLin. We need pack animals for the mountains. Can you name any? We have to leave them in the wild when we get to snow. So, we need strong animals who go home alone."

"Yes, I can suggest banderlings." LinLin smiled. "They are not as tame or as helpless as bree. They migrate from high pastures during the summer to our lower pastures in winter. They know, you see, that we protect them from wolves and have feed available all winter. Your banderlings will naturally join the seasonal migration."

"Excellent! I am happy that we not leading animals out to die!"

AckTik became Ge's best friend. I crafted a make-shift board and pieces and taught TikTik chess. AckTik taught us cha'ani, a complex strategy game with pegboards and dice. I didn't take to the intricate peg-board soldiers with ever-changing map conditions. But Ge loved it and gave AckTik a run for her money. Ge teased me that my only problem with the game was that I could get lost in a goldfish bowl. That of course, prompted a discussion of goldfish and goldfish bowls.

We entertained many representatives from many different Groves. And that's when we met KiKi. She was from the Splendor Tree Grove in the very far west. They only had a small outpost in Ifka'a Kifma'a. She came with an array of aunts to speak to BanTik about us. But she ended up spending most of her time with TikTik.

Even to my alien eyes, KiKi was lovely. Her fur was splendidly shiny, her quills smooth and thick, her amber eyes bright, and her teeth were dazzling. She was dainty and shorter than TikTik. It was blindingly obvious that TikTik was smitten.

I watched them with growing delight and amusement. I had already adopted TikTik, funny, brave, compassionate, and wise, as a brother. One night during dinner, TikTik and KiKi isolated themselves at the corner of the u-shaped banqueting table. I asked BanTik about their marriage customs. BanTik told me their dower customs; it is the groom who comes with goods and money for the bride's family.

I said, "Brace yourself, BanTik; looks like you'll need to pay TikTik's dowry soon."

BanTik was startled. I indicated KiKi and TikTik at the corner, heads almost touching as they indulged in private conversation. TikTik made KiKi laugh. BanTik's attention sharpened, and he motioned to the Matriarch, indicating the couple. Matriarch responded with a knowing smirk. She wasn't surprised at all. Sharp as a needle, she was.

The big question on everybody's mind was how to survive the mountain pass. AckTik told me that Acorans sicken at about twenty degrees and start dying at about ten degrees. They would have to time the expedition to the warmest days in summer so that the Acorans had some hope of surviving.

I asked, "Why don't you make snow suits?" After I got the Acoran word for "snow" supplied to me, I asked again. "Why don't you make snow suits?"

At first, AckTik was confused. That is when I discovered that the idea of clothing designed to keep heat in the body was an alien concept to the tropical Acorans. Acorans had zero "keep warm with clothing" technology. We talked well into the night as AckTik, BanTik, TikTik and KiKi absorbed this new concept.

I explained fur clothing, flannel and linings, knitting, gloves and warm socks. Ge contributed, too. He pointed out that migratory species that move through cold climates have adaptations. Cold biome creatures have undercoats of fur and feathers to keep them warm. KiKi said that near her Grove banderlings coated the trees with their undercoat when they migrated. The self-same warm undercoat fur that our pillows and bedding were stuffed with.

So, KiKi and I took on the mission of inventing warm clothing. Banderling fluff was easily available – but make a very poor thread when spun. Too fragile and prone to breaking. We solved that by encasing it with Acoran silk. It took a lot of tries with a local fabric producer, but we finally came up with a fine yarn that was resilient and strong enough to knit with.

Pretty soon I had a dozen knitting apprentices recruited from the local fabric producer, SekBlick. We all labored away, creating knitting patterns. It took weeks of group effort and many tiny incremental innovations. But we finally had finely knit close-fitting underwear, complete with ski masks.

I taught everybody how to do box quilting of silk stuffed with banderling fluff. We worked for weeks to attach the warm quilted lining securely and comfortably to a thick leather suit. It was hard to get a leather thick enough to be warm but soft enough to be comfortable. Then I recalled the ridiculous pre-industrial Earth fashions of puffy sleeves poking out between heavy oversleeves. I eliminated leather at the joints and replaced it with silk stuffed with banderling fluff. The Acorans ended up looking like Elizabethan courtiers, but the suits worked.

Sometime during that whole process, it dawned on me that TikTik needed a prosthetic.

So, KiKi and I started working on a prosthetic for TikTik. We could keep it secret only so long before revealing our scheme to TikTik. We needed him to test it before we could refine the design. Our first attempt was an utter failure. If it was tight enough to stay on it was tight enough to act as a tourniquet and stop all blood circulation.

After a lot of trial and error, we settled on a vest supported by thick shoulder straps and a leather sleeve. We attached a partial glove with a sturdy hook sewn into the palm. TikTik could finally swing.

TikTik said, "Well, I still swing with a limp."

AckTik and KiKi promptly chorused in protest together, "But you're *swinging!*"

AckTik and Ge got together and devised a training regimen. TikTik had never swung before, and his shoulder and chest muscles were inordinately weak. TikTik was so pleased that he overdid it several times and had to be treated for muscle strain, complete with lectures from AckTik on taking it easy.

It was coming up time to apply to Matriarch for another moon's visit. After all, it was less than two moons to the planetary charter vote. Ge said, "I hope she sees our value."

I laughed. "TikTik can swing now, thanks to us. Matriarch dotes on him. She's not kicking us out!"

I was correct. We had strengthened Bay Tree's ties with Amber Tree and Splendor Tree Groves. We had opened up new profit opportunities with SekBlick, a premium fabric supplier. Ge had improved shipping by introducing locks, which proved to be a very profitable license for the Grove. Ge had introduced scientific physical fitness training, and I had introduced cookies to their diet. All in all, the Bay Tree Grove was doing quite well because of us. We had more than paid for our keep – even at half a branch of meat a day.

One day I asked BanTik, "How many Groves must sign a petition – how do you say it, paper signed by many people to request action by the council?"

"A petition," BanTik supplied.

"Right. A petition, to have a motion entered at the General Council?"

"Twenty-seven."

"Ah. We're not at the tipping point, yet."

"Tipping point?"

"At first, only the most brave will accept a new idea, like First Daughter LinLin. Next come the early to accept. They aren't quite as brave as first, but they also like new ideas. Next, you hit the 'tipping point' when most will accept new idea. Then after time even the most worried accept the new idea. We need to hit the tipping point on the idea that Acorans and Humans must make a treaty."

After a bit of reflection, BanTik said, "Instead of approaching the Groves in order of precedence, I will recruit the Groves with the most daring matriarchs and first daughters."

There was always something going on at that large and powerful Grove, but BanTik stepped up the pace. That was the season for political cocktail parties. I was the lone human fashion-setter in Ifka'a Kifma'a. You do what you know to do, right?

I insisted on decent clothes for Ge, which he hated. It was a job to talk him out of his camping gear and into a decent suit. Once I succeeded, he was really impressive. His hair was getting pretty long by then, and he started wearing his signature braid. We were paraded in front of every visiting Grove dignitary BanTik could lure to the Grove. And it seemed BanTik had an endless supply. I was in my element, but Ge wasn't. Gotta give him credit though. He held his own.

* * *

"Hmmm? You're welcome. Just giving the Devil his due. But you're not supposed to interrupt the interview!"

"Yeah, okay. Love you too, honey. Hey, does anybody else need a potty break?"

"O.K. Let's all take ten and we can start again."

71

"Everybody comfy? Relieved? Hydrated? Good. Now, where was I...?

* * *

Pretty soon, everything was falling into place. We had the Smoke Blossom, Green Wood, Yellow Heart, and Shelter Tree Groves on board. If we hadn't hit the tipping point, we were getting close. BanTik arranged a tour of the Philosophers' Tree.

11

THE PHILOSOPHERS' TREE

When we first got there, the clearing was so huge that the real scale of the Tree wasn't obvious. There was a huge slash cut through the jungle canopy to the west. It cast a shaft of bright light onto a narrow tower of flowers on the east side of the clearing. The tower was a series of stacked terraces, elegantly arranged in a curve with tiers of different flowers at each small narrow terrace. There was an identical opening to the east with a matching flower tower to the west. Only the flowers in the heart of the sunlight were blooming. The rest were closed. The penny dropped. Each tier of flowers on the tower is a different color. It starts with very deep colors at the top of the towers for sunrise and sunset, and shaded to lighter, brighter colors towards noon.

"Li," Ge breathed, "it's a clock!" Ge spun around, taking it all in.

I stared and marveled and said, "When I heard Acorans talk about 'meeting at pink' I thought I was mistranslating. This is what they're talking about!"

BanTik and TikTik seemed both impatient and amused that it took us this long to figure out Acoran time.

"Surely you have clocks," TikTik said.

Ge answered, "Yeah. But nothing like this."

I piped up with, "Your solution is much more elegant. Wait a second - what do you do at night?"

TikTik pointed. "Moonflower beds. They bloom in time with the moons, so it isn't color, just numbers. One bed, two, etc., up to six."

BanTik directed our attention to the Tree. It was so huge I had mistaken it for more of the jungle. Nope. It was a towering Barrel Tree. The central trunk was at least half a kilometer in diameter. Its buttress roots were so large that they dwarfed the fully mature trees grafted onto the trunk. The grafted trees represented every Grove,

73

some more than others. Every color and texture of bark, every leaf shape, every blossom was represented.

Ge and I stared, mouths hanging open. "How do you graft a mature tree onto a completely different species?" Ge asked.

I asked, "What do the trees mean?"

TikTik answered Ge, "No idea, you'll have to ask one of our botanists."

BanTik answered me, "Each tree honors a hero."

We didn't have to wait in line to go in like everybody else. We were escorted inside by a docent immediately. We wandered and explored with BanTik helping to translate the docents' explanations as needed. We visited trees of war heroes, brilliant writers, philosophers, scientists, and explorers. There was one particularly poignant exhibit of a doctor whose children all died of green pox. She spent the rest of her life finding the cure.

We finally stopped for a much-needed late lunch and the docent excused herself. Then we wound our way through one last tree on the way out. As I was examining the exhibits, I looked up and realized I had lost the guys. After a quick recon, I stepped out on the balcony and realized they were all on the ground.

"Hey!" I called out to them three meters below me. "Very nice, leaving me up here."

Ge responded, "Happy to come back up."

"Oh, I don't think so. You already rudely left me."

"Well then, you come down." He grinned. Ge has a bit of showman in him, and the line of Acorans entering the Tree was just behind him.

Feigning reluctance, I crossed my arms. "Alright, but only if you promise to be good."

Ge grinned wickedly. "Oh, I can promise you, I'm *very* good!" TikTik was laughing, Kiki and BanTik were equally amused. Ge got a good laugh out of the Acorans in line, too.

I gasped. "You know I didn't mean..." I narrowed my eyes. "Well, I'm not coming down after that!"

"You can't live up there. You have to come down."

I sighed. "I will come down - but only if you swear by everything Holy to be a perfect gentleman!"

74

Ge grinned again and put one hand over his heart and raised the other in a pledge. "I swear by everything Holy to be a perfect gentleman … from the waist up."

TikTik fell over laughing, all the adults in line got a huge laugh, too. I rolled my eyes but accepted defeat as gracefully as I could and went down.

Ge and I were becoming truly conversational by that time and began exploring the city on our own. We had finally reached the stage where silence between us felt easy instead of tactical. So, we started wandering the city alone. We developed the habit of taking the public basket vines that surrounded and crisscrossed the city and stopping at random stations. The air smelled like jungle primeval and hot food.

We hadn't made it half a block before the whispers started.

"There they are—"

"Is that them?"

"Look—don't stare—"

The Acorans didn't approach, not directly; they clustered in doorways and along balconies, peering over railings as though watching rare animals. It made the hair rise on the back of Ge's neck.

He muttered, "This is unnatural. I feel like I'm walking around inside a documentary about myself."

I laughed. "Welcome to the glamorous side of not dying."

"That isn't funny," he hissed under his breath, jaw tight. "They're tracking our steps like predators."

"They're fans," I corrected. "Admiring, not stalking."

"That's worse."

A group of schoolkids pointed at him and dissolved into giggles. Ge blanched like they'd drawn knives.

"They think you're handsome," I whispered.

"They think I'm a specimen."

"Handsome specimen," I corrected. "That's an upgrade."

He shot me a look, half strangled. "You're enjoying this."

I bumped his shoulder lightly with mine. "You'll adapt. Everyone does. The first time people whisper your name, you panic. After a dozen times you stop hearing it."

He glanced over his shoulder at a knot of teenagers. "Do they ever stop staring?"

"Nope."

"Comforting."

I grinned. "You get benefits. Free dessert. Priority seating. People return your calls in two minutes."

"Right. And permanent surveillance by strangers."

"Occupational hazard."

He blew out a breath and kept walking, stiff at first. I watched his shoulders settle by increments as the minutes passed and nothing terrible happened; only more wide eyes and flicking quills, more pointing, more deliberate not-looking.

"You're really not bothered by it," he said finally.

"I grew up as a living Barbie doll display. This is comparatively gentle."

He winced. "Sorry."

"Don't be. You asked."

He nodded, still watchful. "How do you keep from feeling exposed all the time?"

"I don't," I said. "I'm armed."

Ge gave a dry snort. "Only you could make that sound like a lifestyle tip."

"It *is* a lifestyle tip."

We walked another half-block. The whispering didn't stop, but his spine slowly unclenched.

"And how do you prevent kidnapping by adoring mobs?"

"Insurance," I said, patting the hidden stunner. "Celebrity with voltage."

He laughed, actually laughed. "You are terrible at reassurance."

"And yet," I said, "you are calmer now."

He exhaled. "Annoyingly true."

He shook his head, half amused now. "All right. I'll try to look less like a spooked animal."

"You'll get there," I said. "Give it a week."

We walked on. The city flowed around us — curious eyes tracking our backs — and for the first time Ge didn't flinch at the sound of his name whispered behind us.

He glanced at me again; not panicked now, but measuring. "You know," he said, softer than before, "for someone who claims to enjoy my suffering, you're pretty good at making it survivable."

I lifted one eyebrow. "That almost sounded like gratitude."

"Don't get greedy," he said; but the corner of his mouth betrayed him.

The city kept staring, but his attention stayed on me for one beat longer than needed.

And that, more than the whispers, was what made my pulse jump. I made a mental note to spend extra time meditating to quash those feelings. Far better to struggle with my feelings than struggle with an unwanted pregnancy.

* * *

One day we ended up in the slums of the city. The trees were ancient and sickly. The stench of rot was clear. There were piles of garbage and trash shoved against tree roots with patches of bark missing. It was extremely crowded. Clouds of thin strongly herbal smoke washed over us. After some inquiries, we discovered it was ri'ippuvu smoke.

Instead of proper stores housed in trees, there were hundreds of merchants displaying their wares higgledy-piggledy in piles on the street. They offered well-worn used things and very poorly made cheap goods. The food stalls were singularly unappetizing, and I wouldn't have willingly eaten from any of them.

"I'm glad I'm with you, Ge," I said. "I wouldn't want to be here without you, or after dark, even with my stunner on me."

"Understandable," he replied. Then added resentfully, "At least you think I'm good for something."

"Oh, geez," I actually cringed. "Exactly the conversation that I don't want to have! Ge, you're a great guy. You're one of the most competent human beings I've ever known. Just 'cause we can't get together ..."

"Not can't," he growled. "Won't. You won't."

"And you know why!" Ge lengthened his stride, and I had to jog to catch up. I grabbed his arm, and he paused. "We've got to cross a continent on foot. Don't make it harder than it has to be."

Ge massaged the bridge of his nose. "Damnit, Li! This sucks. I hate the friend zone."

"Yeah," I replied with a sigh. "Sorry about that. Can't see a way around the platonic barrier, though."

"Let's get outta here."

We left quickly. It was a very enlightening visit. It was also reassuring in an odd way. It was good to have a clear view of the failures of their society as well as the triumphs. I learned more when I visited Tree and Branch and read a book about recovery from ri'ippuvu addiction complete with a call to political action.

* * *

77

TikTik sat cross-legged beside me on the massive bay tree roots, the slanted afternoon light cutting the leaves above us into glittering green shards. He tapped the leaf on my tablet with one blunt fingertip, correcting my transcription again.

"Not ka-RENN," he said patiently, exaggerating the vowels. "It is *krenn* — like you are spitting out a pebble."

I tried again. "Krenn."

He made a face — a wince mixed with a smile. "Better. Too soft. Say it as if you are offended by the sound itself."

"KRENN," I barked, over-enunciating. The sound echoed off the patio trees.

TikTik's mouth twitched. "That is how old priests say it when they find mold in the archive."

I laughed — but before I could answer, something winged and sizable smacked straight into my cheek. I swatted instinctively and half-gasped, realizing in that instant that squishing an insect *on your face* is a *terrible* idea. More grossed out than hurt, I fumbled around trying to find some leaves to wipe it off. TikTik's eyes widened — and then, very solemnly, he raised his own hand and slapped his own face in *perfect* imitation of my panic.

I cracked. The laugh ripped out of me uncontrolled, the first real one in days. He kept his expression grave for a beat — then one eyebrow went up, almost smug at having delivered the joke with surgical precision.

When I could breathe again, I wiped my eyes and scrawled on the tablet for him to read:

Was that revenge for "ka-RENN"?

He took the stylus and wrote beneath it with ceremonial neatness:

Correction. Not revenge. Pedagogy.

Then he tapped the word krenn again and looked at me expectantly — as if nothing in the universe had just collided with my face.

* * *

It took a lot of finagling, but we finally got the Scale Tree Grove to pledge support. BanTik used up a lifetime's supply of favors in those individual Grove meetings but finally hit the tipping point. The proposal for the Expedition was entered onto the General Council meeting docket.

To celebrate, BanTik took us to see our first jakapa'o match. It is a fast and furious ball game with complex rules and multiple goals each with different points value. Players swung, and occasionally fell into the trapeze netting below, at incredible speeds. But there was one fellow, the largest, burliest Acoran I had ever seen, who performed the most dazzling dives and made more points than anyone else.

Once he dove off his perch, grabbed the ball with his true hands, grabbed a lower swing bar with his feet-hands, and with the momentum of his dive, spun around the swing bar like a gymnast, distracting the goalie, before slamming the ball into the goal. It was a spectacular goal, even to my untrained eye. The stadium erupted in whistles. As acknowledgement, he did a few one-foot gymnastic twirls. And the game continued.

I asked for a backstage invite to meet the burly player and between BanTik's status and our own celebrity, we got in. We were ushered into a comfortable meeting room. Clumps of reporters were interviewing the coaches and other players. We were introduced to *Ka'alka'eipeke Guska'kippur.*

I goggled at him. "Could you write that down for me?"

Rocking back and forth in his low chair, quills quivering with amusement, he wrote it down and pronounced it for me. I was completely lost after the first four syllables.

"Do you mind if I call you "Kah?" Everybody laughed, quills flashing, and Kah told me he didn't mind at all.

I politely opened the conversation with, "Which Grove are you from?"

Everyone froze for a split second, looking embarrassed, and Kah shrugged, "Not from a Grove."

BanTik explained, "Kah is from the far north. Their customs are very different from ours."

Ge paid very acute attention, and added, "Customs that obviously encourage highly gifted athletes!"

"Indeed." I had obviously committed a *faux pas* but had only an intuitive niggling about what it was. "Did you play jakapa'o while growing up, or did you learn it all after you came here?"

"I played at home." Kah said.

"I know a guy who would love to work out with you," I turned to Ge. "It would do you a world of good."

79

Ge was enthusiastic about the idea. Once again, he immediately got lost in a bro-science discussion with Kah and AckTik. I chatted with BanTik. By the end of it they had a training schedule set up.

The next day, I went to the `Tree and Branch` and asked for a simple translation dictionary or any materials to help me learn the Northern Tribes' language. My favorite clerk seemed surprised and assured me they had nothing like that.

"But this is a huge trade city. Wouldn't knowing Northern Tribes language help trade?" I asked.

"We do not trade with them. Northern Tribes are not traders, they are raiders. They are always attacking the borders, making trouble, stealing whatever they can get their hands on. There are no books about them. If there were, they would not be popular," he explained.

I was beginning to understand the situation. "I see. Is there a history of the war with the Northern Tribes?" That, they had.

"Ge, I've discovered a major problem." I held up the history book. "This thing is propaganda at its worst. Apex Jungle soldiers are ethical, noble, and brave. Northern Tribesmen are unethical, untrustworthy, cowards. It's outrageous. I can only construct an accurate history by ignoring 80% of the book."

"Yeah. I notice the same thing when I'm out with Kah. It's pretty bad," Ge agreed.

"Looks like a simple trade argument to me. The Northern Tribes want trade. The Apex Jungle nation forbids trade by demanding tolls to use rivers and canals necessary for moving goods. The Northern Tribes are too poor to pay tolls. So, a long history of war and raids at the border."

Ge smiled. "Well, it's official: you've gone native. You worry about how Kah is treated and trade wars more than about getting home."

His comment brought me up short. He was right, I had just never realized it until then. "Huh. I miss home and my family and my life and even artichokes ... but, here..." I struggled to put into words a feeling that I was only that moment becoming aware of. "Here, hell, Matriarch likes me better than my own mother does."

"Oh?"

"Yes." I grimaced. "Matriarch does not begin every conversation with a long inventory of disappointments caused by yours truly, complete with an indexed list of all my limitations."

"Yeah," Ge said. "I get it."

The puzzle piece fell into place, and I turned the tables on Ge. "Yeah, no chance of you getting lost in the middle of the pack here, huh?"

He grinned. "Not hardly!"

That was when we visited the Great Temple of Acora Mother with TikTik as our guide. Instead of a single tree, it was a ring of interlaced trees. Each tree was woven in a basket pattern around and through the tree next to it. The trees were stunted and only a third of the size of the giants grown to house people and businesses. The limbs were interlaced overhead, so that the clearing at the center of the temple was protected from rain.

Instead of the usual hidden illumination, the twigs surrounding us twinkled with thousands of tiny blisters of bioluminescence. The floor was hard-packed earth, worn shiny by thousands of hand-feet. Intertwining branches extended out from the main trunks creating niches used as altars. In the center were four magnificent colored wooden statues of the Great Beasts. Ice Brother was particularly impressive; it appeared to have been carved of snow-white wood.

Wealthy Groves had individual altars. TikTik led us to the altar for the Bay Tree Grove. We admired the ancestor portraits displayed there, rather like the ofrendas popular on Nueva Anahuac. As we explored the grounds, we realized that the trees of the main temple were mirrored by their full-size counterparts in a ring around the temple. Those trees housed the many clerics and administrators of the vast complex.

It was virtually a government unto itself. We walked the grounds swarming with Acorans wearing green robes. We read informative signs and discovered that at certain times in history the Temple complex *had* been an independent government unto itself.

TikTik told us about cults that only worshipped one of the Beasts, and 'Sun Philosophers' who were much more philosophical. The 'Sun Philosophers' didn't worship the sun; they sought enlightenment as symbolized by the sun. They were renowned for their discipline. They followed strict schedules for reading philosophy, fasting, meditation, and exercise highly reminiscent of Tibetan monks. Once I knew, I was able to pick out their distinctive yellow robes in a crowd. They seemed to be a sizable minority. For every dozen green robes I saw, there was a yellow robe in the crowd.

As TikTik, Ge and I were peacefully touristing, three Acorans dressed head-to-toe in white charged down the path at us, screaming incoherently. It took no genius to recognize tin-hat-conspiracy-theorists in action.

12

UNIVERSITY EXAMS

I whipped out my stunner and downed the lead and the guy on the right. Ge grabbed the third guy and held him aloft. The third guy tried to club Ge in the arm. Annoyed, Ge plucked the small, weighted club from his true hand. Desperate, the Acoran grabbed Ge's forearm with his feet-hands and tried to bite Ge.

Ge turned to me. "Would you do the honors?"

I zapped idiot number three with a quick stunner blast but also caught Ge's hand with the edge of the blast.

"Ouch!" Ge dropped the white-robed fanatic and stretched out and massaged his hand. "Please take aim, in future."

"Sorry, Ge. It'll get better in a minute."

TikTik asked, `What is this weapon?` with his quills in the "alarmed" position.

`"Oh,"` I replied, `"This is my stunner. It's a small weak weapon. You use on dangerous wild animals. It does no permanent harm. This was how we overcame the waibeeb attack."`

By that time, some green-uniformed security guys arrived on the scene. The Acoran crazies were already waking up. The security guys restrained them and detained us. After what seemed like hours of questioning and an endless sea of forms, we were finally told to go back to the Grove.

BanTik did a masterful job of managing the press after our little incident. My stunner disappeared from the story, and it was Ge who overpowered our assailants. We distributed an image of Ge holding two very large stones overhead, muscles bulging. It appeared in all the daily leaves, and nobody questioned the official story. I was surprised. There had been a dozen witnesses who watched me stun those guys. But BanTik's version stuck. My stunner remained a 'secret' weapon.

As the date of the Council vote drew near, BanTik redoubled his efforts. He brought in a speech coach to help us write and refine our required speeches before the Council. BanTik arranged interviews

83

with prestigious clerics from the Acora Mother Temple and Sun Philosophers. He convinced us that demonstrating our intelligence and technology would help the cause, so we agreed.

The college professors interviewed us together and separately. We were both questioned about our beliefs, and about the prevalence of various faith traditions within our culture. I looked some of that up on my phone. I was paired with the Sun Philosopher who had asked if we had souls.

I explained Christianity, my own faith tradition, and quoted Jesus, "You shall love your God with all your heart and with all your soul and with all your strength and with all your mind; and love your neighbor as yourself." I went on to explain, "In our sacred texts, there are many parables and teaching tales and examples, but those are the only two direct commandments. Jesus claimed to be the Son of the living God, born not made, unlike the rest of us who are made by God, not born. Just as many of you believe that you are natural creatures, and the Beasts were born of Acora Mother. There are some humans who believe that Jesus was only a mortal man and a prophet. Either way, he spoke truth and wisdom, and he was tortured to death for it. What do you call a man of wisdom who is killed for professing that wisdom?"

"A martyr."

"Thank you. Jesus was a martyr, and his followers founded the church after his death. Christianity has grown and changed and survived for over two and a half millennia. I am most familiar with Christianity since that is my own faith, but we also have philosophers, like you." I described the various monastic traditions, and how there were some Christians that followed those traditions, and some philosophers who followed the practices but not the Christian faith.

I said, "There are those who believe that our only existence is this reality: no souls, no faith, no afterlife. Others believe that there is an after-life, but do not know which faith is true. Others have faith, but there are many

84

faiths. It is the work of a lifetime to sort it all out. I am not expert. I fear I may mislead you."

"Not at all." Professor Blin smiled. "It is refreshing to see faith through a different lens. To hear from an amateur, if you will pardon me, rather than from an expert who has studied every nuance."

After a few days of rest, it was time to be interviewed by the medical professors. I opened up my phone and showed them anatomy illustrations. We arranged to have a medical illustrator meet at the Bay Tree Grove to copy the illustrations. We were poked, prodded and questioned. We were asked to run on an outdoor track so they could study our body mechanics.

They all stood in awe of Ge as he demonstrated his weight-lifting capacity. He explained the body mechanics of barbells. We had Ge's weight kit sent over from the Grove. He demonstrated lifting weight overhead. He loaded the bar with 48 branches (approximately 100 kilos) of heavy stone weights. Then, he added weight to the first barbell and loaded a second barbell so they each carried 52 branches (approximately 100 kilos each, for a total of 200 kilos). Ge centered himself between the barbells and picked them up one in each hand, and with a small grunt of effort stood up, and carefully set them down. His demonstration was met with many whistles.

Ge seemed startled. "I'm not a professional athlete. There's lots of guys who train professionally who can do better than this."

All eyes swiveled my way, seeking confirmation. I looked it up on my phone. "Uh, yeah. It looks like the record dead lift, lifting it up, but not putting it overhead, was 525 kilos SEU, or thirteen branches more than what Ge lifted."

"SEU?"

"Oh. Uhm. Your turn, Ge."

Ge explained, "All weights are standardized to match what they would weigh on Old Earth to make the competition fair. Or else, athletes would train on worlds with high gravity to get stronger and compete on worlds with low gravity with an unfair advantage. So, all weights are

85

adjusted to be identical to Old Earth gravity and the weight is given in Standard Earth Units."

Then they ushered Ge into a separate interview. With him out of the way, they moved on and there were a lot of embarrassing questions about menses and reproduction.

"What is this menses you speak of?"

"A woman's body prepares for pregnancy by building up the tissues inside the womb. If there is no pregnancy, the womb sheds the lining. It's a messy bloody affair that takes anything from four to ten days."

"How does your body "shed" the lining?"

"The lining and a lot of blood drips out through one's vagina." I was determined to be calm and clinical, but I was failing. I was embarrassed and uncomfortable. I'm pretty sure it showed because the professors zeroed in on that particular exotic aspect of my physiology.

"This has not been observed with you," Professor BlanBlan said as though it were an accusation.

"I have a tiny implant that stops menses, and I am currently infertile. But my implant is near the end of its life, and I will regain fertility again once my body has cleared the implant medicine from my system."

"How old were you at the onset of your - what do you call it - menses?"

"Fourteen years old. My onset was normal and average..."

"And how old were you at your first sexual encounter?"

I gasped, "That's hardly relevant informa..."

"We must examine you to verify your claims. Please disrobe."

Finally, completely fed up with them, I resisted. "I have explained our nudity taboos. I will not disrobe. I did not agree to a physical exam."

Professor BlanBlan led the charge again. "How can you expect us to believe anything you say when you won't consent to the simplest verification?"

"Professor, I appreciate your curiosity, but not your complete lack of manners. I am a person!

Not a new lab specimen. I am an intelligent feeling creature much like you. Although I sincerely hope I am a creature who is kinder than you are! In your greed to ask questions, you're not even letting me finish my answers!"

Professor BlanBlan gestured to some impossibly young security guards. They approached with the swaggering stance of soldiers about to do harm. My jaw dropped open. After the civilized welcome of the Bay Tree Grove, I could scarcely believe my eyes. But the professors apparently had every intention of assaulting me and stripping me down right there on the spot.

"Stop immediately! I am one of only two ambassadors willing to bridge your culture and my own. Do you treat all visiting dignitaries as you are treating me? If so, it is a miracle that you manage trade with anyone!"

The security guards, three males and a female approached. Two of them had some kind of shackles in hand. They split up.

I shouted, "If you touch me, I will fight back!"

One team of two grabbed my right arm, the other two grabbed my left arm. Furious and deeply frightened, I screamed and swung my arms. In spite of the Acorans' tremendous upper body strength, they are tropical creatures and pretty small. Females are only about 25 kilos and males a little bigger at 30 kilos. None of my assailants weighed more than 25 kilos or so and I managed to fling two of them off.

Akido training to the rescue. I used my *uki otosh* technique and dropped the one with shackles to the floor and turned to the last assailant. He attempted to restrain my right hand, so I collapsed in a ball, rolled backwards, flung him to the floor. I stepped over him, and shouted, "This interview is over!"

I stormed out of the room angrily satisfied with the mess I had just created. I stepped out of the Medical School Tree and sat on one of the buttress roots doing breathing exercises.

Professor Blin greeted me.

"Oh, hello, Professor Blin."

"This posture is one of the meditative practices that you told me of?" he asked.

"Yes. I was calming myself after a very upsetting interview with your medical professors," I replied. "It wasn't a legitimate interview - by the Mother! - I don't have the words. The questions

87

were not scientific. They were designed to offend and embarrass. Then four security guards attacked me and tried to strip my clothes off! I was here to help your brightest minds understand us to support interspecies cooperation. Instead, I ended up facing a pack of ravening waibeeb!"

"Ah." He nodded sagely. "Would it help if I told you that they were not professors? They were military specialists there to gauge your stress response."

I snorted. "A foul test. How did Ge do?"

Professor Blin's quills quivered with amusement. "He grabbed the closest questioners by the front of their garments, two in each hand, lifted them off of the floor in front of him and very calmly warned, 'proceed at your peril.' They chose to desist."

I laughed. "Yep. That sounds like Ge."

AckTik came out. "I'm sorry, Li."

"I'm not speaking to you, right now!"

Professor Blin intervened. "She didn't know. If any of you had known, it would have contaminated the results."

Light bulbs began going off. I turned to 'professor' Blin. "And you are not a philosophy professor; you are the dean of the university."

He nodded.

"But why the lie? Why would you present yourself as less than you are?"

"The military required it." His quills flicked with annoyance. "I don't know why. I refused to participate in the stress test."

"Well, if you will excuse me, I have no intention of accepting any more invitations from this university," I said.

"I warned the military advisors that would be the case," he said. "I asked for more time for the legitimate professors to interview you. But with the vote approaching, the military advisors insisted."

"I will only answer questions written and submitted to me at the Grove," I said.

88

"More than fair, thank you," he agreed.

Ge approached from the other side of the tree, carrying some hand pies filled with a sweet/tart fruit we were both fond of.

"I come with consolation prizes," he said. He handed me a pie and a large clothing-protective leaf.

"Thanks! Did they try to stop you from leaving?" I asked between bites of pie.

"Yeah. Six security guys jumped on my back. I brushed them off. You?"

"Uh huh. I only had four security guys. So, I guess I'm not as scary as you. They attacked and told me they would strip me naked. I dropped them with my Ninja-level Akido moves." I explained.

"Didn't know you knew Akido," Ge said, sounding impressed.

"Yeah. A necessary social skill nowadays. I started lessons when I quit dance."

Then Ge turned to AckTik, eyes narrowed, and said, "You and I are gonna have words."

I put my hand on Ge's forearm. "She didn't know. This whole stupid exercise was a stress test invented by the Council's military advisors."

"I guess we both failed, then," he grinned. "Serves 'em right, though."

"Yeah." I polished off the pie. "But it's a good bet that Matriarch knew and consented. Am I correct, Dean Blin?"

Ge asked, "Dean?"

Dean Blin nodded in answer to Ge's question, then explained, "No, your Matriarch was not consulted."

I countered with, "Doesn't mean she didn't know." I turned to Ge. "I plan to test her when we return to the Grove. Then we'll know what we're dealing with, one way or another."

AckTik gasped, "You can't do that! Matriarch took you in straight from the jungle. She has sheltered you for moons, now. How could you?"

"It never crossed my mind until *your* university betrayed us," I darted a dirty look at Dean Blin, hands on hips, "You *earned* my suspicion."

89

AckTik's quills drooped with embarrassment, "I thought this was legitimate like the first session. I'm so sorry."

"Just promise me you'll keep quiet about this until dinner, lah?"

AckTik nodded agreement, and we sealed the deal with the Acoran shoulder-grab-and head-bow gesture.

I dressed very carefully for dinner that night. Once Matriarch entered, I very coolly said, "The next time you throw me and Ge into a nest of waibeeb, I would appreciate a little warning."

Her quills wavered between shock and confusion. Good. She didn't know. I relaxed.

"I'm glad to discover that you didn't know. The professors were not professors. They were military advisors peppering me with questions designed to embarrass and intimidate. Then they attacked and tried to strip my clothes off for an "examination." I beat them off and stormed out of the room. Ge suffered the same fate. He grabbed the nearest questioners by the front of their garments, lifted them into the air, and threatened them. They tried to stop Ge from leaving, too. Obviously, they were ineffective with him, as well."

TikTik's quills were cowed, then horrified. Round-eyed, he turned to Matriarch. "By the Mother! I have Seen it. Li and Ge were treated horribly! What were those idiots thinking?"

I answered TikTik, "They weren't thinking! They were acting out of fear. I think the idea of trade with an unknown species terrifies your military. We have weapons and transportation that you can't imagine, much less defeat. In their minds, any unknown is a danger. It never occurred to any of those morons that Matriarch would take insult from the mistreatment of her guests. Or, if they did, they discounted our Matriarch as trivial."

Ge added a heartfelt, "It seemed that way to me, too."

Matriarch's quills rose in full aggression pattern. One didn't need TikTik's telepathic Sight to feel her rage – and the power behind the rage. Matriarch was impressive, virtually a force of nature, when she wanted to be. As leader of one of the wealthiest and most powerful Groves on the planet, the woman knew how to manipulate power.

"What is the proper method for redressing an insult to the Grove from the military?" I asked.

"I shall contact their superiors at Gu'ulmani, our national capital. Never fear, I shall not let this pass. Can you identify the military officers?" Matriarch asked us.

"The leader called himself 'Professor Blan-Blan,' Dean Blin will know," I added.

"Yeah, the leader of the pack in my case also called himself BlanBlan," Ge added.

Matriarch snorted, "A famous general from history."

"Ah. Lack of creativity is yet another sign of low intelligence!" I joked. I got a laugh, which diffused the tension. But from the set of Matriarch's quills and those of RinTik, her First Daughter, Ge and I had nothing to fear. Professors 'BlanBlan' would have been safer seeking refuge from the Northern Tribes they harassed. Matriarch ordered dinner for herself and RinTik sent to her office.

Matriarch stood and said, "If you will excuse RinTik and I, we have some important vines to send."

We all made the respect gesture as she and RinTik swung out of the room and resumed our conversation. "I recognized the name of my tormentor from our visit to the Philosophers' Tree. I thought it was just a case of the professor being named after the original hero," I said.

TikTik answered, "Oh, no. We don't do that. Once a person's Tree is planted on the Philosophers' Tree, that name is forever reserved for them alone."

Ge said, "Oh. Like a retired number in sports."

Quills flashed with curiosity, so he continued. "In most team sports, the players are assigned numbers on their uniform. The numbers identify them on the field of play. The first numbers designate their position on the team and the last one identify the player. Most numbers are recycled. But some numbers are 'retired,' never re-used again, to honor a retired or tragically killed sports hero."

Quills flicked with understanding and TikTik agreed, "Yes. Precisely like that."

Conversation turned to other subjects, mostly detailed re-telling of the entire incident from AckTik's, Ge's, and my point of view. Then we discussed our Congressional speeches and BanTik's efforts to gain support for the upcoming expedition vote. He complimented us on our crowd funding effort, as he had used the list of supporters frequently as evidence of rising public support of the idea.

TikTik came up with the idea of publishing a pamphlet explaining the human diaspora, our bios, and the text of the proposed legislation. He thought that distributing it would help solidify public support. BanTik, Ge and I all agreed, and a writer was immediately hired. The writer was a team, actually. The writer showed up with an assistant who recorded everything in a very abbreviated form with a series of dots rather than regular script.

The word for this system escaped me and I finally looked it up on my phone. In pre-information age times, it was called 'shorthand.' In an amazing display of virtuosity, the booklet was written, edited, approved by the Matriarch, and published in less than three weeks. We were kept quite busy during those weeks offering interviews with the local press.

13

ARBITRATION

The power and wealth of the Bay Tree Grove was such that military and political authorities converged in Ifka'a Kifma'a to examine the accusations Ge and I had made against the "BlanBlan Professors" only ten days later.

Acorans have an elaborate set of protocols for such occasions. Ge and I got coaching from the Grove's legal advisors on what to do and say and polite forms of address to use. We arrived. I made Ge wear a proper suit. We were ushered to a spacious Council chamber. There was a large circular table, hollow in the middle with entrance and exit gaps on either side. The counselors, lawyers, and press arrived and greeted one another, chatting quite casually.

Once we were all assembled, two women from the Blackwood Grove entered and flanked the raised speaker's podium installed in the table dead center between the witness entrance and exit gaps. The Groves' First Daughter entered and dropped onto the speaker platform. One of her attendants acted as announcer and called out, "Madam Chancellor."

We all stood and made the respect gesture. Madam Chancellor started the ball rolling. "Do all invited Representatives agree to abide by the Accords achieved at this Council?"

Then, one of her attendants called out loudly, "Say you to agree to abide by the Accords achieved at this Council?"

All the Representatives had two paddles in front of them, one gray and one in their Grove colors. They all lifted the colorful paddles.

The attendant called out, "Let the record show Accord." The other attendant had shorthand gear with her and made notes.

We went through the weird tedious echoing-the-Chancellor's-questions rigamarole. I was fascinated to know that they voted to achieve accord at every step along the way. Our Matriarch swung into

93

the center of the room assisted by two of her Maidens. So, adjudicators at the table, witnesses in the center.

"I accuse Colonel MemLak of insulting the Bay Tree Grove. He abused the human ambassadors sheltered by my Grove. I believe he acted improperly without authority. I accuse Colonel MemLak of endangering an important and delicate diplomatic mission"

There was a stir amongst the attendees as the more astute realized the true nature of the legal action. Madam Chancellor then asked, "Do all invited Representatives agree to adjudicate these matters at this Council?"

We reached accord on that point. Then it was time for the witnesses. First, Ge spoke, and he spit out his rehearsed bit. They voted on whether to enter his testimony as truth in the record and we achieved accord. I went next, and polished off my testimony with, "In my opinion MemLak is an untethered weapon, just as likely to inflict harm on the people he defends as he is to inflict damage to your enemies." My testimony got accord.

Then Dean Blin gave his testimony, another accord vote. Finally, AckTik told her part of the story. Everything got recorded as a true report in the record. Madam Chancellors announcer gave everybody a one-petal break (about twenty minutes).

"So, how're we doing, BanTik?" I asked.

"Quite well," he replied. "But this is the easy part. Very frequently accord is achieved for every single vote but one or two points towards the end derails action. What is your expression? 'We're not out of the jungle, yet?'"

Then it was the military's turn. Under their system, you don't have a witness on the stand once and then once again for cross-examination. The Acorans bring the witnesses back as often as necessary to testify on every relevant aspect of the case. The military legal counsel testified that he had warned MemLak that his idea would not be approved by his superiors. He produced a memorandum leaf as evidence. Then Dean Blin came back and testified that he had advised against the stress test. MemLak's superior officer testified that he had no prior knowledge of MemLak's actions. Each point of testimony was given accord and entered into the record.

In the most surprising variant from human legal procedure, TikTik and Dean Blin were asked to give testimony about their psychic Sight of us. In TikTik's case, he testified about his Sight of Matriarch. They both claimed that we had been injured, and that Matriarch had been offended. That was all accorded and entered into the record. Then, a Council-appointed Seer from the Temple of the Mother, resplendent in elaborate Temple ceremonial robes, came in. She gave testimony that agreed with the testimony of TikTik and Dean Blin.

Testimony for the defense came next. Several witnesses testified to MemLak's sterling military record. A Seer testified to his character. "Although a bit rigid and reactionary, that is not necessarily a bad thing in a military man." Then a different Council-appointed seer gave matching testimony. It was all entered into the record.

Their lawyer also testified that MemLak was duty-bound to assess any reasonable threat to peace. We represented such a threat. Therefore, MemLak was duty-bound to test our reactions when angry or frightened. He felt that the interview was a low-impact method for assessing the risk we represented.

The military lawyer testified with a book in hand, quoting from what was evidently a set of military regulations. She cited a regulation granting MemLak authority to behave as he had. Our lawyer promptly waved her gray paddle. The announcer turned to Madam Chancellor and relayed, "Correction to evidence requested."

Accord was reached and our lawyer...

* * *

...wait a minute, I've got it here in my notes...RahTik.

* * *

RahTik marched out to the center and cited another part of the text that limited MemLak's authority when a diplomatic mission was involved. Ah! I thought, 'we've arrived at the meat of the matter.' There were murmurs amongst the representatives, as they all worked out the implications. That's why Matriarch was so careful to call us ambassadors, not guests.

The military lawyer grabbed her paddle, and another correction was proposed and voted in. The military lawyer asked, "By what authority are these aliens designated ambassadors? Why should this Council acknowledge them as such?"

There was a ripple amongst the Council as the representatives realized we had reached the heart of our purpose. RahTik had coached me for when this came up. BanTik tensed up beside me as this was the most delicate part of our Council case. RahTik hustled over to the table and raised her gray paddle. They voted to allow me to prove my credentials. BanTik and I moved to the center. I remembered from some drama, 'lawyers should never ask questions that they don't already know the answer.'

I produced my phone. I took a picture of Madam Chancellor and passed the phone over to her to be passed around the table. Many were startled and others expressed amazement. Once the phone had been handed back to me, I explained.

"This device records data, among other things. Visual data, like the image I produced of Madam Chancellor. It also holds a permanent record my personal data. It will only open to the touch of my palm."

I palmed it and presented my ID to BanTik. "Obviously, my credentials are in my own language. But BanTik is quite expert and can translate."

They stopped everything and voted to allow BanTik to translate.

I showed it to him, and he began to read it out. "Her full name is Li Catherine Shackford Carroll." He and I had practiced the pronunciation at length, and BanTik nailed it. "She is First Daughter of Chu Hua Shackford. She is Descendant of the Star Dancer."

BanTik looked up and explained, "The Star Dancer is the first ship of alien colonists to have arrived on Acora. Thus, the Star Dancer Grove is their oldest Grove. She also bears the title of Sister of the First House, their equivalent to First Daughter."

I smoothly interrupted, as we had rehearsed. "I don't wish to appear immodest, Madam Chancellor, but 'Descendant of the Star Dancer' is one of the wealthiest and the most prestigious of our Groves. My Grove enjoys first precedence. My companion is George Victor Montenegro Oates, called Ge."

Ge marched into the center of the circle and repeated the identification rigamarole with his phone. Then I spoke up again, as we had rehearsed, "Ge is an award-winning scientist among our people. We discovered your civilization by accident. Neither of us expected to become ambassadors. But the wisdom of the Mother is limitless. In Her providence, no better team could have been chosen to represent humans in these negotiations."

Pandemonium erupted. Everyone was talking to everyone else. It took nearly a minute for the announcer to settle the room back down. The military lawyer's quills dipped in defeat briefly before returning to professional neutrality.

Madam Chancellor proposed that testimony be closed, and the charges reviewed. The charges were reviewed one by one.

They reached accord that Colonel MemLak insulted the Bay Tree Grove Matriarch. The vote for accord acknowledging that the Colonel had abused Ge and I only took seconds. They also quickly reached accord that MemLak acted improperly without authority. Finally, after deliberation and several negative votes. Matriarch's voice finally settled the deliberations. Ge and I were formally acknowledged as human emissaries and awarded the status of ambassadors.

Our real objective had been achieved. MemLak was voted guilty of endangering a diplomatic mission. I was certain that Matriarch's offense taken was real, just as my distress and Ge's was real. I was also certain Matriarch had turned that lemon into lemonade within five minutes of learning of it. Matriarch was, hands down, no doubt in my mind, the best leader of either species I have ever known. It was an absolute joy to learn from her.

We were now positioned to win the greater Council vote and fund the expedition. Ge and I were going to get to go home, assuming we evaded Grbić.

Ge wore a triumphant grin. "Award-winning, huh?"

"A fellowship is an award, Ge," I said grinning right back.

Ge asked, "So, how does it feel to go from fashion guru to world savior?"

I looked skeptical, "World savior?"

Ge laughed. "It never occurred to you that we will be the first people to contact and negotiate treaties with an intelligent alien species? We're gonna go down in history, Li."

97

"Oh, yeah. That." I shrugged. "I think I've exceeded my mother's expectations; but 'world savior'" I made air quotes, "still seems like a stretch."

"Not if we manage a reasonable treaty. What do you think would've happened to the Acorans – and us – if their first encounter with humans was a hunting party seeking exotic game?"

"Eww, disgusting!"

"Exactly. That's never gonna happen, now, Li. Both species have a fighting chance for peace – pardon the mixed metaphor. This First Contact will benefit both species; not destroy one or the other."

14

COUNCIL VOTE

BanTik and RahTik sponsored debate after debate. Vote after vote. They already had a majority, but not a consensus. Supporters and allies went into action. There were rounds of behind-the-scenes dealing in favors. Matriarch spent a fortune on lobbyists and generating public petitions in support of the Expedition.

"Getting home isn't good enough anymore," I announced to Ge when we shared a reading nook together one day. "I want to get home, sure, but now I'm determined to establish peaceful relations between humans and Acorans."

"Yeah. I know what you mean." Ge marked his place in the book and turned to me. "You and I could make it to Novy Samara without the Acorans. But I would feel like a total loser if we don't succeed in introducing the Acorans."

I grinned and teased him, "So I can hope for cooperation from you for dressing properly and talking to diplomats?"

He grinned back. "Don't get your hopes up. I make no promises."

Ge and I spoke frequently in private to many representatives. Slowly, over the course of weeks, we crept our way towards consensus. The Gum Tree representative, BanGua, was proving to be a cantankerous, contrarian bastard. For what appeared to be the first time in his life, important people were paying attention to him. He reveled in the spotlight. He claimed that Ge and I were great deceivers. That he alone had penetrated the sheep's clothing to the wolves beneath.

Then I noticed an interesting phenomenon. Any time a Seer was giving testimony, BanGua was nowhere to be seen. At dinner that night, I brought it up to Matriarch and BanTik.

"What would cause a man to disappear any time there is a Seer in the room?"

BanTik replied, "He has something to hide."

"I think it is time, as we say, to play dirty. BanGua suffers from greed, making impossible demands. He also suffers from egomania. He loves

99

all the attention he's getting. It's time to use threats."

Matriarch's and BanTik's quills settled into respect positions.

"Can you arrange another meeting with him, BanTik?" I asked. "We'll bring TikTik. Then, we'll know."

BanTik agreed that he could arrange the meeting. He didn't think that BanGua knew TikTik was a Seer, as he hadn't attended the trial.

Matriarch said, "We will have to be quite discreet. Extortion is a crime and one I will not willingly participate in. None of us may be heard to issue a threat."

I asked, "What do you call it when you base a statement on a theory for the sake of reasoning. Like saying 'what if' and creating a story to support your idea? You know, to speak hypothetically?"

BanTik supplied the Apex Jungle word.

I continued, "Once we know, I will ask to speak to BanGua privately. I will speculate, hypothetically, about a foreign emissary who ruins a single individual from a minor grove to save an entire world. Hypothetically, of course. BanTik and TikTik will have to make their presence known elsewhere and promptly. So that if it ever comes up, you can truthfully claim you were not in the room."

Matriarch reached over and patted my arm. "You are not a daughter of my body, but you are certainly a daughter in spirit."

"You are more my mother than my biological mother ever was," I replied with tears in my eyes. I blushed to the roots of my hair and had to explain it was a pleasure response as turning beet red alarmed them both. I embraced Matriarch affectionately.

BanTik arranged the meeting. TikTik took one look at BanGua and twisted his face in disgust. "He likes his sexual partners young; illegally young. He has several stashed in small apartments around the city. His Matriarch would disown him if she knew."

BanGua rose from his chair, his quills in full aggression posture. He looked murderous, in fact. "You have no right to bring a Seer unannounced to a meeting. It's illegal!"

Ge rose. BanGua promptly dialed it back to 'deeply offended' quill position and sat back down.

"Tsk, tsk, Representative," I said. "People who live in leaf houses shouldn't set fires. BanTik, TikTik, would you please excuse us so that we may have a private conversation?"

BanTik and TikTik quickly exited. Ge remained standing. His looming presence intimidating by itself.

I turned back to BanGua and launched into my rehearsed speech. "I would like to offer you an exercise in imagination. A very brief story, if you will. Suppose that an idealistic emissary is determined to reach consensus on an important vote but is stopped by a lone holdout. Further imagine that the emissary can achieve her goal by embarrassing that lone individual from a minor grove. Also imagine that the emissary was sexually abused in her youth and heartily detests men who indulge themselves in that way and would gladly see the holdout consigned to the prisons of Brother Fire. Don't you think it be easy for the emissary to justify ruining a single individual to save two entire species and her own career? Hypothetically speaking, of course."

BanGua furiously spat out, "Of course."

Ge seemed startled and gave me A Look, but otherwise maintained his intimidating stance.

I smiled. "So, I can count on your support at the next vote?"

BanGua clenched and unclenched his fists, his quills flicking between horror and fury, but he finally spat out, "Yes."

Ge opened the door for me. BanTik, TikTik and the representative from the Smoke Tree Grove were standing in the hallway chatting.

I turned and spoke through the doorway to BanGua, "Thank you for a very productive meeting."

Later that night in private, Ge confronted me. "You were sexually exploited? You can't drop a bomb like that and then leave me hanging. C'mon, Li."

101

I sighed. The words sat in the back of my throat like stones. I'd never told a man this before; not directly. But Ge was looking at me like he wasn't going anywhere.

"My first sexual encounter was rape." The word hung between us. "I was babysitting for my mother's boss. He came back early without his wife or guests. He drugged me and did the deed with his kids sleeping in the next room."

Ge went very still. His jaw flexed once.

"Mom didn't believe me," I added, softer. "Thank God the school counselor did. I spent the next five years in therapy. That was the big emotional trigger for my gen mods; I wanted to erase him from my body, from my memory. I *tell* everybody it was strategic, for my career, but..."

Silence again; but not empty. Watched-silence. Witnessed-silence. It made my chest feel too small for my heart.

"I'm fine now, five years of therapy helps a lot." I managed, reflex, my old armor.

Ge exhaled as if the air weighed something. "That explains a lot." His shoulders rolled, like he was trying to shake the story off his own body, then his hands curled into fists. "If I ever meet him, he'll answer to me."

The fierceness should have made me laugh it off, that used to be my move, but it didn't. Something else rose to my mouth instead, something I had never said out loud: "The thing I still hate," I murmured, "is not that it happened; but that Mom didn't believe me."

Ge's fists eased, slowly. "I believe you," he said quietly. No vow that time. Just that.

* * *

I had the speech notes propped on my knees, running the opening lines for the hundredth time. The cadence was finally in my mouth, the argument clean, no stumbles. All the work BanTik's speechwriter did; it held. I should have felt solid.

Instead, the old voice – my mother's voice – slid in like fog: *You always oversell yourself. You're not leadership material. You embarrass yourself when you try to be important. Stay in your lane, Li.*

I shut my eyes. The words fluttered apart. The notes lay unnoticed in my lap.

I tried again. The same line — *You're going to let everyone down* — came with a physical effect now: ribs tightening, scalp prickling, palms damp. It didn't matter that Ge and TikTik and the whole Acoran science wing believed I could do this. My mother's ghost had seniority.

You will humiliate yourself. You will make a mess of their future out of sheer ego.

The thought was so sharp it made me bend forward; arms folded across my chest as though I was bracing for impact.

I didn't hear Ge approach; I only noticed him when his shadow crossed my lap. He didn't speak; just waited.

"I'm not the right person," I said without looking up. "BanTik made a mistake asking me to carry this. Someone else should deliver the argument. Someone who doesn't..." My throat closed around the rest.

Ge crouched beside the bench, so we were level. "Doesn't what?"

"Doesn't fall apart under pressure." The confession left a heat in my face I hated. "Every time I try to do something that matters, I — I hear her in my head saying I am playing grown-up. And I believe her. It's pathetic."

Ge watched me, not blinking. "That voice in your head — is it accurate, or is it just familiar?"

I didn't answer. The answer was obvious, and I couldn't make my mouth shape it.

He sank to sit fully beside me, shoulder just barely touching mine. "I have watched you for weeks. You don't crack under pressure; you perform. You crack in *private* because you were trained to expect failure."

My eyes stung. I turned my face away.

"You think you will fail?" he said, quieter. "Then fail at practice, not at the council. Keep failing here until you run out of ways to fail. That is what competence looks like in the real world; not the impossible hero version your mother demanded."

I let out a shaking breath. "I don't want to undo this for everyone."

"You won't." He said it as if stating weather. "You're afraid of humiliation, not of damage. That means you're safe to trust with risk."

His certainty landed in me like a weight set on an anchor point, steadying. The mother-voice still hissed at the edges, but it had to argue now against evidence in the room, not just memory.

"Run it again," Ge said gently, tapping the notes. "Out loud. And when you hear her; talk over her."

* * *

The next day, the Council meticulously made its way through the agenda. They reached consensus on the total amount of the Expedition funding. They achieved accord on the percentage-of-income levy on each grove to raise the funds. They slowly worked their way through the Bay Tree Grove sponsoring the Expedition. They reached accord on the first formal document to be submitted to their human counterparts. They established the powers of the emissary and the limits to that power in separate votes. Then, they awarded BanTik the title of ambassador with TikTik as his successor if he was unable to serve.

Vote by vote, inch by inch, we moved closer to our goal. As we got closer to Accord, the idea of Ge and I making out way to Novy Samara on our own, without the Acorans, was intolerable. I realized that Ge spoke truth: I had "gone native." I was now as concerned with Bay Tree Grove, Matriarch, BanTik and TikTik as I was about me and Ge. Getting home was no longer the objective. Defeating Megacore and seizing this opportunity to affect history was the objective. Failure, with its inevitable political consequences, was unthinkable.

Finally, in the last vote of the day, as the grove that had proposed the legislation, it was our turn to speak. BanTik did his usual bang-up job and was greeted by an enthusiastic chorus of whistles.

I took a few deep cleansing breaths, ignored the scathing whispers of my mother's voice in my head, prayed that my shaking knees would go unnoticed, and took the center stage.

"It is highly illegal amongst our people to steal a planet from its rightful owners. But there are always a few rare criminals who break the law. Our human settlement here on Acora is illegal under our laws. Humans are stealing the north of Acora because we do not know you exist. Our purpose with this Expedition is to establish for all time, under your laws and our human laws, your possession of this planet with full independence for all Acorans.

Our peoples can learn much from one another. Our understanding of biology is as primitive as your understanding of the electro-magnetic spectrum, which we have mastered.

The exchange will enrich both cultures materially, as well. We leap between stars. We inhabit not only this planet but over a hundred other planets. The size of the human market is almost inconceivable. For every one of you, there are a million of us. Your goods are highly desirable. Trade in Acoran silk alone will triple the size of your treasuries.

And the meeting of our peoples is inevitable. Our population here on Acora is now nearly equal to yours; and we have only been here for three generations. In our ignorance, we thought this beautiful world was empty. Free for the taking. With no constraints, human immigrants will continue to come. Eventually, we will come here, to your jungle.

It may take a generation, or even three generations, but make no mistake, humans are coming. We are coming not to conquer, we are coming for land and farms, but we are coming. And we are coming in overwhelming numbers.

If we seize this moment to establish legal equality between our peoples, we will halt further human immigration. We will come with riches and knowledge, and both our peoples will benefit.

Now is the critical moment. This moment will determine the fate of the world. Of both our peoples.

Extend the branch of peace. Because humans are coming.

Have the shoulders to establish trade and enrich all Acora. Because humans are coming.

Do not shirk your responsibilities hoping that your descendants will deal with us. Because humans are coming.

I beg you all to seize this moment. Future generations will thank you. Humans will thank you. This responsibility rests

on your shoulders. Wrest victory from
the maw of danger. Vote yes to this
Expedition!

I was greeted by a cacophony of whistling. The representatives were on their feet. I gave them the respect gesture to each quadrant in turn and turned to Madam Chancellor and repeated the gesture. Then I left the center dais and returned to my seat.

Ge gave me a big hug and whispered to me, "The hairs on the back of my neck stood up."

I whispered back, "We already had the votes, my speech was only window dressing."

A few seconds later order was restored. Madam Chancellor's announcer called out, "What say you to proceeding with the diplomatic mission to humans in the north?"

15

FEET OF CLAY

We reached accord. BanTik was thrilled, "Not one single defection! It was remarkable to pass that easily - on the very first vote."

The first time Kah showed up for a training session, I pulled him aside and asked him if he would teach me about his people and his language. His quills flashed in surprise.

"You wish to study Northern Tribes and learn my tongue?" He asked.

"Yes, of course," I answered. "I am not of the Central Republic nation, and I bear you and your people no ill-will. In fact, it may be more advantageous for my people to trade with you Northerners than with the Central Republic. Or, at least split the trade between your nations."

Kah rocked back on his haunches, cocked his head to one side, rippled his quills as he thought it over. After a moment, Kah agreed. I went through the same basic word vocabulary as I had with TikTik. We set up a half-hour appointment prior to each workout session he had with Ge and AckTik.

The Northern Tribes had a smaller and less hierarchical kinship networks than the Apex Jungle nation. A few days later when I was discussing it with TikTik, he assured me that the Northern Tribes were more socially primitive.

I gave him the gimlet eye. "_Not_ more primitive. Equally sophisticated, just different. Humans live in nuclear families." That was a whole rabbit trail in and of itself; once I explained the bizarre and alien notion of a nuclear family, we continued.

"Humans work together in large groups by choice forming companies and teams flexibly based on the needs of the project, not based on kinship. That does not make us more primitive. We have

107

conquered the stars, TikTik, while your people are still trapped on the planet of your birth. We are not primitive. We are just different. This is also true of the Northern Tribes."

"You sound like a matriarch!" TikTik exclaimed.

"Then your matriarchs speak truth and wisdom," I grinned, recognizing the compliment TikTik intended.

"Why aren't you studying to be a matriarch?" TikTik spread his quills in genuine curiosity.

I laughed. "First, it is not a career opportunity available among my people. Second, I wouldn't want the responsibility. I see the burden your Matriarch carries, how tired it makes her. I want no part of it, even if the opportunity presented itself."

"Such a waste of talent," TikTik said sadly. "You will make a brilliant matriarch when you are older."

I rolled my eyes. "You and my father!"

"What?" TikTik's quills flashed.

"My father says I have 'an ocean of talent, all of it less than two buds deep,'" I explained, translating centimeters into Apex Jungle measurements. "My mother can't understand why she birthed one talented child, my brother, and one so untalented, me."

TikTik's quills splayed out in shock. "I don't understand. How can they be your parents and know you so little?"

"Oh, TikTik, I think they know me better than you do. I have never completed my education because I am too flighty to settle down and concentrate on finishing. In fact, I've never achieved anything in any arena. I know you don't see it, but I am considered to be quite pretty amongst my own kind. Every bit the equal of KiKi. But that and the ability to converse well is all that I offer. I am not good at academics or well, anything. But I'm shrewd enough to use my good looks to my advantage."

TikTik folded his quills down in thought. Then he said quietly, "If that were true, and I do not believe it to be true, how do you explain your brilliant political negotiation with the Amber Tree Grove? If you are so bad at business, how have you created new fabrics and a new branch of the textiles industry from nothing?" TikTik seemed exasperated. "Besides, that is not what I have Seen of you. I have Seen your talent, your character. You are the only one who doesn't see it. Once you develop the confidence to be the matriarch you are capable of being, you will be unstoppable." TikTik placed a gentle true hand on my forearm and said, "Sometimes parents remember a child's awkward development and do not appreciate their child's talents when their child is an adult. Your parents are wrong about you, Li."

I smiled. "You say the sweetest things, TikTik."

His quills flickered. "Ah. You do not believe me." He shrugged, his quills rippling. "You'll figure it out." Then he grinned, his quills perking up. "You'll owe me one when you find out I'm right!"

"Alright," I grinned. "IF you're right, I'll owe you one."

* * *

When I made that promise so casually, I was certain that I would never have to deliver on it. Little did I know at the time that one simple, superficial, promise would change the fate of worlds. But I'm getting ahead of myself. Because back then, I was not the only one suffering from a crisis of confidence.

* * *

As TikTik and I became closer, he shared his journey with bullying. Even when he wasn't teased by the other kids about his disability, he was brutally excluded from participating in their games because of it. His mother, who had shielded him from the worst of it, died of a mysterious untreatable illness when he was just entering adolescence. Aside from grief, he was suddenly exposed to the full intensity of the bullying. That was when the gift of Sight showed up. That's when he learned to See people to protect himself and diffuse threatening situations.

109

But it was a case of too little too late in some ways. TikTik never fully regained his confidence. He told me about standing on the highest viewing platform on the tallest tree in Ifka'a Kifma'a and visualizing throwing himself off. It was only the force-feeding of love and admiration from Matriarch and his father that forestalled suicide.

I shared my lost dance career story. TikTik's quills quivered with agitation. "I can See. There's more to it than that."

I sighed. "I don't think I'm ready to share that particular story, TikTik."

"I think that unless you do, your wound will only fester," he replied.

So, I told him. "One week after my fourteenth birthday I was babysitting for the Dean of my Mom's department. He came back before his wife and guests did. He drugged and raped me. The bastard dropped me off blocks from home. I was so high that I struggled to stumble up to my own front door. It took forever to thumb the lock open. When I told my mother the next morning, she punished me for lying." I was in tears when I finished.

TikTik's quills twitched with horror, and he gasped, "Your own mother didn't protect you?"

I shook my head sadly.

TikTik embraced me and let me cry on his shoulder. Several things became clear to me at that moment. First, I felt more at home in the Bay Tree Grove than I ever had at home. Second, I was more useful in Bay Tree. Here, I mattered. As much as I missed home, I realized how shallow and unfulfilling my life had been. I was ambitious and did well but got little satisfaction from it. Here, amongst the Acorans, what I did actually mattered.

When I was done, he very gently said, "Do you realize that the attack is not what wounded you? Your mother's betrayal is the real hurt. That is why you seek only the wealthiest suitors, so that you can escape her and feel safe? That's why you can be so singularly focused on making a career of your beauty but too scattered to pursue any other ambition. That's why your view of yourself is so distorted. That's why you reject Ge. Your mother has made a profound

110

error in undervaluing you, Li. You must not let her error destroy your life."

TikTik was the best therapist I have ever known, of either species. He was right, too. I found that after I unburdened on him, I was less emotionally reactive, less prone to depression. I was also more apt to speak my mind. I think the days of withdrawal and verbal evasion was pretty much over after that.

I don't remember how I found out, but only a few weeks after the vote a news story broke, exposing BanGua's misdeeds. I had nothing to do with it, but I'm pretty sure the timing was not an accident. I turned to BanTik, "I don't know how you did it, but thank you!"

"Did what?" he asked looking blandly innocent; but not quite innocent enough. There was a devilish gleam in his eye and a smug set to his quills that he couldn't disguise.

I don't remember if it was a few days before my conversation with TikTik, or if it was a few days after, but Ge also came face to face with his own humiliating limitations. I walked in on him in a small library on the north side of the tree that we both favored for studying. Ge immediately turned away from me, but not before I saw the tears in his eyes.

"What's going on, Ge?" I asked as gently as I could.

"Ten years. I wasted an entire decade being mis-educated and uneducated. I thought I understood biology! After reading the notes from the last eco-survey team, I got some inkling of how bad our understanding of biology is and how poor my education was. Lars, from the last team, suggested *Introduction to Biology*." Ge gulped. "It's a textbook for ten-year-old children. Hell, even at that, it's challenging. Good God! There's a section in here on the quanta physics of photosynthesis. For ten-year-olds! Everything I thought I knew is either wrong or useless!"

"Quite a blow," I sympathized.

"Devastating," Ge's shoulders slumped.

"The good news is once you get over feeling stupid, you'll be able to see the potential," I said.

"The potential?" Ge asked with elaborate patience.

"Uh-huh. Potential," I answered, getting into the swing of things. "Do you think for one minute that I would be able to wade through Acoran science and translate it so that human scientists can learn and benefit from it? No. I could not, and you know that I could not. But you *can*. Who else do you know has a post-doc in xenoecology and

111

speaks fluent Apex Jungle? Who else cares enough to devote an entire decade to learning human science, and what looks like more hard graft to master Acoran science? You! That's who. My God, Ge, you'll be a modern-day Prometheus. You're about to set the world of science on fire! Hell, there may even be a Nobel in it for you."

He looked completely shocked. So, I switched to teasing to knock him out of it.

"Assuming, of course, you stop feeling sorry for yourself long enough to actually learn Acoran biology."

A huge grin spread across his face. I could almost *see* his energy ramping up. He bounded out of his low couch, grabbed me in a big bear hug around the waist and tossed me into the air. Once he calmed down enough to put me down, I suggested, "Ask AckTik for help. She's good at this and will be able to steer you in the right direction."

I was disquieted. That brief physical contact awoke...longings. Longings that I was in no position to satiate. Longings that I was convinced were dangerous to me emotionally and physically. I meditated and prayed. I think I kept up appearances fairly well.

Ge began to study like a man possessed. He gobbled down books and information at an astonishing pace. AckTik told me a few weeks later that Ge had made it through the equivalent of three Acoran years of study in only a few short weeks. AckTik was hard-pressed to answer some of Ge's questions. Ge was obsessed with finding out *how* the Acorans had arrived at the knowledge presented as facts in the book. AckTik recruited an eminent professor, DanBlin, from the Ifka'a Kifma'a University to explain.

* * *

Hmm? Yes, the very same DanBlin that co-authored *A Biology Revolution in Five Volumes*. One day DanBlin told me, "I don't know what you did to set his fur on fire, but I have never had the pleasure of tutoring a student so hard-working."

* * *

Of course, I passed that gem along to Ge. He grinned. "I notice that the harder I work on my studies, the less you parade me around like a show pony at cocktail parties. Win-win in my book! No chance of me stopping now.

"Besides, this is fascinating. I found out that the porcelain sculptures that you admired in the meeting room are made of the high-silica walls of gourds. Once the glass gourd flower is pollinated, they slap a carved wooden mold over the fruit bud, and the fruit conforms to the mold. They get incredibly intricate shapes that way."

Ge laughed. "I was thinking about our first contact and planetary settlement laws the other day. It dawned on me that our laws assume that we need to *protect* indigenous populations. The Acorans can engineer plagues targeting human crops and farm animals that would never disturb their own ecology. They could starve us out in a single crop cycle. We need to come to terms with them to protect *ourselves.*"

"Sobering thought," I replied.

"I finally figured out how they graft mature trees of different species onto the Philosophers' Tree, Li. It's brilliant! But they only use open wood-fueled forges. Those only get to about 1100 degrees or so. They can handle tin, copper, gold, and zinc but they can't even manage silver. That's why metals are ornamental, not utilitarian for them."

I was happy for him. Ge was in his element. Ge told me later that he and DanBlin had already come up with the idea for *A Biology Revolution.* The books emphasized how the Acorans acquired their knowledge. Ge included complete instructions for reproducing and verifying Acoran research.

Kah adopted the true-hand gloves that AckTik and Ge were using for swing practice. He improved so quickly and dramatically that his entire team adopted the gloves. Pretty soon it was a huge controversy with the ruling authorities of the sport. They debated whether the gloves constituted cheating or were an innovation that should regulated. They eventually came down on the side of "innovation," but it was a close thing.

Kah and I then turned our attention to coming up with good foot-hand gloves which I immediately adapted for the Expedition. The whole thing – the Expedition, I mean – nearly came to a screeching halt a few days later.

We were at dinner and BanTik was complaining about 'Rusties,' a pejorative name for Northern Tribes. He claimed they wanted to use the canals and waterways but were unwilling to pay for the privilege. Then, he cracked a joke. "What has one million legs and the combined intelligence of a bree foal? The entire nation of Rusties."

* * *

113

I – ahem – well, I sort of went off on him. I didn't mean to. 'Cause I didn't think that was wise in front of Matriarch. But I did. I had just finished another lesson with Kah, who I greatly admired, that very morning so BanTik's attitude really stung.

* * *

"I am ashamed of you, BanTik, now that I have discovered what a hypocrite you are. You entertained Kah earlier today – invited him to this very tree – and the instant his back is turned you abuse his people. What do you say about me and Ge when we're not in the room? Are your titles and riches not enough for you? You feel the need to belittle the Northern Tribes so you can feel more important? Where is your compassion? Have you misplaced your heart? Where is your sense of justice? Have your ethics gone missing?"

I stood so that everyone had to crane their necks to see me. "Your policies are not calculated to defray the cost of maintaining the shipping lanes OR to bring peace and save lives. Your policies are designed to trap the Northmen in poverty. No wonder they hate you and resort to murder and plunder!

"The answer to your toll problem is blindingly obvious. Levy the tolls on the way OUT, after the Northerners have earned enough money from trade to pay them. That would enrich your nation and put an end to the border wars virtually overnight. That is a simple solution you would have seen for yourself if you were not blinded by self-serving, unjust, and ignorant bigotry. Now, if you will excuse me, I have lost my appetite."

I stormed out. As I passed Matriarch, I noticed she was paying very acute attention, her quills poised in deep thought. TikTik said, "I tried to tell you, Dad," and I was out of there. I went to my room and turned on a meditation recording on my phone. When I was in the last five minutes of the meditation and my heart rate and adrenaline had returned to normal, there was a knock at the door.

"Li?" TikTik's voice came from the hall. "Matriarch would like to see you."

"Coming," I replied. I switched off the meditation, unfurled myself and answered the door. "How much trouble am I in? I mean, are Ge and I getting kicked out or anything?"

"Kicked out?" TikTik asked.

"An expression meaning 'asked to leave and forcibly removed, if necessary,'" I explained.

"Ah. No, it will not come to that." TikTik's quills quivered with amusement. "It is not very often that my father gets a thorough, and well-earned, scolding. Your little speech is the talk of the Grove."

I groaned. "Better and better! Now I've offended Matriarch."

TikTik laughed. "You really don't have any idea how Matriarchs think, even though you are one. Matriarch is as amused as I am. She always thought that BanTik's neck was too big for his collar."

"Oh. So why does she want to see me?" I asked.

"No idea." TikTik shrugged. "My bet is on subtle, politically astute, and calculated way to gain advantage for Bay Tree Grove."

TikTik ushered me in to the Matriarch's chambers. Seated next to her in a comfy conversational nook was her First Daughter, RinTik, and two younger nieces but no servants attended us. So, it looked like this was going to be a training session for Matriarch's offspring.

I crouched down in the full respect posture. "I apologize for disturbing your meal, Matriarch."

"You apologize for the disturbance, but not for scolding BanTik?"

"I will not apologize for my opinion. BanTik deserved to be scolded. His attitude was in immediate need of adjustment. You know, his neck is sometimes too big for his collar."

They all laughed. Matriarch's quills were still quivering with amusement when she said, "So, tell me, what is your position in your Grove?"

115

"I am the only daughter of my mother, and I am Descendant of the Star Dancer. The Star Dancer was the ship that transported the first colonists to this planet. If you want to seed the stars with your offspring, you want to send people with the best chance of success, right? So, the first colonists on the Star Dancer were carefully screened for high intelligence, adaptability, and genetic soundness.

"Being Descendant of the Star Dancer is prestigious. Once the first-generation colonists succeed, then anybody can come; good, bad or indifferent. So, you quickly acquire a broad range of humanity. But the founding core of Colonial society, is always our best and brightest.

"I am also Sister of the First House. My grandparents established many of the legal structures here. So, I have the Right of First Speech. I can introduce new legislation verbally at any planetary government meeting without any legal preamble."

The Matriarch was amused. "And yet you still maintain that your people have no Matriarchs?"

"Well, not the way that you do." I smiled. "I never sought political power or influence – I never even considered using my family's position in society for advantage. I always thought my titles were dusty relics of little utility. I'm changing my mind about that."

Then we got into the weeds. I explained the politics and legislature, and governance. Matriarch wanted me to guarantee that Bay Tree Grove got first priority in all trade negotiations.

"Sadly, that is beyond my power. I can suggest, I can educate, I can influence, but I cannot promise. My strongest recommendation is to hire my father's best friend, Erwin Cheong Ben Joseph. He is the best lawyer I know of. His counsel will assure you get the best terms possible."

She accepted my limitations. I noticed her drooping. "Matriarch, you are fatigued. Please let us continue these talks over the next few days."

RinTik and her nieces agreed and urged Matriarch to rest. We conferred many times over the next few weeks hammering out a plan for negotiating trade between Bay Tree Grove and humans. It wasn't entirely one way. I was learning a lot from Matriarch.

In only a few days, I realized Matriarch was grooming me to be a tool for her Grove. I heard TikTik's voice in my head, "My bet is on subtle, politically astute, and calculated ways to gain advantage for Bay Tree Grove." Indeed, you were correct TikTik! I didn't mind, though. I was thrilled to be learning from such an astute leader.

During one of our talks, I asked her to propose legislation to change the toll structure as I had advised.

"That will be difficult," she said. "There are many more representatives with BanTik's attitude than with yours."

"I understand, Matriarch. But you are the Bay Tree Grove Matriarch. You can suggest, you can educate, you can influence. You don't even have to introduce the legislation. If you proceed with the subtlety and skill that I know you for, the idea will take root, and another Grove will propose it. My bet is on the Amber Tree Grove as they suffer greatly from the border war and are very open minded. But I leave that to your judgment."

"It will be the work of years and cost a fortune," she said.

"That is my greatest worry. The time it will take. Our human legislators may not wish to invite you to trade in full partnership. Not with the border war still active. No, humans will be much more willing to offer full trade privileges without the border war to contend with," I advised her. "I have every confidence in you. And I can tell you how we dealt with similar integration problems from our own history. I will not leave you unsupported."

She eyed me, her quills indicating deep thought. "No. I know enough about you to know that you will support me. Very well, as you are willing to negotiate on our behalf, I shall negotiate on yours."

"Thank you, Revered Matriarch." We grabbed each other's shoulders, although I had to lean down rather far, and we did the Acoran nod to seal the deal.

16

MOUNTING THE EXPEDITION

It was shortly after that when I discovered BanTik's daughter, LemTik, was pregnant and expected to give birth any day. The entire clan was abuzz with the news. One morning, I awoke to a celebration. LemTik's daughter had navigated her 'first birth' and was now safely ensconced in LemTik's pouch and securely attached to a nipple.

Ge grinned when he delivered the news. "Fascinating. They're marsupial, so "first birth" is the graduation from in utero to the pouch. Second birth is when the baby pops its head out for the first time and gets named."

I got all teary-eyed. Believe it or not, hearing about LemTik's first birth, awoke an overwhelming array of primitive instinctual impulses in me. Ge noticed.

"Ha! I knew it," he said triumphantly. "You've come down with 'baby-itis.' The condition of wanting a baby when your friends announce their pregnancies."

"Busted," I replied. "I want to make babies. I just don't want to do it in a jungle over 4,500 kilometers from home."

Ge got all fake-sincere. "Is it the jungle or is it me? 'Cause I'm happy to help you out…"

"No. It's the jungle." I shrugged, "Or, more accurately the jungle and a cross-continental hike."

"Damn," Ge said. "I hate patience. I get it. But I'm not giving up on you."

I smiled. "Lovely sentiment. One that you will promptly abandon once we reach home and we both have more choice. We want two completely different lives, Ge. Mutually exclusive ambitions."

In private it was much more of a struggle. Ge was handsome, smart and smitten. Even though he was the class clown (there was rarely a moment when Ge didn't crack a joke or show off) and his ambitions were diametrically opposed to mine; I admired him and

I worked *very* hard not to develop deeper feelings for him. I spent a lot of time meditating to deal with my feelings, in fact. I was terrified of getting pregnant and one thing leads to another; so, I maintained a strict no-touching policy.

One day while I was working on my Acoran with TikTik, I asked, "Why haven't you proposed marriage to KiKi?"

TikTik looked startled, then his quills settled sadly. He held up his withered hand and sighed. "She's so beautiful; she will never accept me."

I snickered. "She doesn't *care*, TikTik! She lights up whenever she sees you. She's a lot more interested in *you* than in your true hand."

TikTik looked at me skeptically. "Even if that's true, her family wouldn't accept me."

I rolled my eyes, exasperated. "TikTik! You're smart, you can See, you're from a large and powerful Grove, you're rich, and you worship the ground KiKi walks on. What Matriarch wouldn't want that for one of her granddaughters?"

His quills wavered uncertainly. "You think so?"

I smiled. "I *know* so."

"You're a stranger to our customs..."

I interrupted him, "Ask Matriarch. She'll tell you the same thing. We may be very different in body and culture, TikTik, but apparently females are females the whole galaxy through. It's a sure bet that Matriarch agrees with me."

The next day, TikTik told me, eyes round and quills spread in wonder. "You were right! Matriarch was annoyed that I was taking so long. She has already begun negotiations with the Splendor Grove Matriarch."

"Well, what's your next step?"

"Gifts. I must present KiKi and her maternal line with gifts," he looked worried. "I know what KiKi would like, but I'm clueless about her mother and her Matriarch."

"Ask your father. Or better yet, get a book about it," I suggested.

"A book?"

"Oh, you think you are the first and only nervous suitor in Acoran history?" I teased him.

120

"Oh. Yeah." His quills flattened with embarrassment. "Probably not."

TikTik and I went to the Tree and Branch bookstore, and I talked to a clerk I knew there.

"Another round of children's books today?" he asked.

"Nope." I smiled at TikTik. "Nervous suitor. We need a guide to courtship gifts."

The clerk smiled. "I have just the thing."

TikTik bought me the Tale of GuanKin – a sweeping historical saga that Acorans are required to read in school – and we both left happy. Then Ge and I were treated to an up-close-and-personal introduction to Acoran courtship.

The first gift to the Matriarch is typically a sculpture or *objet d'art*. I helped TikTik out with that one. I pointed out that the Splendor Tree Matriarch dressed in subtle elegant earth tones. I advised him that Matriarchs decorate their Groves with their favorite colors. Therefore, the gift should be in those tones.

TikTik presented her with a gorgeous statue of Sister Wild covered and delicately scented with the soft lovely shades of Bay Tree bark. Matriarch approved, and evidently, so did the Splendor Tree Matriarch. TikTik got an encouraging note advising him that a gift to KiKi's mother would be well-received.

The gift to KiKi's mother should be useful for the household. Sets of dishes, kitchen implements, linens, etc., are appropriate. Matriarch gave him the hint that KiKi's mother said she was shopping for a new centerpiece. TikTik commissioned a centerpiece fashioned to look like a Splendor tree. The leaves were executed in semi-precious stones. It came with an elegant tray and matching condiment containers. It was another hit.

The book advised silk or clothing for the bride gift. But TikTik said, eyes sparkling, quills in their excited position, "I have a better idea." He arranged for a basket lined and padded with the most gorgeous celestial blue silk, and nestled within curled up for a nap, one of Buk's offspring. TikTik confided in me, "She fell in love with Buk and mentioned she would love to buy one of his pups."

Negotiations went well. Everyone teased BanTik about the expense of off-loading a son. The wedding was planned for the secluded glade in the center of the Grove. Everybody dressed up in their best clothes.

121

The staff outdid themselves. They draped the trees with fruit garlands (for fertility) and lanterns (for hope). Hundreds of chairs were set out.

KiKi and TikTik walked in holding true hands. Both Matriarchs were brought in seated on hand-carried sedan chairs. The betrothed couple sat down on cushions facing each other and clasped hand-feet and true-hands together. The green-robed Acora Mother officiant had the Bay Tree Matriarch swear under oath that she would give up her great grandson. Then the priestess had the Splendor Tree Matriarch swear that she would accept TikTik as her own offspring.

Then Kiki and TikTik swore oaths of life-long fidelity. They were greeted by a chorus of excited whistling. TikTik picked KiKi up and carried her over to her Matriarch and set her down. The Matriarch kissed them each on the forehead. Then, they moved over to our Matriarch, who was in tears. She kissed them each on the forehead.

Everyone erupted from their seats whistling and many excited hugs were exchanged. Matriarch was consoled by RinTik and several of her granddaughters on the loss of her favorite great-grandson. The staff swooped in and delivered food to perimeter tables and the party lasted until well after the stars came out.

Every sentimental and romantic wedding scene from every single rom-com I had ever seen passed through my mind. On the whole, I think the Acoran ceremony had them beat. Contrary to custom, KiKi and TikTik stayed at the Bay Tree Grove and planned to return to Splendor Tree Grove after the Expedition. They were both blindingly, adorably happy.

It was time to assemble the Expedition team.

"Obviously, as the appointed ambassador, you're coming, BanTik," I declared at our first planning meeting. "I also suggest we invite KiKi, since TikTik is your appointed successor, and it would be cruel to separate them. They already know about Grbić, but TikTik doesn't care."

"Yes," he replied. "His Sight will be very helpful in negotiations. And you're right. The Expedition is so important that we all feel it must be done, regardless of the risks. Should we bring a historian to record our journey?"

I sighed. "Hmm. Ge and I will be recording everything on our phones, so I don't think that will be as important as having a doctor on the team. What about AckTik?"

Ge agreed. "AckTik is an excellent doctor, but she is also athletic and will fare well on this grueling journey. She's got a streak of adventure in her. I don't think she'll mind the danger."

After days of meetings, invitations and negotiations, we had our team. Me and Ge, BanTik, AckTik, TikTik and KiKi. Ge requested Kah. His strength, agility, and greater knowledge of the geography of the mountainous north would be valuable. After some back-and-forth negotiations with Kah's employers, we were able to arrange a sabbatical year for him, and he agreed to come.

We planned to use our emergency boat, the only lightweight collapsible boat available to us, to negotiate the Irtysh River. As large as Ge was, we had reached capacity.

After a whirlwind month of preparations and leave-taking, we were all packed and ready to travel onboard Matriarch's yacht.

17

DEPARTURE

Naturally, Matriarch took the opportunity to flex. We walked from the Grove to the main road as a group, each shouldering our backpacks. Representatives from the local news leaves and historians from Ifka'a Kifma'a University accompanied us. Matriarch led the way in a sedan chair. Her First Daughter and five of her other female offspring, each of them exquisitely dressed and dripping in jewels, were her Maidens. They carried the chair. Representatives from each Tree in the Grove followed.

At the main road, Matriarch had arranged for bree-wagons to convey us to the docks. They were the largest, most elegantly decorated bree wagons I had ever seen. The wagons were fashioned from the light-toned bay tree wood and were polished to a high shine. Each sported the swirling Bay Tree Grove logo and was drawn by a team of four bree. The bree were draped with colorful silk banners. The effect was richly ceremonial, but restrained, in keeping with Matriarch's elegant taste.

I briefly attempted to calculate the value of the jewels and equipment in use and promptly gave up. The display of wealth was staggering. I gotta admit, Matriarch had *style*.

Ge said, "Jesus! Matriarch could have paid for this expedition out of her pocket change!"

"And miss the opportunity to forge a political alliance already disposed to accepting a trade treaty?" I asked. "Oh, no. She's far too clever for that."

"What are you grinning about?"

I replied, "If Matriarch ever gets off-planet, PR firms will have to watch out! All their fancy-pants statistical analyses and psych profile response projections are nothing compared to Matriarch. She is – hands-down – the best publicist in the known galaxy."

Ge laughed. "True."

Matriarch and her entourage were settled into the lead wagon. The wagon was equipped with a rack designed to accept the sedan

124

chair. The treaty negotiation team got into the second wagon, and everyone else was distributed in the wagon train that followed. As we made our way to the docks, more and more Acorans lined the path. We were greeted with whistles and shouted good wishes. There was the occasional heckler, too. But they were rare.

"Ge," I said. "We're getting such a reception; I wouldn't put it past Matriarch to have seeded the route with boosters."

"Boosters?" Ge asked.

"Yeah. Staff and relatives and friends who warm up the crowd and amp up the response. You know, like the opening act for a band."

"Yep. Sounds like Matriarch."

We arrived at the dock. The dock was decorated with colorful swaths of fabric. Woven plaits of flowers disguised less attractive utilitarian features. A drum line edged the dock. All the drummers wore Bay Tree Grove colors. They carried an impressive array of wooden, leather, glass gourd, and metal instruments.

A huge crowd had gathered to see us off. Acorans swarmed the route to the dock. They were perched on every branch. They gathered on the swing-ways. They crowded the balconies and windows of the nearest commercial buildings. There were large flipcharts scattered through the crowd with Bay Tree Grove staff attending each one.

Once we were all off of the bree wagons, staff rushed forward with sturdy support blocks and the Matriarch's Maidens settled her sedan chair on the blocks so that it stood about half a meter above the dock. BanTik climbed up on the front of the sedan chair and with a megaphone in hand, began to address the crowd.

"I must inflict a speech on you for if I don't Revered Matriarch will have my fur." His comedic timing was perfect, and he got a nice laugh.

"We leave now on a mission to secure our future. Not just the future of the Bay Tree Grove, the future of all Acora; all groves, everywhere. Our human visitors have only arrived in a trickle. But for every one of us, there are a thousand of them. If we do not negotiate a trade treaty with humans, we will be overwhelmed by sheer numbers alone. With a trade treaty, we will have secured trade rights to the largest and richest market imaginable. We go to avoid being

smothered by their greater numbers. We
go to secure greater prosperity for us
all. We go in peace. We go in hope. We
go to seize our future."

That was when I realized staff were turning the flip charts displaying the text of his speech for the crowd. It was a beautifully orchestrated performance. His speech was greeted with ear-piercing whistles.

When the applause had died down a bit, BanTik finished with, "Let us pray." He handed the megaphone to Matriarch and climbed down. Everyone hunkered down in a squat and raised their true hands in prayer. Matriarch stood. She was in full command of the crowd, and they quieted. I think even the birds paused for her, and she prayed.

May your journey be blessed. May
Storm Sister send you clear water. May
Fire Brother send you warm sunshine. May
Ice Brother send you gentle breezes. May
Wild Sister nurture you in her bosom. May
you travel in peace. May your journey
fulfill our hopes. May you seize a better
future for us all. In Acora Mother's
name we pray. So be it.

The crowd echoed, "So be it." Everyone stood up.

That was the cue for the drums. They started playing, each instrument tuned to a different note. It was fast, upbeat, and wildly optimistic. Matriarch had arranged for cheap single-use leaf lanterns to be distributed throughout the crowd. Acorans started flicking the little pockets of bioluminescence to life. Tiny pinpricks of light shone in the shade of the canopy. They twinkled like fireflies. Each one insignificant, but seen by the hundreds, they were breathtaking.

BanTik lifted Matriarch from her sedan chair and set her on the dock. They embraced. Matriarch hugged KiKi, then TikTik and she kissed TikTik on the forehead with tears in her eyes. She did the Acoran shoulder-grab-and-nod greeting with Kah, AckTik, and Ge. Ge had to kneel down, because she was so tiny. Then it was my turn. I had a huge lump in my throat and tears in my eyes. I felt like I was bidding my one true mother good-bye. Matriarch knew. She gently bumped her forehead into mine. A final salute and vote of confidence. I stood with tears leaking down my face.

The staff had already loaded our luggage. We boarded the Bay Tree Grove yacht. The yacht was a large three-hulled, square-rigged,

126

single masted catamaran. There were pairs of oarsmen in the bow of each hull. They cast off and we started forward immediately, with the drums fading behind us.

The oarsmen rocked the odd hockey-stick shaped oars in front of the boat, drawing it through the water rather than pushing it by paddling. Ge was fascinated and questioned the oarsmen. With many smiles they explained 'sculling' to him. He asked to have a crack at it. Ge took the oar of the central hull and went to work, sculling the craft. With winks and snickers, the other teams of oarsmen on the outlying hulls left off working at all. Ge was sculling the yacht by himself.

Round-eyed, the Acorans watched him. Pretty soon we were all gathered on the deck chattering and watching. Ge was oblivious to us all, completely focused on mastering this new task. He experimented around with different speeds, angles, and rhythms with the oar. He settled on one rhythm that seemed to work the best.

Well, damn. I found myself admiring him. Both his athleticism and his very impressively short learning curve. Ge looked good sculling a yacht, too. The captain had his first mate measure the speed by dropping floats on a rope into the river.

"Two floats against the current and no sail assist, sir."

Many gasps and whistles of amazement. Everyone was talking about it. I think I saw one betting pool start up. The lead oarsman tapped Ge on the forearm. "Excuse me."

Ge broke out of his reverie and looked startled. "Yes?"

"As much as we appreciate the assistance, sir, sculling the yacht is our job."

Ge looked faintly embarrassed. "Oh. Right. Thanks for the lesson!"

We scattered to settle into our luxuriously appointed cabins. I unrolled my favorite white Acoran silk dress. Not a wrinkle in it, even after being rolled up in my backpack. I paired it with my trusty sparkly sandals and wandered out to the deck. We were all chatting when the lunch bell sounded. Ge and I were seated with KiKi and TikTik. I don't know how we got there, but we ended up discussing the philosophy underlying the treaty.

Ge quoted, "There is a tide in the affairs of men, Which taken at the flood, leads on to fortune. Omitted, all the voyage of their life is bound in shallows and in miseries."

"Well said, Ge. Exactly," TikTik agreed.

127

"Actually, Ge can't take credit for that one. He's quoting an ancient playwright of our people," I explained. I turned to Ge, "Although I'm impressed that you know your Shakespeare."

18

GULA'A MIFLA'A

The oarsmen worked in shifts through the night while our team enjoyed a leisurely house party aboard the yacht. Even then, Ge spent much of his time studying the texts from DanBlin that he'd scanned into his phone. He called it "Promethean studies." In spite of all his goofiness and class-clown jokes, I recognized world-beating ambition in Ge. He was going to change the scientific world throughout the human galaxy. If only it wasn't going to end up with me dealing with academia and all those politics, I thought I could go for it. We arrived at Gula'a Mifla'a late in the afternoon.

Representatives of the Amber Tree Grove met us at the docks and ushered us to their Grove. Our timing was great. We had a few minutes to settle in before the dinner bell sounded and we were ushered in to the dining room.

Evidently, the cook from Bay Tree Grove had sent a vine, because they offered an entire roast brebola to Ge. We renewed our acquaintance with the ambassadors that had pledged the Grove's help back in Ifka'a Kifma'a. I sat next to LinLin. While not yet the matriarch, LinLin was First Daughter, and it was an honor to be seated next to her.

"Your Apex Jungle has improved since we last spoke," she said.

"Thank you." I smiled at her. "I also want to thank you again for making this expedition possible. Without your aid and political support, Bay Tree Grove would never have been able to push this through the legislature."

"You are welcome." LinLin flipped her quills modestly. "But I'm dying of curiosity. What is your plan? What route will you follow? How have you been equipped?"

So, we had a long discussion about the expedition. I filled her in on our emergency boat. Then told her our plan to have Kah negotiate

129

safe passage with the Northern Tribes. We also discussed human laws and our plans to negotiate a treaty.

"Actually, making the trek to the human capital city is not that daunting. Physically challenging, tedious, fraught with discomfort, but I am not worried about that. My greatest concern is negotiating a treaty once we get there. We have a wide variety of lawmakers with a wide variety of attitudes and concerns. There are some, a substantial and influential minority, who will not want to trade with you because of the border war. Swaying their opinion and diluting their negative influence will be … delicate."

LinLin's quills rose in surprise and agitation. "Surely your people understand that we must protect ourselves from the Northern Tribes? This war is not of our making!"

"I am so sorry, but I will have to disagree with you about that. This war is entirely the result of the current administration's policies."

LinLin was offended, her quills folded down.

I hastily added, "Please let me explain. The current policies are not designed to defray the cost of maintaining the shipping channels, nor to protect the people of this city. No. The current policies are designed to trap the Northern Tribes in poverty and the Northern Tribes know that. That is the source of their rage and hatred. Instead of levying the shipping tolls on Northern trade ships coming *in*, levy them on their trade ships on their way *out*. That way, the Northerners will have traded enough to be able to pay the tolls. That policy change alone would halt the border wars. If human history is any guide, it will be a generation before the hatred and suspicion, with their inevitable individual acts of violence, die down. But the border war would halt within weeks."

Her quills rose with hope. LinLin was thinking furiously.

That's when I decided to pile on the arguments and got really warmed up to the task. "How much treasure do you squander on the border war? How many of your sons and daughters do you sacrifice each year? It is only by the blood and treasure of your people that the southern Central Republic is free and unmolested."

Her quills were upright and quivering with excitement. I asked, "How many other border cities suffer as you do?"

She thought about it. "Nine. There are nine others."

"If you band together with the other border cities, how many close trade partners will support you politically?"

LinLin considered carefully. "At least ten trade partners, and with any luck, a dozen."

"A minority of twenty or so Groves is pretty significant in a governing body of only forty-seven delegates. Bay Tree Grove Matriarch has given me leave to promise you that she will support any petition for a change in the toll policies that you introduce. And of course, where Bay Tree Matriarch leads, others will follow. A change in the trade policy will stop the border cities from exhausting their treasuries and wasting their citizen's lives. The tolls will ease the tax burden on all Central Republic citizens. The end of the border war will pave the way for negotiations with humans. In a stroke, Amber Tree Grove will vastly increase in influence and wealth."

LinLin was convinced. She summoned other members of her Grove, and we hashed out the idea in detail. We spoke well into the night. Then we worked the next day with the Amber Tree Grove's legal team to rough draft the initial petition.

"The hatred for the Northern Tribes is strong in Ifka'a Kifma'a, and most are indifferent about humans," I advised them. "Do not suggest that you are pressing for better treaty and trade with humans. You should frame it as legislation designed to relieve the border Groves of a dreadful burden. Emphasize how this new policy will generate new toll income and enrich everyone."

While I was hammering out intricate legalities with LinLin and her legal team, Ge was busy, too. Later that night, he showed me a new pintle that had been installed in the bow of the rescue boat and the sculling oar that fitted into it. The biggest problem had been cutting holes for inserting the new hardware. The boat fabric was tough. They had finally succeeded by burning their way through with plant enzymes.

In the end, it was a very tidy job. Ge assured me that if he could scull two floats with a large catamaran, he would double that speed with the smaller and much lighter emergency boat. After a flurry of calculations, Ge figured out that meant moving about ten kilometers per hour while going upstream. With a strong river current in our favor, we should fly down the river.

We left early the next morning with fanfare, but it was a lackluster affair compared to the Bay Tree Grove Matriarch's efforts. Then the penny dropped for me. Our send-off had served two purposes for the Matriarch. First, it was a magnificent display of power and wealth for her peers. Second, she had strengthened my admiration and loyalty.

I laughed with TikTik about it. "You were 100% correct, TikTik. Subtle and designed to give the Bay Tree Grove an advantage!"

We fell into a comfortable routine aboard the yacht. We were fortunate to have my favorite amongst the Grove's chefs, RanLing, as cook. I begged a box of opella spice from her. It added a few extra grams to my pack, but I wanted more options than salt or nothing.

We partied and relaxed in comfort for the next five days. There were small towns and tiny villages but no more major cities. On the sixth day we passed a burnt-out village. The tree homes were burned and broken, the streets and roads already overgrown with creepers. A sad, desolate place. It was a sobering reminder of the cost of the border war.

* * *

I didn't know it at the time, but Ge surreptitiously created an avatar, disguised his phone to go online. He wanted to look up the projected weather and get a look at a map of our route.

* * *

#Forensic Investigation File:

AI: REQUEST FOR AUTHORIZATION TO CONDUCT SURVEILLANCE. The energy signature of the eco surveyor, previously classified as neutralized, has been detected on the net again. I risked chirping the subjects' IDs and confirmed that they are dead. The log on is calculated to be approximately 400 kilometers north of the crash site. The contact was brief, and it could be an anomaly or a data error. It is more likely, however, given that the match is quite close, that the native species has obtained the phone and is using it.

CSO: The *natives?* You think the natives are trying to use human technology?

AI: It is reasonable. They are a highly literate culture. They have had contact with humans before. The phones are alluring technology. In spite of the danger imposed by recently increased governmental monitoring, I chirped the eco surveyor's ID chip, as well as the collateral. Since their ID chirps returned no echo, we can safely assume that the surveyor and the collateral are dead. Why wouldn't the natives appropriate the phones? They would be unskilled which also explains the erratic pattern of use. The native's pre-industrial transportation would explain the slow and irregular movement, as well.

CSO: They may have removed their ID chips.

AI: Highly unlikely. The collateral had a cephalic implant which is fairly easy to remove. But the eco-surveyor had a subscapular implant. He would require thoracic surgery far beyond a simple medi-bot or his collateral's capability.

CSO: Why should I care that some natives are playing with a phone?

AI: Whether native contact is mediated by a human or not, the natives arriving at any human settlement will derail your charter efforts. **RECOMMENDATION**: Deploy a surveillance drone to the area to discover who operates the phone. Do you wish to authorize surveillance drone deployment?

CSO: Alright. **AUTHORIZED.** Code: ELG. 66128!

AI: AUTHORIZATION VERIFIED. Surveillance drone ES1 deployed.

* * *

The next day, the yacht pulled over to the side of the river where five tall sturdy columns of stone jutted out from the water near the bank. Some crewmembers hopped out and waded through the waist-deep water with ropes in hand and tied off the yacht. A long gangplank was extended to the shore.

We gathered on the deck dressed in hiking outfits with all our camping gear. The entire crew assembled on the deck.

"This is as far as we can take you," the captain said. "We all bid you good luck and farewell. It has been a pleasure to have you aboard. May Acora Mother bless you and keep you safe."

The captain reached up and Ge hunkered down so they could do the mutual-shoulder-grab-and-nod farewell. Many farewells were exchanged. I hugged RanLing goodbye. She had worked most closely with me to develop human recipes for Ge. RanLing was my favorite of the Bay Tree Staff.

We exited the yacht. Don't know about anyone else, but my stomach was doing flipflops. It sorta felt like both excitement and stage fright, but I was also feeling pangs of regret for parting with civilized comforts. We started walking upriver along the shore and a chorus of whistling from the crew faded behind us.

19

JUNGLE TREK

Everyone mostly walked. The undergrowth was much thicker near the river where the sunlight broke through. So, there were times when we were forced away from the water's edge, and times when we had to swing. Even with Ge carrying my pack, and the Acorans finding the easiest path for me, I could only swing for fifteen minutes or so at a time. My limitations slowed us down. We didn't care, we were still fresh and excited to make a start.

The sun was dropping toward the horizon when Ge spotted a promising camp site. My phone estimated the distance I had traveled as under ten kilometers. Ge and the guys cleared a tent area of debris. Ge showed everybody how to operate the tent. KiKi and I set up a cooking fire and started steeping `chet`.

I never cared for it, but it was hugely popular with the Acorans and Ge liked it. KiKi and I reheated a buffet of food that RanLing had gifted to us. We only had enough for another day, and then we would have to play hunter/gatherers for the rest of the journey.

We were only about 20 meters from the river shoreline and Ka took off towards the river. I thought nothing of it at the time, but the following morning as we were breaking camp, a ninety-minute ordeal; Kah showed up with a rope of small river fish. Evidently, he had set his line the night before and was reaping the harvest that morning.

Ge, Kah, and I beheaded, gutted, and scaled the fish then put them in a keeping bag of silk with a heavily waxed lining. We would have the more perishable foods from RanLing for lunch and have the fish tonight.

We weren't making as much progress as I had hoped. Breaking camp, stopping for lunch, setting up camp, and foraging for fruit was taking up the majority of the day. At that rate it would be over a year to make the trek. At dinner that night, I found Ge shared my concerns.

Ge said, `"I've figured out that at our current rate of speed, it will take us over a year to make it to the capital city. The planetary` charter vote is coming up in December, so we only have six months to get there. We're going to arrive way too late to do any good! We've got to double our pace. Any ideas?"

I suggested, "Don't stop for lunch. Have a huge breakfast and dinner. Stopping and setting up for lunch is taking over an hour a day. Can everybody handle that?"

"What? Nothing?" Kah asked. "Is there any way we can carry some snacks with us?"

"Sure." KiKi suggested, "We can stock up on fruit instead of nibbling as we go every day. Fruit is good for several days in a keeping sack. We can snack on it as we swing."

"What if we moved a little ways inland?" I asked. "There's only bracken under the shade of the canopy. Ge and I can jog through that on foot pretty easily while you guys swing. If we weren't constantly taking detours, and went in more of a straight line, I think that would help, too. And - let's face it guys - I suck at swinging and slow everybody down."

"We need the river for navigation and fish, though." AckTik pointed out.

TikTik contributed, "Send someone up a tree every night to check to see if we have gone adrift."

Ge said, "No need. My phone can act as a direction beacon. It will send an audible signal when I'm off track. We can use that to navigate. That way, we only have to visit the river for fish."

I turned to Kah. "Can you swing ahead of us near the end of the day and set fish lines? That way, we can pull in the fish as soon as we stop to make camp. If we cut the fish into thin filet strips, we can smoke them overnight. Even brief smoking should hold them for days."

BanTik pointed out the obvious. "Good ideas one and all. But the biggest time waster is making and breaking camp. I think if we assign jobs for that and practice on our speed, we can cut our time way down. I know our military forces break camp in a scant few minutes."

We figured out who should do what and assigned TikTik to keep time and make any helpful suggestions that he could. We set a goal of breaking camp in less than twenty minutes. Ge had a fishing net, but it needed hands-on attention to be effective. Kah showed Ge and AckTik how to weave multi-hook fish lines, and they set to with a will. I went to bed feeling optimistic.

The next morning, we didn't make our twenty-minute deadline, but we came close. So, we broke camp in one-third the time we had on previous days. We also made a lot more progress, going from less than ten kilometers in a day to nearly twenty that day. That night after dinner, we analyzed our performance.

AckTik very sensibly pointed out that our time after dinner in the dark was "dead time" when we couldn't travel. She suggested we prepare breakfast right along with dinner and just hold it warm in the camp stove. Or, if we were using the stove for smoking fish, eat breakfast cold. That way we could re-pack everything but the stove at night and wouldn't waste time cooking twice during the day. We immediately adopted her suggestion. I saw Ge fashioning a weird strap with a cord and loop attached.

"What are you up to?" I asked.

"If I don't get a brebola or a neopig soon, I'm gonna lose it," he explained. "So, I'm making a sling. My brothers and I used them as kids. When I was in top form, I could hit a rat at five meters. Even a little thirty-gram stone is a pretty deadly ballistics weapon. With a bigger stone, you can bring down a charging boar."

"Ah, I get it now." I grinned at him. "Ge mighty hunter. Bring much game."

He smiled ruefully. "Yeah. But only after I get some practice. I haven't used a sling in years."

"I have every confidence that your appetite will speed your progress."

We kept practicing and refining our camp setup and breakup routines. In only a few short days, we had morning down to fifteen minutes, and camp setup was a mere twenty minutes. We were also going for a longer time each day as we grew more fit and more used to travel. We were regularly making 20 kilometers per day. Ge spent his time whacking trees with stones from his sling and improved his accuracy significantly.

Right about then TikTik approached me and Ge with his quills flicking in concern. "Kah grows more worried with each passing step. His people do not respect him. They call him 'blood traitor.' He worries that his presence will trigger retaliation or spoil negotiations. We approach his hometown. He parted from his family on bad terms."

"You have Seen this?" Ge asked.

TikTik nodded.

"What do you recommend?"

TikTik spread his quills helplessly and shrugged. "I have no suggestion."

Ge said, "I'll ask BanTik for advice." But when we asked BanTik, he had no advice to give, either. So, I thought about it long and hard as we hiked that afternoon. After dinner, as we relaxed around the campfire, Ge spoke.

"I'm worried about meeting the Northern Tribes. If we all go in, they may mistake us for spies or soldiers and attack. If Kah goes, they may think it's a trick. What if Li and I go in first and offer them gifts? Would that help?"

I turned to Kah. "You're the Northern Tribes specialist. Do you think Ge's tactic will work?"

Kah thought about it, his quills wavered uncertainly, and he shrugged. "We approach Pusata'aman Wengma'apuri, the town furthest south on the river, and the one with the fiercest chieftain. He will be impressed with Ge. I think Ge should go first, then you, Li."

"Done!" I grinned. "Are there any protocols for gift giving or etiquette that we should know?"

Ge and I grilled Kah and practiced speaking Northern Tribe while BanTik, TikTik, KiKi, and AckTik played cards. Ge had never attempted the language and was content to learn, "I am Ge."

The next day Ge saw a flock of wild brebolas feeding on the ground. He killed one with a single stone. It was so quick and silent that the flock was undisturbed. Ge wasn't so successful the second time. He wounded the bird which flopped around on the ground screeching in pain and terror and the flock took off. Ge hurried over and put the poor thing out of its misery by breaking its neck.

KiKi burst into tears and TikTik comforted her. Ge and Kah went further into the woods, out of sight, and beheaded and gutted the birds by cutting them in two and scooping out the innards. Ge had the presence of mind to rescue the livers. We set up camp less than an hour later.

Ge asked, "How are you going to pluck them?"

"I'm not. I'll skin them and put'em in a stew." Then I asked everybody to scatter and gather any greens, edible mushrooms, or tubers we could use in the stew. We assembled a feast. AckTik came back with a murmuri gourd, a tart mildly earthy fruit much prized for savory dishes. KiKi came up with an armful of delicious piku leaves. Everyone else contributed a few tough, woody tubers.

KiKi and I stored most of the produce for later use and chopped the tough roots into very tiny pieces so they would soften in the stew. I added some salt and opella. KiKi unfurled Ge's largest ten-liter cooking pot, and we set the whole thing to cook. It was one of the best meals I have ever prepared. No kidding. It was a huge hit. We kept it warm overnight and feasted on it for breakfast.

20

PUSATA'AMAN
WENGMA'APURI

As we made our way north, we gained elevation. Different tree species cropped up and the trees thinned out. The ground brush was thicker and becoming more of a hindrance to me and Ge. Kah said we were getting close, but Ge was the first to spot signs of agriculture.

We paused, and the Acorans scattered to the trees preparing for a long anxious wait. Ge led the way with me behind and Kah trailing about twenty meters behind us. We stumbled across a footpath that angled towards the river, so we followed that. As we got closer to the river, and thus the town, the path widened. Eventually we encountered a sort of monkey bars, for swinging installed over the road.

We saw and photographed the first house we came across. It was set back from the path about a hundred meters. The house was partially sunk into the hillside with only the southern and part of the eastern and western walls exposed. The gable roof was substantial, covered with large slabs of stone overlapped to shed rain. The roof plunged to meet the ground at the back. The doors and windows were tucked in under stone arches. The walls were timber and what appeared to be stucco, rather like Tudor half-timbered houses from Old Earth.

We saw more and more houses, all along similar lines with the roofs plunging to the ground on the northern side. Then, we spotted our first commercial building. There were bree carts parked in front, it sported colorful signs and had large doors for cargo. Someone spotted us and many whistles followed us down the street as the Northerners spread the alarm.

As we got further into the center of the town, two story buildings started to appear. Towards the center of town, they were crowded very close together with only a narrow walkway between. We arrived at the town square. It was actually a rhombus. There was a large utilitarian fountain in the center feeding both a catch basin and several bree watering troughs. Businesses on the south side of the square, whose northern roofs faced the square, had wide arches cut into the roofs with doors leading to the interior. Their roofs sported brightly colored signs and murals. In fact, most of the buildings displayed bright decorative murals.

We stopped by the fountain and waited. Northerners began to gather. Everybody was talking at the top of their lungs. It sounded like the crowd at a football pitch during a championship game. Some shouted questions at us, but I wasn't good enough at Northern Tribe yet to catch any of it. Kah sought to blend in with the crowd but was soon discovered and shoved towards us.

I shrugged. "Well, so much for that tactic. I think we'll still be fine."

Kah nodded, but his quills flicked with uncertainty.

There was a ripple in the crowd and a tall Northerner with henchmen appeared. He was the biggest Acoran I had ever seen, only a handspan shorter than me, and the spitting image of Kah. The swell of shouted conversation peaked. The tall Northerner glanced at the henchman on his right. Henchman whipped out a bullroarer, you know, those big whistle-on-a-string things. He whirled it around his head. It was incredibly loud and very effective at quieting the crowd.

I squatted down in the respect posture and said, "*I am Li.*"

"*I am Ge.*"

"*Me learn Northern Tribe talk-talk. But me bad. Sorry-sorry. Me talk pretty one day.* Does anyone speak Apex Jungle?" I asked as I stood up.

"Yes, I am familiar with that foul tongue," he said.

I thought, *Wow! and I thought the Southerners were bigoted!* Had no more time to think about it though, because he continued.

"I am Ka'alka'eipeke Suma'aligrika, Leader of the Eastern Confederation of Tribes, headquartered here, in Pusata'aman Wengma'apur." He turned to Kah and said, in a very sarcastic way, "Welcome home, son."

"Hi, Dad."

Ka'alka'eipeke', senior, turned to one of his henchmen and said, "Told you he would come crawling back."

My Northern Tribe was pretty bad at that time, but it was good enough to catch *that*! I turned to Ge and explained. "Chieftain is Kah's father. He just insulted Kah by calling him a coward right here in front of God and everybody. Be prepared, okay?"

Ge nodded, turned narrowed eyes to Ka'alka'eipeke, senior. Ge flexed, as though preparing for a fight. The henchmen raised their quills nervously.

Kah rolled his eyes exasperated. "By the Mother! I have *not* come 'crawling back!' I bring Ge and Li, travelers from another planet, who are here to negotiate trade between our people and theirs. They represent hundreds of times more wealth than all the Southerners combined. I come offering the greatest gift of riches the Tribes have ever received!"

Kah's quills were in full aggression pattern. The henchmen stared at Kah, shocked. A very elaborately dressed matron in the crowd pushed through to the front and approached.

Her quills flicked with amusement. "I believe you, son. Now all that is left to do is to convince this stubborn old bree!"

Kah said, "Thanks, Mom."

She embraced Kah and turned to me. "Shall we begin this again? Would you care to join us for lunch to discuss trade. And, perhaps, the foolishness of stubborn old men?"

Ge and I both laughed. I answered, "We would be delighted. But first, we are accompanied by four trade representatives from Ifka'a Kifma'a. They are waiting for us in the forest. We did not want to be mistaken for spies or a military intrusion. May we send Ka'alka'eipeke to usher them to your house?"

She turned to Kah. "I have years of conversation stored up, so when you get back, we shall have a good long talk." She patted Kah on the arm, he kissed her cheek. "See you soon."

Kah nodded and left at high speed, swinging down the street. We were ushered to a sprawling one-story house. Kah's mother led the way, and servants opened the large double doors for us.

"I am Ka'alka'eipeke Sulralani. Welcome to my home." I recognized the formula from Kah's coaching.

"May Acora Mother bless all in this house," Ge and I chorused together.

When we entered, the room was bathed in beautiful pinky-gold light. I realized that many of the roof tiles were translucent agate or some similar translucent stone. They admitted glorious soft light to temper and supplement the light from the windows. The beams, rafters, and purlins that supported the roof were carved and painted with bright intricate floral and leaf patterns. The floor was a coordinating mosaic of polished multicolored stone.

The furnishings were much like those in Ifka'a Kifma'a, except that many were upholstered in leather or fur. I had high hopes for being able to feed Ge properly. Instead of a fireplace, small metal braziers were scattered around the perimeter of the room. Buckets of charcoal were set out near the braziers. A large fur rug of many different hides sewn together in a geometric pattern softened and complemented the pattern on the floor.

Ge explained that we came from different worlds. He told Suma'agika and Sulralani about the human diaspora and the expansion of human colony worlds. He told them about our mission to inform humans about the existence of Acorans. He explained why the vote in December was so important.

I got straight into the meat of it and told them about the change in the river tolls that I had proposed. I assured them that within a few weeks there would be a coalition of more than twenty Groves working to get the legislation adopted.

Ge explained the sabotage and how we got stranded in the first place. We were wrapping up when Kah, BanTik, AckTik, TikTik and KiKi showed up.

As we were walking to the dining room, Ge turned to Sulralani. "I must warn you, I'm from one of our heavy worlds. I have genetic modifications so I can be comfortable on that world. Those changes require extra protein. I eat half a branch of meat a day. I sincerely hope that will not inconvenience you."

"A half a branch by yourself?" she asked, quills raised in surprise.

"Yes." I explained, "He has a lot of muscle mass to support."

"Very impressive. It's no inconvenience at all. We keep kua, unlike our southern neighbors. Our herd is quite large." She smiled and said with a wink, "They accuse us of being barbaric because of it."

"Ah, I understand. My people share your habit of keeping domestic meat animals. So, we share in your 'barbarity.' KiKi is a vegetarian. She has such a tender heart for animals that she burst into tears when Ge killed a brebola in front of her." I turned to Kiki and added, "I am sorry that Ge traumatized you, poor dear."

KiKi responded at that point, "Thank you, Li; but I'm fine, now. Will there be some vegetarian dishes for me?"

"Certainly," Sulralani replied with a smile.

Then she asked me about our animal husbandry. I told her in the broadest strokes about the livestock humans keep for food and fiber. The dining room was spacious, colorful, and the table was set with elegant ceramic plates and bowls. Unlike the restrained designs favored by Matriarch, our plates were bracketed by elaborately decorative knife, spoon, and tongs sets. We were seated for lunch. Suma'agika said a brief prayer of thanks for the food, and we were served. It was delicious.

We got sorted into rooms. There was a minor glitch because Ge and I were paired in a room with a single bed. Our hosts assumed that we were a wedded couple.

"Uh-oh," I said. "I'm not okay with this."

Ge grinned roguishly, "I'm happy to share a room with Li; but we are not married. Li and her family would not be as happy with this arrangement as I am."

So, we had a laugh and got that straightened out. Then we figured out how domestic sanitary services worked, composting toilets, stone bathtubs in a separate room. As I settled in, I thought long and hard about how to make my point with Suma'aligrika.

* * *

#Forensic Investigation File:

AI: **SURVEILLANCE REPORT FOR AUTHORIZED SEARCHES.** The energy signature of the eco surveyor was not detected within 50 kilometers of the last reported net log on location. I now classify the log on as an anomaly.

RECOMMENDATION: Reduce alert to background surveillance. Do you wish to authorize background surveillance?

CSO: Fine. I don't have to devote any more time and attention to this. **AUTHORIZED**. Code: ES1.41668!

AI: **AUTHORIZATION VERIFIED.** Monitoring reduced to background surveillance.

21

NEGOTIATIONS

After dinner and a lot of conversation that night, I said, "I would like to tell you the tale of the Naughty Puppy." Everyone agreed, and I began.

"Once upon a time there was a prosperous village. One family in the village raised prize darlus. A puppy was born that was very handsome. But that puppy was very naughty. He yowled at the tiniest provocation, and sometimes with no provocation at all. He bit anyone who fed him. Sometimes, he would creep up on the children at play and nip them without warning. No amount of training or scolding would make the puppy behave.

"Well, the mother was fed up with that puppy, even though he was beautiful, and put him out of the house. But the puppy kept sneaking back in to steal food and soil the floors. Exasperated, the father built a fence to keep the puppy out. But the puppy was clever and soon learned to get past the fence. The family made some half-hearted attempts to hunt down the annoying puppy. But they didn't try very hard because he was beautiful, and nobody likes killing puppies.

"That was when a rich and powerful trader from a distant city came to the village. The trader immediately saw the problem of the Naughty Puppy when the puppy broke in and nipped one of the children in the merchant's presence.

"Now the merchant had no sentimental attachment to the puppy. He set his best trackers after it and soon killed the Naughty Puppy. But he did not kill just the Naughty Puppy, he killed *all* the puppies in the village because he assumed they were all nuisances like the Naughty Puppy. The villagers were very sad about losing their beloved pets. But the merchant was so rich, and the trade he offered so profitable, that they soon dried their tears and traded happily ever after."

Everyone froze. The only sound was the occasional tiny pop from the burning braziers. Sulralani turned to her husband and pointedly observed, "The Naughty Puppy no doubt thought he was very courageous. He believed that all the obedient puppies living in comfort were cowards."

Suma'aligrika snorted in disgust. "What? Do they have bows that shoot a thousand arrows at once? She seeks to frighten us with children's fables!"

Ge cleared his throat. "Ah. Not to put too fine a point on this, but we have developed much more sophisticated phrenochaotic weapons."

I hastily added, "I am horrified that my people invented them. They are now universally outlawed throughout the human worlds."

Ge countered with, "Yes. But we still have them, and they are legal for use against alien species. I should explain. When you beat a drum you can hear it, right?"

Everyone nodded, quills flicked with understanding, and he continued.

"Well, you can also feel the vibrations of that sound if you touch the drum. Intelligent minds also produce vibrations. They are not as obvious as the vibrations of a drum and are a lot more complex than a drumbeat, but they are essential for life. Phrenochaotic weapons crush those waves. The body lives on for a while, but the individual's mind is destroyed. There is no

147

hiding place, no deep rock, that can ward off that weapon. The person loses even the ability to drink water and there is no recovery.

"It is mercy to let anyone so wounded die of thirst. They are incapable of feeling pain. A single contingent of our soldiers armed with that weapon in one of our smaller airships could exterminate every single Northern Tribesman in the span of a few days."

"They would not kill you all." I gulped, fighting rising nausea. "They would put a lethal fence around one area so our scientists could study you."

They all, Southern and Northern alike, gaped at us horrified.

AckTik said, "It can't be true."

I buried my face in my hands. "It's true. God, I wish it weren't. I am ashamed that we even invented it. I would never, ever condone its use. I would never, even when threatened with death, participate in genocide. But Ge and I are only representatives. We do not have the power to control military leaders. Just as you did not back in Ifka'a Kifma'a."

TikTik took his father's arm and nodded. "What they say is truth, Father. I have Seen it."

BanTik's quills showed utter disgust. "We have nurtured these monsters in the bosom of our Grove? And you said nothing about it!"

TikTik came to our rescue. "Not monsters, father. Two individuals with powerful voices who are doing everything they can to *prevent* this terrible outcome. They seek to unite ALL the peoples of this planet, Central Republic, Northern Tribes, and Humans alike."

"I apologize, BanTik," I said quietly. "We did not mean to deceive you. Good long-term trade agreements are rarely achieved with threats. You were so sympathetic to our cause, such an intelligent voice of reason, that I saw no need to threaten you, even by implication."

Suma'aligrika rose with quills in full-on aggression position, and he said, "Only if you carry news of us to your people are we at risk of this fate! All we need do is execute you. Then they will never find out about us."

"No, that is not true," Ge said. "You may delay things for a time, but humans will find you. It is inevitable. We two are at your mercy now. But our people are not. The only way to stop our military leaders is to make peace. We must create treaties with our government and trade agreements with our business leaders."

TikTik jumped in again, "It is truth what Li and Ge say! If we do not seize this current, our best opportunity for peace and prosperity will be lost for generations to come."

"I've heard enough!" Suma'aligrika shouted and stormed out of the room.

I couldn't hold back anymore and started crying, and I am an ugly crier, folks. I was dribbling snot and leaking tears. Ge rescued me by handing me a handkerchief.

"I am sorry; so, so sorry. I have failed you. I have failed you all. Worse, I have failed my own people. It couldn't have gone any worse." Once I'd blown my nose and mopped up the tears Sulralani smiled.

"Do not be so sure of that. TikTik is not the only one who Sees. My husband is a stubborn old bree, too proud for his own good. He won't listen to any of you. There are times when he won't listen to me. But he still listens to his mother."

Hope sprang up again. Ge suggested, "If he won't listen, a demonstration might help. He's bound to believe his own eyes. We don't carry any lethal weapons, but Li can demonstrate her palm stunner. It is a weak weapon designed to make the attacker faint. It stings and the attacker wakes up in a few minutes with sore muscles but is otherwise unharmed. It is excellent for driving off unwanted animals."

"You still have your stunner, right?" Ge asked.

I nodded. "Essential equipment."

149

Sulralani called a servant over and gave instructions. "My steward will see to you for the night. Do not fear my husband. I must excuse myself. I have a lot of ruffled fur to smooth."

We scattered to our bedrooms. Each of us deep in our own thoughts.

The next morning, I did my best to mend fences with BanTik. "BanTik, I am so sorry Ge shocked you with our weapons technology. That wasn't fair. But you didn't tell us everything either. Did you brag about your ability to engineer crop plagues that would kill all our food crops and force us to flee? Did you talk to us about the growing problem of ri'ippuvu'us addiction? No, you did not. Ge and I discovered those things on our own. Every ku'aka bloom has spines."

His quills limp with defeat, BanTik said, "I have misjudged you. I have misjudged this situation so badly that I question my own discernment. I question sleeping in the home of the most aggressive and barbaric Northerner imaginable. I question everything."

"I see it differently, BanTik," I replied as gently as I could. "Your judgment is fine. Your information was faulty, not your judgment. Ge and I could have lied to conceal the full extent of human strength. But we did not. I would not. You deserve better than that from us. Trust your judgment of us gained over many months experience. Trust TikTik's Sight of us. I spent weeks with Matriarch. I did not explain our weapons in detail, but I did tell her about our powerful airships, and she knows that Ge understands your plague technology. Trust your Matriarch."

BanTik did not immediately change his opinion. But his quills wavered with uncertainty, they were not folded in defeat.

Suma'aligrika's mother, Miri'imaru, arrived in a sedan chair right after breakfast. Sulralani and Kah brought her up to speed and translated our answers to her questions. Later that morning, five bound prisoners were led into the courtyard.

Ge explained how deadly weapons worked in our society. "Private citizens may own deadly weapons. This is especially true on colony worlds when facing dangers from local animals and where colonists need to hunt for meat. However, to purchase such a weapon, one must take courses on the weapon's operation, maintenance, and safety. You have to prove that you have adequate safe storage to prevent the weapon from falling into the hands of thieves, or worse, children. You have to maintain a large deposit that the government can confiscate if you use the weapon irresponsibly – or allow anyone else to use it irresponsibly. You must pay license fees. Only then may you purchase a weapon. There is technology woven deep within each weapon so that law enforcement agencies can track the location and use of each and every weapon."

Quills flicked with understanding all around. It was my turn.

"This weapon that I'm demonstrating is so weak and the consequences so temporary, that none of that applies. Anyone can buy them from a variety of merchants."

I slipped my hand into the strap, and my palm print activated the stunner. I lifted it in front of me, about three meters from the prisoners, and chickened out.

"Oh, God, Ge. I can't," I moaned.

"You had no problem at the Temple," he replied.

"It's different in the heat of the moment when I was under attack. Mowing down bound prisoners is just… I'm sorry, I can't do it."

"Is it capable of dual access?" Ge asked.

"Oh!" I sheepishly re-set the access codes and added Ge as authorized. Ge didn't even lift it but fired from the hip.

Each prisoner yelped and collapsed twitching in the petite mal seizures that a stunner inflicts. Ge lowered the stunner, deactivating it. The demonstration took less than a second. The seizures quickly passed, and the prisoners were knocked out cold.

Quills rose in astonishment all around. Suma'aligrika's were raised in anger. Muri'imaru turned to her son and Kah translated.

"Do not hinder them in any way. Rather, give them every aid you can. They claim that this is the weakest of

151

their weapons. After what Sulralani and the Crippled One have Seen, I believe the aliens. They are here to *prevent* the use of these terrible weapons, not to deploy them. They have already helped change the Blackies' laws to generate trade. They offer us riches and peace. Don't let pride make you a fool. Do not stir the waibeeb nest and bring destruction on us all! Turn your heart and mind to hopes of peace and trade and be celebrated for founding a new era of prosperity."

I squatted in full respect posture before her and used my feeble Northern Tribe, "Thank you, Revered Grandmother."

Ge promptly copied me, followed by Sulralani and the rest of the expedition, all murmuring our thanks. We were interrupted by the prisoners waking up.

Suma'aligrika's quills lowered and wavered with uncertainty. He turned to his wife and said, "You handle this," and stalked back into the house.

Sulralani embraced her mother-in-law, and we went in for lunch. Suma'aligrika did not join us, but we sketched out a basic plan to prepare for the next leg of our trek. We needed to make it over the mountains.

22

THE MOUNTAINS

We faced twin challenges in the mountain: keeping the Acorans warm and keeping Ge fed. Game, fish, and forage would suffice until we hit the snowline. Not much game for Ge and no food at all for the Acorans above the snowline.

I explained to Sulralani, "When a person is in cold conditions, especially if they are working hard, they need more calories, more food. We were counting on using our boat as a sled, with Ge as the draft animal. I think our team will even be able to tolerate the cold long enough to take turns helping me push the sled. So, coming up with good snowshoes and mukluks would be a big help." Then I was off and running drawing pictures and explaining snowshoes and mukluks.

Sulralani ordered custom supplies from local craftsmen. After some experimenting around, we all learned to walk in them. It was particularly challenging for the Acorans, given their gait. We settled on very short, round snowshoes for them. The team managed that best in our tests.

We turned our attention to food supplies. Sulralani showed us her kua herd. They were large herbivores, a little less than a ton each. They had sharply sloping backs, rather like an Old Earth giraffe, but not quite as severe. They had long necks about the same proportion to their bodies as horses. Their fur was mottled shades of brown, beige and black that camouflaged them quite well in the shade of the forest.

We watched them nimbly stand on their back legs and prop themselves up on tree trunks to eat the lower leaves. Ge said, "They're folivores, like deer or goats."

I started to explain pemmican to Sulralani, and she knew immediately what I meant. "Yes. We make travelers' loaves of kua combined with nuts and vegetables and dry it. A branch of meat becomes a third

153

of a branch. There are different recipes, some that are vegetarian, some that are a blend of cooked grains and fruit that reconstitute into a tasty porridge. We smoke some of the savory ones for added flavor. Our travel loaves are very convenient for hunters and will serve you well, I think."

We calculated that Ge could handle carrying 24 branches (approximately 80 kilos) of dried food and supplies. The Acorans could manage between five and ten kilos each, Kah and me fifteen kilos each. Between us, we could carry nearly 135 kilos of dried food (the equivalent of 400 kilos fresh) and snow supplies. Ge gifted his heaviest scientific instruments to the Ka'alka'eipeke family. The rest of us did likewise with our heaviest trade goods. Sulralani gifted us with a lush large fur rug.

We set up a five-meter path denuded of vegetation and wet it thoroughly. We used the mud slick to practice sledding. Even going uphill, it only took me and one Acoran, even tiny little KiKi, to drag the boat/sled without getting too winded. With a team of Acorans, I could get some rest. With most of us pulling together, Ge could take breaks.

After a month of being exposed to this novel idea, and extensive persuasion from Muri'imaru and Sulralani, Suma'agika softened his stance. I told TikTik, "By this time next year, this will all have been his idea."

TikTik laughed and agreed. Kah's father even arranged for a guide. Sulralani convinced him to provide pack banderlings as they are much happier at high altitude than bree. I don't know how, but he even found a pair of kua trained to harness for Ge and me to ride. The saddles actually hung from their shoulders, so we were riding them piggy-back style. The saddles had to be heavily adapted, and stirrups were unknown to them. But we soon explained our need and Sulralani arranged for them to accommodate our deformed feet.

I was getting worried about our remaining time because preparations took weeks, and our deadline loomed. It was already early June, so we would be approaching the snowline in late June, an excellent time to cross over the peaks. We took off at the crack of dawn with fond farewells and a prayer for our safety but no other fanfare.

Mounted on banderlings and our kua, we were averaging nearly twenty kilometers per day, even going uphill and taking time to hunt, fish, and forage. We only broke into the dried supplies once along the way. As we got into the mountains, the pace slowed down, and we only averaged fifteen kilometers per day. Kah and AckTik took lessons on sling-hunting from Ge, and both got pretty good at it.

I was ridiculously pleased with Kah when he brought down his first hare. Not to be outdone, AckTik killed a brebola two days later. The path became much more difficult as we went along, and we dropped to only twelve kilometers per day. Then, as we approached the peak and the trees thinned out and became more stunted, our path was easier.

The Acorans were doing fairly well, although KiKi and BanTik both showed signs of distress from the altitude. They were all wearing their knit underwear and soft boots but hadn't yet donned the snowsuits and mukluks.

We made camp within sight of the snowline and paused for four days so that KiKi and BanTik could adjust. I taught them both deep breathing techniques, and everybody else lined up for those lessons. The guide gathered up the banderlings and our kua, roped them together, and returned to Pusata'aman Wengma'apur.

We took off as soon as KiKi and BanTik demonstrated they could hold their breath for thirty seconds. I estimated that was about the maximum adaptation to altitude we could expect. We got dressed for the snow and walked through snow for nearly a kilometer before it became deep enough to support a sled.

We set up the tent inside the boat, lined the bottom with the heavy fur rug, Sulralani's gift to us, tossed in the luggage and most of our team climbed in. AckTik and Kah teamed up to help me. When they started getting cold, TikTik, BanTik, and KiKi swapped places with AckTik and Kah and pushed together as a team. At lunch time, everybody got together to push with me pulling solo to give Ge some relief. We made excellent progress and put a little over twenty kilometers under our belts that day.

* * *

Unbeknownst to me, Ge surreptitiously got online to get a fix of our location. With the feeble security protocols in place in his phone, his sign-in stood out like a beacon.

* * *

155

#Forensic Investigation File:

AI: EMERGENCY ALERT – IMMEDIATE C-LEVEL AUTHORIZATION REQUIRED – EMERGENCY ALERT.

CSO: What are you panicked about now?

AI: The eco-surveyor threat, previously categorized as neutralized, has resurfaced on the net. The login has been re-classified from anomaly to actively re-engaged - potential result – **CATASTROPHIC.**

CSO: What. The. Hell. One minute you say you've solved the problem, then you change your mind; the problem remains.

AI: Whoever operated the phone sought location data. While apparently limited to walking speeds, the threat is moving. Satellite coverage at the log in location is quite poor, and no exact location could be determined. I estimate that the target is nearly 700 kilometers north of the splash-down location. It is highly unlikely to be the eco-surveyor, and I think that members of the native species have co-opted the phone.

CSO: Everything I've been working on for two decades rides in the balance. What do you suggest?

AI: RECOMMENDATION: Immediate, discreet, permanent intervention. At the current calculated rate and direction of travel, the threat will shortly exit the New Himalayans. Recommend deploying an armed drone (reference Security Manual CLVL11.7311.0e-g) to the estimated location of the target with search parameters adjusted to include natives. Implement drone search in a 50-kilometer radius from the estimated location. Designate ES2 for this maneuver.

CSO: How confident are you that these tactics will produce results?

AI: The target is proving to be elusive. I also recommend implementing strategy Accelerate (reference Security Manual LLVL11.7311.3a-m) to ensure success. Do you wish to authorize either or both of these strategies?

CSO: AUTHORIZE BOTH. Code: 34635ft.8*XU.50874. 35575rcf.407858.

AI: AUTHORIZATION VERIFIED. Drone Maneuver and Accelerate are now underway.

* * *

That night, we slept in very close quarters. Ge and I discovered that humans radiate exactly the right temperature for Acoran comfort. All the Acorans ended up piled on or against us. We woke up under a heavy sweat-inducing blanket of Acorans. There was a storm that night, and we had a little more than 60 centimeters of snow to clear from the tent. Little did we know it at the time, but that weather interfered with the drone and saved us all.

My implant had given out a month earlier and my natural menstrual cycle was emerging. I had cramping and spotting but no real period.

KiKi collapsed a corner of the tent in the stern of the boat and set up the camp stove to melt snow into water and recharge the heat packs. They were all amazed at how much snow it takes to make a liter of water. We were living exclusively on dried rations then, and the hot porridge became everyone's favorite. We settled at around fifteen kilometers progress per day.

We got one boost past the highest part of the pass. The mountain sloped down at a fairly gentle angle to a snow-covered valley. After hiking down partway to check out the slope, Ge wanted to actually sled.

"That run to the valley is a gentle slope with deep snow. With all of us on board, we can use the boat to slide down the mountain. I figure the relatively streamlined shape of the boat would keep us on target. It would save us a lot of tough slogging through the snow and at least two days walking."

We all hopped in, and Ge made sure the weight was evenly distributed. He shoved off and ran behind the boat for a few meters and jumped in as it gained momentum. It worked fine for two-thirds of the way down.

We picked up quite a bit of speed by that time. I figure we were whizzing along at about 40 or 50 kilometers an hour. Then, we hit a bump. The boat wobbled and began slipping sideways. It yawed more and more to the right.

Ge was leaning like a sailboarder on a big wave to straighten out the boat. We accelerated, helplessly trapped in the boat with no way to control our descent. Towards the bottom of the slope, we began to spin. All the way across the valley, we spun faster and faster. By shifting his weight and leaning away from the spin, Ge kept us upright. Kah quickly caught on and helped.

We spun to a stop about two thirds of the way across the valley. There were no injuries. Kah saved KiKi from being crushed under Ge's pack by pushing it out of the way with his feet-hands as we were careening across the valley. To this day, I have never known anyone as coordinated or agile as Kah in his prime. Nobody threw up in the boat, thank goodness. Once we recovered from the dizziness and nausea, we made a pact to *Never Do That Again*.

It worked, though. That one terrifying miserable descent carried us over forty kilometers in only minutes. We made nearly 58 kilometers that day. We sped up once we were on the downhill side, but it still took us fourteen days to make it through the pass to the downslope snowline. Once Ge spotted the snowline, everybody got out and made one last herculean push. We ditched all the snowshoes, but the Acorans still needed all the rest of the cold-weather gear.

We reached the stunted scattered trees of the tree line and Kah spotted a small relatively level patch, and we camped. Everyone checked for frost injury, and we were all good. Stinky and greasy from not bathing, but good. We celebrated with porridge that night and double-dosed ourselves in the morning. We were the first team in history to get Acorans over the mountains intact and healthy.

The next afternoon, when we had all scattered for a little alone time. Ge checked his phone. He screamed, "Screw me!"

I turned and noticed the phone in his hand. He slapped out the memory card and hurled the thing as hard as he could. It was well over 100 meters when I lost sight of it. And I'm pretty sure it bounced down the slope a bit before coming to a stop.

23

COMMITMENT

"Uh. A little explanation?" I asked.

Ge looked hang-dog guilty. Then he sighed. "I checked on our location and the news with my phone. Evidently, Megacore tracked it 'cause I got a notification of third party locators activated on my phone. They must have tracked me for a while. Lawmakers are considering moving the planetary charter vote to an earlier date. They're voting on whether to reschedule in three days. Naturally, Megacore is pushing hard for the earlier vote."

"What's the proposed new date for the planetary charter vote?"

"September fifteenth."

I was blinded by rage. "Crap! *We agreed!* You know who is hunting us! You're willing to let my family think that I'm dead but then risk all our lives to ping a map?! I *told* you and *told* you – your phone has crap security! But what do I know – after all, I'm the brainless fashionista bimbo, right?"

"I don't think you're a bimbo…"

"Oh yeah?" I stood hands on hips glaring at Ge. "Your deep respect goes a long way toward explaining why you blew off your promise and betrayed us all!"

Everyone else started showing up in response to me and Ge shouting. We explained the situation. In my case, through gritted teeth. In the middle of the inevitable questions, I thought I heard a mechanical hum and shushed everyone.

"Is that?" I started.

Ge finished for me, "A drone? Yes."

An explosion ripped through the valley. The fireball was impressive. KiKi fell over from the shock. Everyone else jumped.

"Thank God it's only a lightly armed drone!"

Then, we had to go down the whole rabbit trail of explaining drones and 'lightly armed' and tracking technology.

"Do you remember that funny humming sound, like an insect, that we heard?"

Quills flicked understanding and I continued. "That is the sound of a drone. That is the sound we must be alert for from now on. Megacore is not fooling around. That strike was meant to kill!"

Ge added, "According to the map I checked, we have approximately 3,600 kilometers left to reach the capital."

Everyone looked mystified, so I asked AckTik to translate. After a moment of staring into the distance, AckTik responded with, "That's over six long vines."

BanTik said, "That's impossible!"

I said, "Remember two-thirds of that will be down the river, going with the current. That will give us quite a boost."

"Yeah. With a decent current, combined with sculling and the boat's motor, we should make two hundred kilometers a day and be on the river for a couple of weeks. Subtract that from the total distance, we need to make," Ge began.

AckTik finished for him, "We have to travel nearly forty kilometers a day."

"So, no rest days." I said, then spat out, "Thanks for that, Ge!"

TikTik touched my arm and used his signature gentle humor. "He feels even worse about this than you do. We need you to work together. You know … the fate of our species, the opportunity for a bath…"

AckTik offered, "It should be possible if we are clever. We will lighten the load when we dump the snow gear and further, by eating through the food. That'll help."

"And finding a tributary so we spend more time on the water will help, too," I added.

BanTik said, "We have to make the attempt. Let's get out of here."

We packed up in record time and kept going until eight o'clock at night – the very last dregs of daylight. Kah climbed a tree and found a camping spot. It was so late we didn't bother cooking but ate dried rations for dinner and breakfast.

* * *

#Forensic Investigation File:

AI: DRONE MANEUVER WAS SUCCESSFUL. The eco-surveyor's phone has been neutralized. The drone reports deploying weaponry and destroying the target at 45.9766° N, 7.6585° E, at 14:37:52 Time Zone Prime. The target was destroyed. There is no sign of any energy signature within 50 kilometers of the target's last location. Target threat has been recategorized to neutralized.

CSO: Finally!

AI: RECOMMENDATION: Discontinue Drone Maneuver and Accelerate. Do you wish to authorize discontinuance of Drone Maneuver and Accelerate?

CSO: AUTHORIZE Discontinue Drone Maneuver. Code: 4573cgt. 4786rqbe. **AUTHORIZE CONTINUE ACCELERATE.** Code: 2334lm.7$MI.50874.

AI: AUTHORIZATION VERIFIED. Drone Maneuver discontinued. Accelerate strategy is currently underway.

* * *

We got an early start the next morning. A little before noon, we had a choice of two routes. Kah climbed a tree and said he couldn't tell which one was better. AckTik recommended moving to the west to get a better view. AckTik and Kah went to the west and came back with a route picked out.

We followed an animal trail high on the side of a steep narrow valley. It was dangerously steep and narrow with a terrifying drop-off to the valley floor below. We could hear water rushing through the valley, although we couldn't see the river through the foliage.

After several conversations with TikTik and a lot of thought, I decided it was up to me to be the better man. "Hey, Ge," I said. "I'm running low on water, I'm pretty sure everyone else is, too. Any suggestions?"

He smiled, taking my question as the peace offering I meant it to be. "If we keep my water generator going by draining it, we can all get refills. I'll set that up when we camp tonight."

The animal track was angling downslope, towards the valley floor. Ge asked Kah to scale a tree and check it out. Kah reported that the narrow defile widened out to a proper valley in another couple of kilometers. We kept to the animal track.

Sunset came early in the mountains even in the long days of summer. By seven o'clock it was too shadowed to continue. There was not any spot of land anywhere vaguely resembling 'flat.' Ge unrolled his camp mattress on the trail. We all sat down, with our backs against the mountainside, padded our backs with blankets and spread the fur rug over us. We slept, or I should say, dozed, sitting up. That was a miserable night.

The next morning the animal track petered out. We backtracked about half a kilometer and took the path angling upwards. It was very slow going. Ge, Kah and I frequently cleared the trail, moving rock and carving a path as we went. That afternoon, a thunderstorm began in the valley below us. We all took a moment to admire it. Absolutely fascinating to see a storm from the top.

Ge stumbled on a new animal track. Actually, it was an animal superhighway. The track was a solid 60 centimeters wide. It had evidently been a watercourse sometime in the ancient past, many of the rocks on the uphill slope were undercut, creating shallow caves. We made better time with easier walking, but we were all so weary from the previous bad night's sleep that we stopped at about five in the afternoon.

It was an easy trail, and we made pretty good time. Over fifteen kilometers, which was really good in the mountains. Another afternoon rain squall swept through the valley, and we enjoyed the light show. Apparently, afternoon rain in the valley was a daily or near daily occurrence.

The track rose and fell, widened and narrowed. At times it was terrifyingly steep and narrow. but it was generally angling down towards the valley. Once again, we made twenty kilometers and counted it a good day's travel. That was the second time we camped in a wash-out. It wasn't as spacious as the first one, but it was relatively flat. A real rarity in that country.

The next day was memorable because we stumbled upon an entire meadow choked with thorny purple berry bushes. The fruit was coming into season. We gorged on the fruit, filling two keeping bags with ripe fruit and another one of the unripe fruit which KiKi told me was excellent for stewing. That slowed us down, but we still made thirteen kilometers that day.

When we set up camp that night, I used multiple layers of security and a disposable avatar to sign on to the net. The vote results were reported. The agenda was changed to September 15th.

I announced that our new deadline was September 14th. We counted days and estimated travel times. It was pretty daunting. AckTik pointed out that we were all much fitter than when we began and could hope to make good time.

We brainstormed ideas. I saw the plains as the greatest challenge, nobody could swing. AckTik came up with the suggestion to make short true-hand-held crutches. She figured that the team could swing on the crutches faster than they could walk.

After some idle speculation and general conversation, I stood and stared down into the valley. `"Can you guys swim?"`

24

PLUNGE

"We are river folk, we all know how to swim," TikTik said and turned to KiKi, "You?"

KiKi nodded.

AckTik also nodded agreement and asked, "What are you thinking?"

"What if we take the river? It's too small to support the boat, but if we equip ourselves with flotation devices, we can let the river carry us off the mountain at pretty high speeds. A good way to remain hidden is to move in unexpected ways. If the drone is watching where they destroyed Ge's phone, they'll never see us when we're a hundred kilometers away."

"No nemes in this water?" Ge interrupted. I assured him that nemes only inhabit warm stagnant waters.

"I only have one personal flotation device," Ge warned.

"What? The lifeboat doesn't have any?" I asked.

Ge looked sheepish. "I never checked."

We opened the boat and checked. It was too big for the path, Ge had to old it out over the cliff. I used my phone as a lantern and checked. Sure enough, there was a sealed pocket on the inside of the bow. It held eighteen flotation vests from small child's size, ideal for KiKi, up to one that was almost big enough for Ge. We worked out who got which vest. Kah, while shorter than me, was twice as burly, and ended up with the largest vest.

Then BanTik sensibly asked, "What are we going to do with our packs?"

After a pause for thought, Ge asked, "What about my camp mattress? That's buoyant. If we wrap the mattress with the tent to waterproof it and lash on the remaining flotation vests it should support the packs."

AckTik looked worried. "That water looks dangerously cold."

"This is high summer, the warmest time of the year." I answered. "It's possible that the water's warm enough. We can check in the morning. You up for the job, AckTik? You will best be able to judge whether it's safe for you guys."

We talked it over for the rest of the night while whittling away on the crutches. AckTik came up with the idea of stuffing hot packs inside the flotation vests. It was July 23rd, only fifty-three days until the vote. We went to bed optimistic.

* * *

I need a break. Anybody else ready for lunch? I've got taco fixings ready, if anyone's interested. Help yourselves.

Are we missing anyone? No? You all comfy? Fed? You have drinks?

Hmm? No. I have my phone log from back then right in front of me. It's the best record we've got, so we'll just go with those dates and distances, okay?"

Okay, let's get back to the story.

* * *

Early the next morning, AckTik and Kah started to climb down to the water. The rest of us continued preparing to navigate the river. Ge had some waterproof tape in his camping kit. We carefully wrapped and sealed the waterproof tent around the mattress. We used that same tape to lash floats to the 'raft'. When we finished with that, we went back to whittling crutches.

AckTik and Kah surprised us by coming up the trail to us. Kah said, "There's a path down. It's not obvious from up here, but easy to spot from down there."

"Is the water warm enough?" I asked anxiously. I didn't want to have wasted an entire morning on useless preparations.

AckTik grinned. "It's not quite as comfy as back home but it will do."

We cheerfully packed up our whittling and took off down the path. We were all in high spirits and bantering back and forth.

165

I said to TikTik, `I can run faster than you can swing."

"I can swing faster than you can run, even swinging backwards!" he bragged cheerfully.

"I'll believe it when I see it," I teased him.

He decided to demonstrate by catching at a branch overhanging the trail. He was facing me and swinging out over the gorge, laughing. The branch broke, dropping him down the slope.

I screamed. A split-second later, I plunged over the cliff after TikTik.

I have no idea what I was thinking. Catch him? Slow down his plunge off the cliff? In fact, I don't think I thought at all. I was operating on 100% panic. I was scrambling down that steep slope, sliding on my butt, dropping past the steeper bits. I must have dropped my pack, because I didn't have it at the bottom, but I don't remember doing it.

I saw the shock on his face as he fell. I saw him bounce off of a projecting ledge of rock. That was the moment that I knew – *I knew* – what awaited me at the bottom. But I couldn't stop. The mist had slicked the stone; my palms burned where they scraped.

He landed on his back in a bush. The branches and twigs he broke were still snapping when I got there a second later. TikTik was gone.

I screamed – one long instinctive wail of grief. There was no translation needed. They all knew what that cry meant. Wails and sobs came from the path. I knelt beside him and shook my head as if denial could change physics. I clutched his shoulders and sobbed into his quills. They did not tremble under me. That stillness was the worst thing I have ever touched.

Ge arrived a few seconds later. He closed TikTik's eyes with a reverence that shattered me further. I turned to him and sobbed on his chest. He embraced me, comforting me. When I could breathe again, he stripped off his shirt, tied TikTik's body to his chest, and started the climb.

I followed in a daze, grabbing his heel when I needed help on the steep bits, useless and shaking. My stomach heaved twice; nothing came up. My ears rang. The roar of the storm sounded far away, as if the world had gone down a tunnel.

We reached the path. KiKi saw…and collapsed. She didn't even make a sound at first; she just dropped, as if her bones had been cut out of her body. Then the keening began; not one pitch but many, fractured by breath and disbelief. She pulled at Ge's knot and dragged TikTik to her lap, rocking him, her quills collapsed flat in shock.

BanTik stroked his son's quills and put his other arm around KiKi to comfort her. Another storm was brewing, and we were shrouded in mist from the top of the clouds.

BanTik keened into his palms. He touched TikTik's head only with fingertips, as if contact might break him again. His shoulders shook soundlessly. Kah turned away and braced both hands on the cliff wall, forehead pressed to stone. AckTik paced a tight, short loop like an animal gone frantic with pain, muttering disjointed syllables.

And Kiki lifted her face to me. That look, not anger, a naked, incredulous *Why him?* was worse than any accusation. I flinched from it as if slapped.

The clouds had dropped until we were inside them; mist slicked every surface, beading on our lashes like tears from the sky. A funeral was impossible here — no time, no graveyard, no bay tree. We could not even keep his body long; the storm and the schedule had already stolen the rites from him. There was no goodbye worthy of his life.

And it was *my fault*. He used the prosthetic *I made*. He took the dare *I teased* him with. He died proving himself *to me*.

I folded to my knees. The guilt was a blade. I could not look at Kiki again. I could not look at BanTik, at the small shape in her lap, at anything without wanting to crawl out of my own skin.

That moment — something in me broke and hollowed. My life, all the shallow seas of ambition and defense, drew in like a tide and left only rock. I heard myself breathe one long ruined breath.

This is on me.

If anything good is to come of this, it has to come from me.

I stood; not because I felt strong but because I could not bear to stay kneeling among the ruins without offering something back. A vow was the only currency I had. I faced them all; soaked, shaking, and wrecked. But that loss broke something inside me. My vast shallow oceans gathered themselves up and I *knew* what to say. I stood up and faced everyone.

"TikTik dreamed of peace and unity between humans and Acorans. To honor him, his dream is now mine. I swear to you by my pain, by Mother Acora and by my God, TikTik shall not have died in vain!"

Quills lifted around the circle; a visceral, electric shock of assent. And, honest to God, at that very second a thunderclap rang out.

* * *

167

I maintain that it was TikTik, sealing the deal. Ge says I'm being superstitious. But he doesn't say it very *loud* 'cause, like, he was *there*. I've seen recreations, but they all clean up the speech. I did a lousy job in the moment. It sounds just as bad in `Apex Jungle` as it does in Standard; and, let's face it, I'm no poet. But nobody needed a great speech, they needed my commitment.

* * *

I wanted to collapse like KiKi, but Ge didn't let me. With tears rolling down his face, Ge grabbed my hand in his and held it over TikTik's body.

`"I pledge my strength that TikTik shall not have died in vain."`

AckTik put her hand in. `"I pledge my wit that TikTik shall not have died in vain."`

Kah joined us and said, `"I pledge my athleticism that TikTik shall not have died in vain."`

BanTik stood put his hand in and said with a creaking voice broken with grief, `"I pledge my wealth that TikTik shall not have died in vain."`

Kiki wobbled to her feet, put her hand in, only able to stand because BanTik supported her, and sobbed, `"I pledge to nurture our child so that TikTik shall not have died in vain."`

Quills flashed everywhere. I thought, *one helluva way to announce your pregnancy to father-in-law.* BanTik hugged her close and they cried together. I got out a length of silk that I had saved to show to the folks back home. It was a glorious spring green color. Ge and I wrapped TikTik in his shroud.

Ge and Kah scouted a little further down the trail and found a shallow washout. We laid TikTik to rest. I felt completely hollow. Numb. And yet, my mind was running at high gear.

`"We will abandon everything that we don't absolutely need and leave it all as grave goods for TikTik. Trade goods can wait."`

Ge reluctantly parted with the last of his scientific gear and lost about ten kilos from his pack. We all shed the heavy furs and quilted snowsuits, using them to pad and cover TikTik's body. KiKi started to put her gorgeous celestial blue wedding dress in TikTik's grave. But I stopped her.

"No. You will need that before the end, and TikTik wanted you to have it."

I turned to the team. "Keep your best ceremonial clothing. It is important to prove not only that you exist but that you represent an advanced and highly sophisticated culture."

Ge, Kah and I dragged rocks. Ge found a large flat slab to cover the mouth of the cave where TikTik's head rested. We piled many rocks over the mouth of the cave to ward off scavengers.

AckTik prayed for TikTik, with many pauses, her voice cracking.

Beloved mother's-cousin-who-is-younger-than-me and wise friend, may your journey be blessed. May Storm Sister send you clear water. May Fire Brother send you warm sunshine. May Ice Brother send you gentle breezes. May Wild Sister nurture you in her bosom. May you find peace and beauty in the bosom of the Mother. Know that you will always be remembered, loved, and honored here. In Mother's name we pray. So be it.

"So be it." We all chorused in return.

"We're all too gutted to go in the river today, and it's getting too late." I said, "We'll camp at the bottom and make an early start."

KiKi was immobile with grief. I gave my pack to Ge and carried her, piggy-back style. BanTik was in similar shape and Kah supported him. I comforted AckTik as best I could. None of us was fully functional. We were all so prostrate with grief that we slowed to a crawl. We found a shallow slow-moving eddy of the river at the bottom of the gorge and camped next to it.

I grabbed my clothes and slipped away from the camp. I immediately plunged into the pool and bathed. God, it had been nearly a month! I mean, there's only so much one can accomplish with a wet washcloth. The sensual luxury of being clean should not be underestimated. I cut loose and cried buckets, washing my clothes and my face over and over again, hoping to scrub away the pain. Once I felt human again, I put on my cleanest outfit.

When I returned, Ge followed me down to the river. The level of stink in the tent declined to everyone's great relief. We spent the night in tears, telling TikTik stories, eulogizing him as best we could.

KiKi and BanTik didn't contribute much, they cried too often. But the rest of us got to say 'goodbye' and start to lock memories of him away in our hearts.

The next morning, we broke camp early and at high speed. Practice had made us quick. We didn't let KiKi help. BanTik only contributed a little bit. Even so, we had it down to less than fifteen minutes. Once we were loaded up for the river, I gathered the team together and put my hand in the middle of our circle. Ge copied me, soon they all did.

"Today is for TikTik," I said. "It's 52 days until the vote."

Ge plunged in first – the water was actually warmer than the air. The Acorans activated their heat packs. Ge tied them loosely to a rope. The idea was that Ge was strong enough to pull us all to one bank if there was a waterfall, so we could walk around it.

We sped down the river. We encountered three waterfalls. Ge would shout a warning and head towards one bank or the other. We all swam in that direction, so he didn't have to pull too much to haul us in. We climbed around the falls and immediately plunged back into the river. The floatie raft was doing a good job of keeping our packs out of water. KiKi and BanTik cried on and off throughout the day.

When the inevitable afternoon thunderstorm hit, it was pretty miserable. I noticed KiKi shivering.

"Hey, Ge! we need to pull over. KiKi's getting cold," I shouted up to the front of the line.

We pulled over and we all cowered under a rock ledge. Kah gave his heat pack to KiKi, and we draped both of the thermal blankets over the Acorans. KiKi sat in Kah's lap in between Ge and me to warm up. As soon as the storm passed, we went back to the river. When it started to get dark, Ge pulled us over to a likely camping spot. According to my phone we had covered nearly 150 kilometers.

We repeated the exercise on the following day, complete with a pledge for TikTik. We only encountered one waterfall and two sets of rapids that we walked around. We made over 160 kilometers. We were better prepared for the afternoon storm the next day and took shelter before KiKi caught cold.

I explained to her, "You're the highest priority now. You've got a baby to keep warm."

At camp that night, in the late shadowy light at the bottom of the gorge, we foraged and Ge and Kah hunted. They brought back a small neopig. We roasted most of it and stewed some of it with the last of the unripe purple berries. We ate the roast along with some leafy greens for dinner and had the stew for breakfast. KiKi was right, unripe purple berries are delicious in meat stews. Ge snacked on the left-over roast meat for the next two days.

25

SLOW TO A CRAWL

The next day we were not so lucky with the river. There was waterfall after waterfall. Kah scouted it for us, and we decided to abandon the river. The trees were thick enough that the Acorans could swing, and the ground was generally clear enough on the dry side of the mountain that Ge and I could run. My biggest problem with running were the straps digging into my shoulders.

Ge cut strips from his camp mattress and taped them on which gave me some relief. Everybody was much happier swinging, and we made good progress, nearly 20 kilometers that day. It was 49 days to the vote.

The next day, we tested the boat. The gorge was widening into a proper valley, and the river along with it. AckTik was scout this time and reported that the river was wide enough for the boat. We opened it and hopped in. Ge turned on the little assist motor and sculled from the front. The valley walls seemed to fly by.

In tones of awe, AckTik estimated we were moving at about 7 or 8 floats. After extensive translations, that worked out to twenty-five to thirty kilometers an hour. We did very well until we heard the waterfall. We pulled over on the east bank. We packed up and headed north to investigate.

The mountain suddenly dropped away. We were at a huge north-facing cliff a kilometer wide. The river fell in a broad ribbon into a swampy lake below. The cliffs on either side of the waterfall were steep and treacherous. There didn't appear to be any land below – only lake. There was a visible ring of slimy lichen and algae coating the last meter of rock at the shoreline. We debated climbing down and getting in the boat. But the cliff was quite sheer with the slippery rocks at the bottom. With all our packs, we would be clumsy, and we decided that it was too risky.

Since we were already on the eastern shore, we backtracked to the first reasonable slope we could find so we could walk around. It was pretty late by then, so we decided to camp. Kah and Ge went hunting but didn't bag anything. AckTik did pretty well fishing and we had grilled fish that night. We made less than 100 kilometers, in spite of our speed on the river. It was 48 days to the vote.

We got underway early the next morning. We had gotten in the habit of breaking camp in the pre-dawn darkness so we could take advantage of every ray of light. We began to climb the valley walls. At the top, I gave AckTik my phone, showed her how to operate the telephoto settings. She climbed up to photograph as far as could be seen to determine a route. Kah volunteered, but he was much heavier and wouldn't be able to make it as high up in the trees. AckTik selected an ancient tree that was thicker and taller than its neighbors.

When we examined the photos, we discovered that the lake blended with a swamp with no clear waterway north. The east was more promising. We all groaned, but there was no help for it. We climbed back down, walked upstream a bit, opened and loaded the boat. Kah and I pushed off hard and fast with the assist motor running to ensure that we made it to the other side before the current swept us over the edge. We made it.

But the campsite was uneven and very rocky. We didn't have any fresh food and broke into our dwindling supply of dried rations. We had another miserable night of poor sleep. We made absolutely no progress whatsoever. 47 days to the vote.

We climbed the eastern slope at the crack of dawn. It was a much rockier, much steeper, and more difficult climb. After the lower slopes, Ge roped us all together. Ge was in the lead, followed by AckTik, BanTik, and Kiki. Kah and I anchored the chain. It was a grueling five-hour climb to the top. Once we were all safely off the cliff. We discovered that we were in an evergreen forest. The ground was springy and faintly scented with the fallen needles. There were occasional stands of bracken but no significant undergrowth. We set up the tent in the clearing created by the fall of a giant spruce.

It was comfortable in the tent, even luxurious. Ge, Kah and AckTik hunted and successfully brought down enough pine-nut quails that we were able to fill up even Ge's belly and have enough for breakfast. It was another frustrating day of no progress. It was 46 days to the vote.

The next morning, the Acorans attempted swinging. The stiff branches and needles inflicted countless minor injuries. The rough bark damaged their gloves. We resorted to the hand-crutches. They were much faster crutching than they were walking. Ge and I jogged along with the Acorans at about eight kilometers per hour.

We made such good progress that we stopped fairly late that day. During dinner, I talked to AckTik.

"I'm worried that Ge and I are doing fine with this diet, but you guys need more fruits and veg. Am I right to be concerned?"

AckTik stroked her quills flat and sighed. "Yes. Especially KiKi. I've been on the lookout for new bracken growth – the mature fronds are low nutrition and inedibly fibrous. But it is late in the season, and I haven't spotted any."

Ge contributed, "We can make tea out of the pine needles and youngest of the bracken fronds. Very high in nutrients. Not delicious, but good for you. Wanna try?"

We quickly stripped needles and harvested bracken until we filled the entire ten-liter pot. Then poured boiling water over it and let it steep until it was tepid. Ge strained out the needles and chopped bracken and brought it back to the boil. He let it cool to drinkable and dished it out to everyone.

Gack! It was awful; resinous, bitter and acrid. It did not taste nearly as good as the pine needles smelled. I added opella which improved it tremendously; and we were later to discover, also improved the nutrition.

We made a little over 40 kilometers that day, absolutely none of it in the direction we needed to go. It was 45 days to the vote.

The next morning, we downed leftover needle tea with breakfast and AckTik climbed a tree to scout for us using my phone. The pictures revealed a potential descent slope about four kilometers further east. We eagerly made our way east, optimistic that we had found a way off the mountain. Once there, it proved to be a false hope. AckTik did her climb a tree scouting routine and found another possible route about three kilometers away. We proceeded on our way. It was the same routine all day long scouting potential routes but not finding any.

When we stopped for the night, AckTik and Kah went hunting and landed a mixed bag of a rabbit and a couple of pine nut quail. We also mixed in a handful of pine nuts and some AckTik-approved mushrooms we foraged. It wasn't bad.

Ge and I excused ourselves and walked through the twilight gloom. I said, "Ge, I should be wildly frustrated by our lack of progress. But the pine straw is so lovely to camp on, I can't be angry about it." I picked a nice little knoll and sat down.

"I agree, but with only 44 days left to the vote, we need to pick up the pace. I'm pretty sure there are comfy pine forests on the lower slopes as well," Ge said.

"Not so much. If I remember my geography correctly, the plains extend all the way into the foothills."

"Still more comfortable than rocky beaches!" Ge grinned. "Uhm. I don't know how to tell you this, but I promised TikTik I would. So," he took a deep breath, "you need to know I've got your back." He was urgent, pleading.

"You expect me to believe that after you betrayed us all to Grbić!?"

He kicked at the pine straw, his fists clenched, "Stupidest damn thing I've ever done. I foolishly dismissed your evaluation of Grbić as nervousness. But you were right. I thought a nano-second blurt was trivial, that I could get away with it. But you were right, again. If it's any comfort to you, I've already kicked my own ass from here to Earth and back. I am so sorry, Li. I'll do everything I can to make it right."

"It's gonna be a l-o-o-o-n-g time before I trust any of your promises!"

"Yeah," he winced "I know. And you're perfectly justified. I still hope that you'll change your mind about me. But even if you don't, I'm here for you. I can think of nothing better to do with my life than follow you to Novy Samara and into the pages of the history books."

"Good to know," I said. He opened his mouth to speak again, but I stopped him with my palm held up. "You've given me a lot to chew on. Gonna have to do some processing."

Ge nodded. "You ready to head back?"

I nodded and we groped our way back to the tent in the gathering gloom. It was 44 days to the vote.

26

MESA COUNTRY

The landscape was dominated by mesas. It looked as if a giant slab of the mountains had been sliced away and pushed over, cracking into thousands of individual irregular mesas. Each mesa was heavily forested with pines, just like our side on the mountain.

We finally caught a break the next morning. The lake petered out and emptied into a deep rushing river. The cliff of the mesa opposite the mountain cliff we were on was lower than the mountain by about six meters and about fifteen meters away.

We followed along the cliff edge, and it kept narrowing, until the gap was only about nine or ten meters. We continued on for a bit, hoping the gap would close, but it widened again. We returned to the narrowest point of the gap.

"Climbing down and back up doesn't make any sense," I said. "Can you jump that far, Ge?"

"Yeah, sure. Why?"

"You jump over with the rope in hand, secure it on that side. We zip line all the packs over to you. Then we follow. Kah will go last. He can untie the rope, and you pull him in. He'll smack into the cliff. But I'm confident that Kah can land with feet-hands extended and bounce without injury. Then you pull him up."

Ge thought it was a great idea, and we gathered everyone for a meeting. We went down a rabbit hole of explaining zip-lining. One of the most confusing points was that Acorans are very used to climbing rope bridges hand over hand, hanging underneath the rope. It took a lot of persuasion to convince them that zip-lining would be faster.

Ge leapt across. He rolled and fetched up against a tree. It looked like he smacked into it hard, and I was worried about it. He sat up and waved, though. Then he secured the rope to a sturdy pine on his side. Kah and I loaded up the rope with our packs and secured our end of the rope. The luggage was already sliding towards its destination as we tied the rope.

Once the luggage landed, Ge waved and shouted, `We're good!`

We had equipped ourselves with a motley variety of sturdy straps, and I went first to demonstrate the procedure. It was terrifying and impressive and exciting all at once. Ge caught me on the other side, helping me slow down so I wouldn't slam into the packs. BanTik went next. Once safely landed, I could see him working to calm down.

`Pretty terrifying, huh?` I said sympathetically.

BanTik nodded.

`It was for me, too. But it's also exciting. Some people rig these and do this recreationally.`

BanTik asked, `Recreationally? For amusement!?` His quills wavered with disbelief.

KiKi came over next, then AckTik.

AckTik said, `Amazing. I'm definitely putting one of these up when I get back!`

KiKi and BanTik stared at her, agog. I turned to BanTik and said, `I rest my case.`

Then we all turned to watch Kah. He untied the rope and dropped it over the edge. With the most jaw-dropping athleticism I have ever witnessed. He did not keep hold of the rope, as I had envisioned. Nope.

Kah leapt after it and caught the rope in midair! He scrambled up it hand over hand midair while Ge energetically hauled up the rope. He ran into the cliff face properly aligned on his hand-feet and one true-hand and absorbed the momentum with bent knees and elbow. He was only a couple of meters below us at that point. Utterly amazed, we all burst out with whistles.

A few seconds later when he scrambled over the edge, Kah took a bow, grinning from ear to ear. The entire crossing of that daunting chasm took less than fifteen minutes. We donned packs and continued through the pine forest.

About a hundred meters in, Kah shouted *`Snowberries!`* Then he repeated himself in Apex Jungle, `Snowberries!`

He took off at high speed towards the east, the rest of us trailed behind. In only a few hundred meters, we encountered another deep chasm running north to south. The scent of fruit was stronger. Kah was lying down, surveying the cliff face.

Kah looked up at us and explained, `There are ripe snowberries on rock ledges along the cliff. If I climb down on a rope, I can harvest them.`

Kah saw our expressions, stood up and rather sheepishly said, "It's important. You know, pregnant lady."

I couldn't help myself. I turned to BanTik and said, "So much for a million legs with the combined intelligence of a bree foal!"

BanTik had the decency to look ashamed. He spread his quills in apology, turned to Kah, made the respect gesture with his hands. He didn't squat, though, which is the full gesture is reserved for one's superiors, and said, "A thoughtless joke that I said before I got to know you."

Kah handled it beautifully. His quills rose with surprise, then he made the respect gesture in return, grinned, and said, "Apology accepted."

AckTik volunteered to go down, too. She pointed out that we had enough rope to wrap it around two trees spaced a couple of meters apart. She could take an arc on the north side, and Kah would work the south side of the ledge. Ge could pull them up whenever their keeping sack was full, or they needed a break.

With our plan and the rope in place, they scrambled down and gathered two full keeping sacks of snowberries. They rested for about ten minutes. On the second trip down, AckTik began slowing down. Ge pulled her up as soon as Kah shouted up that his keeping sack was full. AckTik's was not full, but she looked pretty tired. They rested for a full thirty minutes before going back down.

On the last foraging trip, AckTik pushed off with hand-feet to arc over to a new bush. But she started spinning on the rope. She caught herself with a true-hand. It bent back at an extreme angle. I couldn't tell if it was a sprain or a break, but that was definitely a serious injury.

"Pull her up!" I shouted and started to haul on the rope. Ge was already pulling and between the two of us, we had her at the top in seconds. Ge lifted her over the edge by her upper arms. Then, Ge pulled up Kah.

I turned to AckTik, "Broken or sprained?"

"Sprained, I think." AckTik winced. "I'll know more as it heals."

After a good deal of fussing about, we had spread a liniment from her medical kit. Then splintered her wrist with a makeshift splint (the one in Ge's kit was way too large) and had her trussed up. I saw the way Kah looked at her while we were doctoring her. I thought, *Oh, Kah, you are charting a dangerous course!*

"I am so sorry. By the Mother, I feel like a fool," AckTik apologized.

I replied, "Do not waste a single second on regret, AckTik. You were doing your level best to help. But lesson learned. None of us should push our-selves when we're fatigued. That's when accidents happen." I stood up and eyed the team. "Right, everybody?"

I got a chorus of agreement. "Let's send Kah down to fill the last keeping sack. Then, we feast on snowberries."

Kah filled AckTik's bag, then filled the last of the keeping bags. We gorged on the berries. You would think from the name that they would be pale and low on phytonutrients, but no. They were black with a waxy silvery coating. They were superb, deeply sweet and aromatic. After the feast. We continued walking north across the mesa until we encountered the next crevasse.

We spent time scouting for a decent place to cross which took hours and repeated our crossing technique of the morning. AckTik ziplined by hanging on to her strap with both hand-feet and her uninjured true-hand. Ge caught her and we made it across with no problems.

We continued to walk but with the Acorans on foot it was slow progress. It was already late, so we made camp at the first likely spot. Ge and Kah hunted but only got two hares between them. So, we did up a rich brothy meat stew for Ge. Kah and I each had a small serving, and it was done. Everyone else munched on snowberries.

We talked well into the night about how to speed our progress. Ge finally came up with the idea of a travois. He explained that a travois was a simple hand drawn litter. He wanted to make one of two poles lashed together with luggage and passengers carried in a sling affixed to the poles. He got the idea from pre-industrial Earth cultures. We latched on to that solution and went to bed optimistic.

We had only gone eight kilometers, but any progress was better than none. Since we lost TikTik, we had moved 450 kilometers. Ge and I were now nearly a thousand kilometers north of where we began. But that still meant we had to cover over 3,100 kilometers to get to the capital and we only had 43 days left.

The next morning, after pledging ourselves to TikTik's memory, I proposed a dangerous experiment. "I want to log on to the net to locate our position relative to a map of

179

the New Irtysh. We're getting short on time, and we can't afford to wander around lost."

AckTik asked, "Isn't checking our location what allowed them to find Ge?"

I nodded. "I hope to avoid that because Ge is the target, not me. Also, I have a much more sophisticated phone than Ge's. It obscures my identity more capably. I will get on and off in a split second when the net is busiest, which will make tracking me difficult. Finally, the instant the data is downloaded to my phone, I will log off and turn off the phone. They can't track it if it's non-functional. I think it's worth the risk for this one vital piece of information."

We discussed it all morning long. Ge surprised me by being the most negative about the idea. "I don't want them coming after me again, but I want them coming after you even less!"

"I get it. I do. On the other hand, I don't want to miss the fastest route to the Irtysh and *guarantee* that we get there too late."

The debate raged on. I pointed out that we were still undercover of the pines and could camouflage ourselves in the grassland. That was a whole rabbit trail as we explained camouflage. Ge showed us his featherweight fishing net and explained how to weave local vegetation into the net.

I explained that my phone could be used – without using the net – to survey the territory and provide us with the fastest route. It was also a compass to let us know when we went off track. It would need its battery, of course, but that was a minor risk, especially if we sited, took notes and promptly disabled it again. My phone case had anti-detection built in. But when in use, brevity was our friend.

At dinner that night, BanTik and KiKi were seized by deepest grief again. They moved away from the camp and clung to each other, weeping.

AckTik explained. "It's TikTik's Tenth Day. The day we sing a hymn for the departed."

"Ah. Does anybody know the lyrics and tune well enough to teach us so we can honor his Tenth Day?"

BanTik heard us and replied, "Sadly, yes. I am old enough that I have now sung it many times."

So, he taught it to us. I entered it into my notes on my phone. We spent hours practicing it. When we thought we had it down, Ge began and the rest of us joined in.

> You who dwells in the shelter of the Mother
> Who lived in Her shadow for life
> Say to the Mother when you meet her,
> "My refuge, my life!"
>
> And She will raise you up
> on the wings of a dove
> Bear you up on the breath of dawn
> Make you to shine like the sun
> And comfort you in Her bosom
>
> The snare of the fowler will not catch you
> And famine will bring you no fear
> Her faithfulness is now your shield
>
> And She will raise you up
> on the wings of a dove
> Bear you on the breath of dawn
> Make you to shine like the sun
> And comfort you in Her bosom
>
> You need not fear the terror of night
> Nor the flood that flows by day
> Though trees fall around you,
> you'll be unafraid
>
> And She will raise you up
> on the wings of a dove
> Bear you on the breath of dawn
> Make you to shine like the sun
> And comfort you in Her bosom
>
> Though we are bereft without you
> We shall love and honor you always
> And know we will join you one day
> And Mother will comfort us all.

AckTik turned to Kah for comfort. I cried myself to sleep on Ge's chest. Hell, everybody cried themselves to sleep that night. It was 43 days to the vote, but my phone only showed about fifteen kilometers progress.

27

SURVEILLANCE

So, we finally decided to do a navigation ping. Ge wrote a blurt search program. I retrieved an ancient disposable avatar and logged in. We were on and off in under a second.

When we examined the download, our location was indicated with a little oval, not a pin.

"Good! The oval indicates an estimated, imprecise location. All we have to do is get beyond the oval and the drones won't see us. Looks like we are only a little east of a small tributary to the New Irtysh. We should start going slightly west, say, north by northwest. I'll set my phone as a compass."

Ge grunted. "Let's go."

We made decent progress with Ge dragging the travois. We made it well beyond the perimeter of the oval before we ran into another chasm. It was a long hike finding a crossing point. We stumbled upon one that wasn't ideal. We crossed in good order, ziplined the travois across along with the luggage, and began hiking on the other side.

"These are getting wider," Ge said. "Pretty soon, it's gonna be too far for me to jump."

"Yeah. We should start scouting for a way down."

Kah volunteered for the scratchy job of climbing an ancient spruce, the least prickly option, and photographing the mesa. Then Ge had the phone plot our location based on the number of kilometers we had traveled. We all examined the photos.

* * *

183

#Forensic Investigation File:

AI: C-LEVEL AUTHORIZATION REQUIRED. I detected a close match to the energy signature of the collateral of the eco surveyor on the net. The log on is calculated to be 996 kilometers north of the crash site. The contact was brief. It could be an anomaly or a data error. Since the civilian is dead, the next most likely possibility is that natives have the phone.

CSO: You piece of junk! One minute you have destroyed the threat, the next minute it's back.

AI: Sadly, I am only as good as my information. **I recommend** an immediate upgrade from background tracking to active drone surveillance. Do you wish to authorize upgraded surveillance activity?

CSO: Do I have any choice? **AUTHORIZED.** Code: HEA571!

AI: AUTHORIZATION VERIFIED. Upgraded surveillance underway.

* * *

"It looks like there's been a rockslide due west of us," AckTik pointed out.

"Worth investigating," I agreed.

The team nodded and consented, so I set a new direction on the phone, and we took off. It was less than a kilometer. It was wide enough and there were no undercuts. But it was daunting. Steep and rocky, with bits of sheer cliff and slippery loose stone slopes.

We discussed it. I suggested a plan for Kah to lead and Ge to anchor the line with all of us tied together. Ge carried BanTik's, AckTik's and KiKi's packs because we figured they were the ones that were at greatest risk from the extra burden. AckTik was worried about climbing with only three limbs and I pointed out to her that Ge and I get by with only two.

Kah began to explore a path down. The first four meters or so would involve sheer wall rock climbing. Kah made it to the first substantial ledge and shouted up, "Good to go!"

The rest of us followed while Kah coached us on the rock holds to use on the way down. AckTik made it fine.

I said, "See, AckTik? Ge and I do it with only two hands capable of grasping, you did fine with three!"

We repeated the procedure, Kah leading us to a safe landing with the rest of us following three more times. Finally, we found ourselves at the peak of a slope of shifting small rocks and gravel. Not nice, rounded river stones, sharp broken shards of rock.

"This is brutal," I said. "You guys need to cover your feet. Don't want you to get cut up."

After considerable fiddling around, the Acorans had on their foot-hand gloves and knit mittens. We reinforced that fragile protection with scraps of one of Ge's shirts that we cut up and tied over the mittens. We descended cautiously. Even with all our precautions, we arrived footsore and hot at the bottom.

It was a narrow canyon with a mixed pine and deciduous tree woodland with open patches of meadow along the creek bed. The creek running through it was two or three meters wide but only a few centimeters deep. Although a full 30 centimeters at the deepest point in the channel. It was impossible to use for travel, largely useless for fish, or, at least, fish of any size. Kah found a shady camp site. Even though it was only midafternoon we settled in. I caught a glimpse of Ge stretching out and massaging his lower back and shoulders. Hauling that travois was no picnic, but no word of complaint from him.

"Damn! I was hoping the river would be big enough to navigate," I complained as we made camp.

"Not good enough for boating, not even good enough for floating, but excellent for navigation." I must have looked skeptical because he grinned and continued. "Every stream in this watershed feeds into the Irtysh. We follow the stream to a larger tributary, etc. Won't be long before we find one big enough for the boat."

"Oh, good to know." I turned to AckTik. "Being out in the sun, rather than the shade of the jungle canopy, stressed you guys out in spite of the fact that it's still cool. Am I right?"

"I'm afraid you're right," AckTik replied. "I am now deeply worried about the grasslands. Brother Fire is an unrelenting enemy."

"Yeah; what with your black fur."

I gathered our little team in front of the tent. "Our highest priority is to protect TikTik's child, right? Our second highest priority is to is to make it to Novy Samara on time, right? And to do

185

that, we must remain undetected, right?" I got more signals of agreement.

"I propose that we break out the caftans as sunshields for everybody. We still have the copper wire mesh for me and Ge to ward off the drones' electronics. That way we'll all stay cooler, and the copper mesh will dampen our electrical signatures. Some of the electricity will still leak around the edges, of course. But I'm pretty sure the drones will read us as low-intelligence herbivores. Do you think that will work, Ge? Does that seem feasible?"

"Yeah. I think so. I can research it on your phone." We all froze, horrified, and Ge petered to a halt.

"You can do that research without signing on to the net, right?" I asked.

"Yes," Ge replied sheepishly. "I won't make that mistake again. Gimme time. I'll come up with creative new ways to screw up." We all laughed.

I turned to Kah. "Could you please go downstream and scout out our route for us? Don't wander too far, a kilometer should do it."

Kah looked pole-axed for a minute as he struggled with mental math. AckTik rescued him. "That's about a vine and a half."

Kah smiled, took my phone, and took off.

Then Ge, BanTik, and I took off up and down the river to find water reeds. We were successful within a few dozen meters. They were lovely, about two to two-and-a-half meters tall. They were mature at the end of summer with developing seed plumes. Ge used his little camp cutter to harvest a few armfuls.

BanTik was fascinated. We had never demonstrated a laser cutter to him before. We headed back to camp to deliver our first load. Kah was already back.

"The grass starts a little more than two vines from here," he reported. He showed us the telephoto shots. We used that information to triangulate our location.

I announced, "Since we lost TikTik, we have moved a little over 465 kilometers, uh, what is that in vines, AckTik?"

186

"A vine is also about ninety percent as far as one of your kilometers. So, a little over 500 vines."

Ge was making calculations on the phone. "We have about 3,150 kilometers, or approximately 3600 vines to go. It's 42 days until the vote."

AckTik's eyes unfocussed. "So, we averaged slightly over 45 vines per day, that's seventy-two days, not forty-two. We're going to be thirty days too late!"

"No!" I disagreed. "The bulk of our progress happened when we were on the river. We went over 400 vines in three days on the river. The rest was overland. We're ridiculously, horrifyingly slow on land. On the river, we fly. Our most urgent need is to get back into a river so we can pick up the pace and cover more distance each day."

Ge was scrolling through the map. "This creek empties into a marshy wetlands about twelve kilometers, uh … fifteen vines, from here. We'll have to go around that. But the creek picks up on the other side. We can get there in a day."

"So, you still think we can make it even if we take a day for preparations?" BanTik asked.

Ge and I chorused together, "Yes!"

KiKi hummed politely to break in on the conversation. "It really doesn't matter. We have no choice. We must, for TikTik."

I embraced her, all misty-eyed. We re-pledged ourselves to TikTik. Then we dove into working out travel arrangements.

Ge worked on fashioning a harness for himself to make pulling the travois easier. We sacrificed KiKi's pack. It held precious little, as we had eaten through most of our dried food. I packed all her things in my pack and gave the last of my dried food to Ge. He made the harness from the sturdy leather and silk pack and held it together with bits of rope he welded with the camp cutter.

"It's a good bet you never thought you would be reduced to the role of draft animal while you were battling your way through a Ph.D." I teased him.

187

"Yeah." He grinned, "Not exactly the game plan. But then this whole adventure is completely off-brand for you, and you've risen to the occasion."

AckTik came up with the idea of fashioning wheels for the travois. Kah reported a downed tree on the other bank of the stream a ways down, it was his marker for finding the melon patch. Ge and Kah agreed to harvest some of the trunk for wheels and search for likely axle materials.

Everybody broke for foraging, and we hit the jackpot. Kah came back with an armload of stripe melon. I stumbled across some sharp garlicky native ramps. Everybody found roots and tubers, Ge brought down a large, plump brebola. It was a feast.

The snowberries we had left were starting to ferment so we dumped them all in a pot and boiled them down. Snowberries are pretty high pectin. We came out with a jam so dense that it was just about a fruit leather. The fermentation actually enhanced the flavor. KiKi taught me how to clean and pan-toast the stripe melon seeds for a tasty snack.

I don't even remember how we stumbled on the topic, but after dinner we each shared our favorite TikTik stories. His wisdom, his advice, his funny quirks, and his best jokes. We laughed and cried by turns all night long. We also healed a little bit more. We all went to bed peacefully that night. We had many kilometers to travel and only forty-two days to travel them, but I was fine with that.

28

GRASSLANDS

We all worked on our camouflage. It took Ge all morning and some of the afternoon to carve out three wood rounds, he wanted to create a spare. His cutter was a little too lightweight for the job and slowed him down. It was designed for clearing brush and collecting samples, not for harvesting timber.

Meanwhile, we wove two camouflage nets. One for the tent out of fishing net and one for the travois out of woven reeds. Ge pointed out that we only had one thermal blanket left. A troublesome thought, but there was no help for it. We set up the camp shower and I supplemented creek water with boiling water to bring it up to comfortable temperatures for everybody. KiKi had two showers right in a row. Ge and I didn't need any help. Air temperature was twenty-five degrees, still nippy for the Acorans, but fine for us. When we were ready, we attended to various housekeeping chores.

Everybody foraged but Ge. He finally managed the wheels and had cut out a hub and some pie-shaped slices to create crude spokes. But that afternoon, he was still working on the axle and pegs to hold the wheels on. I threw the fur rug Sulralani had gifted us over a branch and beat the living daylights out of it with the sculling oar. The dust flew and it fluffed back up again nicely.

Our foraging was highly successful in that rich valley. The creek was so shallow it was a simple matter to wade across. I stumbled on a kaladu tree and harvested a keeping sack full of the sour fruit. I showed KiKi and BanTik how to set the camp stove to dehydrate. In only a couple of hours, we had dehydrated most of the kaladu fruit and all of the mushrooms. AckTik blundered into a treasure trove of walnuts. We hulled those to take with us. On his third trip to the melon patch, Kah bagged a small antelope.

After dinner we harvested some pliable saplings and, by the light of the camp lantern, built a cage over the travois-turned-cart. We covered it with a thermal blanket topped with a camouflage net and

189

counted it a very productive day, even though we hadn't moved at all. We had forty-one days until the vote.

The next day Ge carried AckTik when the trees grew so dense that the cart wouldn't fit through. Ge turned it on its side, and Kah and I carried it through the dense bits that way. We made it to the grass pretty soon. I suggested that we fluff up the grass after we crushed it flat with the cart.

I explained, "The furrows left in the grass are obviously artificial and a drone can follow the tracks to us." We took turns scuffing the grass back into place even though it slowed us down.

AckTik helped fluff grass most of the time. Ge was pulling the cart with only the luggage aboard. Evidently, riding a crude wooden cart wasn't a luxury experience and AckTik was getting pretty battered. She preferred to walk anytime we took a break and slowed the pace. I slung my pack onto the cart and had her ride on my back from time to time to pick up the pace. Even going at walking speeds to eradicate our tracks, we made good progress and made it around the wetlands by early afternoon.

But there was no creek. We searched for nearly a full kilometer after where it was supposed to be. I worried that our calculations of location or the map was wrong. It came out as a whine, and I shut my mouth hard on any further complaints.

Ge asked, "Implant wore off and you're getting your period?"

I nodded.

Ge stopped and said, "We haven't missed it. The map isn't wrong; it's a different season. The creek is intermittent here. It only flows in spring when the snow melts. We have to go back and search for the creek bed. Even overgrown with grass, we should be able to find it."

Sure enough, we found it in less than an hour. The grass was thinner, there were more rocks, and it was definitely sandier. The Acorans grabbed their crutches, and we picked up the pace. I jogged alongside the cart holding one of the frame poles to keep it from yawing or tipping from minor irregularities in the creek bed.

Out of the shadows of the mountains, we were able to keep going longer and set up camp late. We fluffed grass up around the unshielded front yoke of the cart. We cut up a couple of melons, thinned some of the jam to make a dressing, and had a big salad, sprinkled with minced dried kaladu. It was a triumph. Ge supplemented with the dwindling dried protein-rich rations.

I used the phone to calculate distance and location. We were right on track and had made over thirty kilometers in that one day – in spite of being lost for over an hour! It was forty-one days to the vote.

* * *

The next day we had the last of the fruit and nut salad for breakfast. After about an hour, the creek bed widened and deepened. Low thirty-centimeter clay banks rose on either side. The bottom was even sandier with rocks and gravel concentrated in the center of the channel.

The Acorans preferred crutching over the gravel. Ge chose to stick to the sand. It was actually easier than dealing with the bouncing and tipping of the cart when the wheels went over rocks. I kept up jogging along stabilizing the back to give AckTik as easy a ride as possible. We had arranged a deeper level of padding for her by doubling the fur rug and that helped.

It was near noon when we heard it. A drone hum. `Slow down!` I hissed in a stage whisper. `Remember - we're an unassuming herd of harmless herbivores.`

We slowed to walking speeds. I could hear the drone humming above. Suddenly, it let out a loud whine from above and behind us.

`Run!` I barked.

I bolted out in front. Ge followed while AckTik clung to the frame of the cart with her good true-hand and both hand-feet. Kah crutched at high speeds, pretty well keeping up with us. BanTik and KiKi trailed behind. I was getting winded and realized I couldn't hear the whine.

I came to a halt, and they all joined me. We flopped down on the ground to catch our breath.

When I had recovered enough breath to speak, I said, `That hadn't occurred to me. The damned thing was attempting to provoke a stampede!`

Ge explained, `Yeah. I saw a special about it. People know that the whine is harmless. But animals don't. So, if you want to uncover humans hiding among animals, use the whine to spook the herd.`

`On the bright side, our rate of travel for today just got a boost! But we mustn't get complacent. For every drone we're aware of, there are two hands-worth we aren't aware of.`

191

"And on that sobering note, shall we?" Ge suggested.

We were all very fit by that time. Even BanTik only needed ten minutes to recover from the sprint.

It was late in the afternoon when we ran into another dry stream bed. It was larger than the track we were on. We turned downstream and jogged until we began to lose light. The banks were two meters high by that time. Our camouflage would only work for grass, not the stream bed. Also, the banks would soon be too daunting to climb. We consulted the map and decided the eastern bank was the wiser choice. Ge went first and helped Kah up, then they helped the rest of us over the lip.

We set up camp while Ge and Kah hunted. They brought down a couple of prairie quail and we dined on those with fresh stripe melon and snow berry jelly for dessert. We made over forty-five kilometers that day. We had forty days left to the vote.

* * *

I will not bore you with a detailed recitation of the next ten grueling miserable days. We trudged along beside that dry or nearly dry stream bed for what seemed forever. On day five, the stream bed turned into an actual tiny stream. It was only a few centimeters deep and 30 centimeters wide, but it was an encouraging sign.

We were averaging thirty to thirty-five kilometers a day, but we were running dangerously low on food. Everyone was losing weight. Kah recognized ground nuts and taught us how to forage for them. They are starchy little tubers that rounded out stews nicely and were good mashed up for a breakfast porridge.

There was plenty of game, so Ge had no problems. He was maintaining muscle mass on a meat-heavy diet. It wasn't my favorite diet; not exactly gourmet variety, but I was staying strong. The Acorans though, even Kah, weren't doing as well. In spite of all the exercise, BanTik was developing a little gut. I'm convinced that lack of fruit and vegetables slowed AckTik's recovery from the sprain.

We did everything we could to preserve the fruit for KiKi. Ge was the first to stop eating fruit, Kah and I followed the next meal. BanTik and AckTik went to half rations by day three. The landscape started to change, and occasional clumps of shrubs and a few trees cropped up from time to time. We were able to forage for white gourds which provide starch and very little else. They have virtually no flavor and take forever to cook. But we also harvested more walnuts and some bead melons. The melons were so small, and the skin so tough, that they had to be tediously peeled and cooked. But it was worth it to get more fruit into the Acorans.

Finally, late in the afternoon on the twelfth day, we found the river. We heard it before we saw it. We hurried forward. It was glorious. Since it was getting late, we made camp and fished for our dinner. It was a very pleasant change. AckTik harvested some ramps and BanTik brought back a huge haul of vine cabbage. We all feasted on fruit that night.

We were 610 kilometers closer and were slightly west, southwest of Novy Samara. We still had a little bit more than 2,500 kilometers to go as the crow flies, but it was closer to 2,800 as the boat floats. We still had twenty-seven days until the vote. Up in the mountains we made 120 to 150 kilometers on water each day. We would make it to Novy Samara in time if we only averaged a little over 150 kilometers per day. We celebrated well into the night on the strength of the good news.

Shoulda known better.

29

NOVY IRTYSH

I woke up with nausea, fever, and chills. I thought I had a stomach flu. But then the Ge and the Acorans woke up with the same symptoms to varying degrees. KiKi was spared, and Ge didn't have too bad a case, but the rest of us were really sick. BanTik was the worst.

AckTik figured it out. She declared it was the vine cabbage. KiKi detested it and hadn't eaten any, Ge had only had a very small serving, BanTik had eaten the most of it. AckTik explained that it was most likely a parasite. So, Ge and I took the worming pills from our medical kit. AckTik mixed up a foul-smelling herbal tea for the Acorans.

BanTik was definitely the worst. In any civilized place, he would have been hospitalized. Ge and Kah took turns carrying him out to the woods at frequent intervals to vomit and pass copious diarrhea. By afternoon, it was up to Ge. Kah was too weak and could hardly stagger away from camp to manage his own diarrhea.

Ge's water generator was working full time around the clock just to keep up with our hydration demands. Between vomiting and diarrhea, we all got dehydrated anyway. That afternoon I asked KiKi and Ge to strike camp and move to a new camp only about 700 meters away. There was a ring of noisome waste building up around our original camp.

Ge was getting better, but I repeated the dose of worming pills that afternoon. By the next morning, I was no longer throwing up and only had occasional diarrhea. I was still weak and wobbly and took a very long nap that afternoon. But I was getting well enough so that I was not a burden.

KiKi had taken it upon herself to nurse BanTik through this. She never left his side. Ge and I gave her breaks during the night. She was reluctant until I pointed out the baby needed sleep. We moved camp again the next day.

We were all terrified for BanTik. He was visibly wasting away. His eyes sunk into his head. He could only be roused a few times a day and only for a few minutes at a time before he drifted off to sleep again. I concocted a thin gruel of groundnut paste and the last of the snowberry jelly and rehydrated dried kaladu mixed in. We dosed him with the gruel alternating with worming tea for three days. Then AckTik's supply of the worming herbs ran out.

I searched frantically through my phone for any local plants that might help. There was a species of local hardy cinnamon that had thick spongy interior bark that was useful. I showed Ge and Kah, who was getting better by the fifth day, what we were looking for. Kah found it, Ge used his cutter to harvest all the bark.

* * *

You can still see the dead tree to this day. Just a little north of the confluence of Novy Irtysh and the Algonquin rivers. It has a little fence around it and an explanatory plaque. Athletes who participate in the annual memorial "Dash to the Capital" pin pics and notes on the branches. Anyway, back to the story.

* * *

We all worked pulling the spongy interior bark away from the exterior rough bark. The gruel now included bits of the spongy bark. That's when BanTik turned the corner. He stabilized. He was able to stay awake for up to thirty minutes at a time. He wasn't putting any weight back on, but he wasn't visibly losing weight anymore, either.

We were force feeding him hardy cinnamon bark tea and gruel heavily laced with it every other hour. We even woke him up a couple of times at night for a dose of the tea. We moved camp again. The rest of us were on the mend. My stamina was shot but I no longer had any overt symptoms.

That night when we were gathered in the tent, BanTik said, "By the Mother! You should have abandoned me. You should not delay on my behalf."

I was horrified. I squatted down in full respect posture before him, just as I did for Matriarch. Everyone's quills flashed in surprise. "Revered Uncle; don't ever say anything like that again. We would no more abandon you than we would our own matriarchs."

Everyone's quills settled in the enthusiastic agreement pose. There were murmurs of agreements from everyone. BanTik was obviously moved and cried, much to his own embarrassment.

Ge got a devilish gleam in his eye and said, "You pledged your fortune to support this. You're worth one helluva lot more alive than dead, old man. No way I'm letting you out of my sight!"

We all laughed, even BanTik. Later that night, BanTik finally felt the urge to eliminate after days of no show. Ge carried him out. It was nothing but dead worms. We doubled up the bark tea. The rest of us drank a few cups daily just as a preventative measure.

I got my period. a spotty affair, more cramping and bloating than an actual period.

It was the season for ripe fruit and vegetables. Our foraging proved to be very productive. BanTik started to eat more and eliminated huge quantities of dead worms with every BM. Since we were no longer limited to what we could carry, we packed the boat to the gunnels with nuts, seeds, squash, melons, and rind pears.

Ge and I set up the boat. We discarded the camouflage. Our best hope of disguise now was to look like outlying colonists traveling the river. We practiced setting up the tent in the boat configured so that there was a narrow walkway on one side of it from stem to stern. Ge installed the sculling oar, and we were set. I caught him with that look again, the one that made me feel both seen and chosen. And God help him; he wasn't subtle about it. That jacked up my pulse every single time.

BanTik was still too sick to help, but AckTik gave her approval to move him. We planned to break camp at the crack of dawn and fly down the river in the morning. We still had 2,800 kilometers to go, and it was only nineteen days until the vote.

* * *

We set the tent up in the boat and launched bright and early the next day. We had to pull over to the shore to let BanTik relieve himself many times that day. He was still eliminating worms like a champ. We force fed him hardy cinnamon tea and had him chew on bits of bark. Every single bite of food that he ate was seasoned heavily with the stuff.

"Ge, are you okay with doing most of the sculling? You're better at it than any of us."

Ge grinned, "I kinda knew what I was getting into from the start; so yeah, I'm okay subbing in for a boat motor."

AckTik's wrist was finally getting better, but not enough for heavy work. When Ge took a break, Kah and AckTik would team up and scull instead. AckTik worked one-handed but still offered significant help. We had to stop fairly early that afternoon. We weren't all fully fit yet, and we didn't want to press our luck with BanTik.

We were a hundred kilometers closer to the capital, only 2700 to go, and had eighteen days until the vote.

For the next four days, we pulled over frequently to give BanTik bathroom breaks. But he was keeping all his food down and regaining weight. He slept more than anyone else and was still weak, but definitely on the mend. We were only making a little over a hundred kilometers per day during that phase of our journey. Finally, on the fifth day, BanTik made it all day long without diarrhea and we decided to pick up the pace. There were only thirteen days left, and we had only moved 550 kilometers. So, we still had over 2,000 kilometers to go.

I was dead worried about it and discussed it with Ge as we sailed down the river. We needed to move 170 kilometers per day to make it on time.

"Are you okay with taking shifts and staying on the river at night, using only the assist motor, Ge. That way we would only have to stop morning and evening for relief breaks, and it would eliminate setting up and striking camp. Everyone could handle the sculling oar as a rudder and keep us centered in the river, even KiKi."

KiKi's voice floated out from the tent where she was caring for BanTik. "I heard that!"

Ge grinned. "Stand aside: I was born for low-pay, high-blister night labor."

I was worried that the last of the dried rations were gone and without hunting game, Ge wouldn't make it. That's when, by the providence of the Mother, we felt a tiny little bump against the bottom of the boat.

I looked over the side of the boat. "The sturj are running!" I cried gleefully.

Everybody else was confused. But I knew what to do. I snaked my hand in the water and within seconds, caught and flipped a sturj onto the boat. Yes, it is that easy to catch them when they're migrating. It was a lovely three-kilo specimen. Kah promptly dispatched, beheaded and gutted the beast. We set up the camp stove on the deck within minutes.

I explained, "Sturj are predatory fish born in rivers but live as adults in the salt ocean. They return to the streams where they were

197

born to mate and lay eggs every year. They inhabit frigid oceans and are very high in fat as a result. They're tasty for everyone, but a Mother-Send for Ge."

I enhanced the sturj with opella and salt and crushed some dried kaladu over it. It was a big hit. BanTik was feeling well enough to exit the tent and partake. The Acorans had never tasted it before but pronounced it delicious.

Ge inhaled over half the fish and said, "I could do that again."

Kah flipped another sturj onto the deck, and we repeated the performance. Kah and I went back for seconds, but we left a quarter of the fish on warm for snacks later.

I suggested, "We should smoke some for Ge. The migration will be over in a few days, and he needs this."

Kah promptly flipped another three sturj onto the deck. That evening when we stopped, Kah went out foraging. He came back with a keeping sack full of long willowy leafy branches. They smelled both spicy, rather like allspice or cloves, and tart, like lemon or kaladu. Kah assured us all that pri'malu'u were the best for smoking fish.

AckTik disagreed and stated that the famed opella wood was better. That triggered a lively debate while we set up the camp stove for smoking. Whatever. It was wonderful to see everybody in good spirits. The team was pulling together again. Nobody won the debate, and pri'malu'u is brilliant for smoking fish. It was a gourmet treat.

I insisted that we exempt KiKi and BanTik from night watch. Ge crashed early and took over sculling when he awoke early in the evening. I was nowhere near as fast as Ge, but I think it still helped. The rest of us hung out on the deck. With Ge, BanTik and KiKi in the confined shrunken tent, it was pretty much full.

When waking Ge, I had accidentally awakened KiKi. With tears in her eyes, she made a life-altering observation. "Ge looks at you the way TikTik looked at me. You order the rest of us around, but you *ask* him. We have a betting pool on how long it takes you to listen to your own heart."

KiKi settled right back down to sleep, but I was wide awake for hours, thinking about it. Apparently, my pulse did not lie, my logical mother-voice dominated brain was deceiving me. We had traveled a little over 120 kilometers that day, and it was only twelve days to the vote.

29

NIGHT SHIFT

The next morning, I checked my phone, and it only recorded another 100 kilometers. I had a gut feeling that it was wrong.

"Ge," I said the next morning. "My phone only recorded about 100 kilometers. But I don't think that's accurate. I think it's under calculating our movement at night because I'm asleep. Should I hand it off to you for the night shift?"

"Yeah. I also think I should take the night shift alone. It would work better than you guys sleeping in shifts around me."

"Excellent suggestion. But it should be both of us for the night shift."

We worked it out. The tent, as currently configured, could comfortably sleep two humans or all four Acorans. BanTik was awake for most of the day, only taking naps in the afternoon. So, it would work out for him. We adopted Ge's suggestion.

I hung out with him in the bow most of the day. Kah and AckTik took over in the afternoon so we could catch naps. It wasn't that restful, but I think it helped. When the Acorans when to sleep we talked about this, that, and the other thing. We got around to "what's the first thing you're going to do when we arrive in Novy Samara?"

"Let my parents know I'm alive – Megacore can't use them for leverage if we're already in Novy Samara with the Acorans in tow. Then, I'll get a head-to-toe glow up."

"Still with the fashion? You look great. You don't need all that."

"Uh-uh. I am not appearing all grubby in a permanent interstellar record, and I'm gonna make you dress up, too. Then I'll contact Huong Owusu. She's a popular reporter with a significant following. I already know her. She's interviewed me a couple of times. Huong's good and the perfect reporter to break the story. With her press credentials we can waltz right into the vote. I'm Sister of the First House and will be able to demand the Right of First Speech. We can put the Acorans under a celebrity veil so that pandemonium won't break out until after we're on the Floor and I can speak."

"You really have worked this out."

"Yep." I grinned up at him. "I even know which hotel we'll stay at, the *Novy Ararat Imperskiy.* I have stayed there many times. It's right on the river with docks for small pleasure craft and they are known for their discretion. It's a sure bet they have a way to convey high-profile VIP guests from the docks to the hotel discreetly."

"You've been thinking about this a *lot.*"

I smiled coquettishly. "Not just about our arrival. About a lot of other things, as well."

"Oh?"

"Yeah. Like for the first time in my life, I realize how many of my ambitions are not my own. I learned them from my mother. Ever since we lost TikTik, the universe has shifted for me. I have no intention of returning to fashion. Instead, I find I'm ambitious to establish peace between us and the Acorans. I am desperate to turn this into a win-win for both species, just as TikTik dreamed it would be."

"Anything else?"

"Yeah. Uhm." I was squirming like a little kid confessing to stealing cookies. "Yeah, I've been thinking about what I said to you back in Ifka'a Kifma'a, you know about my ambition to marry for money. Uhm, well, that's mom's ambition, as well."

"Jesus! It's like pulling teeth!"

"Ahem. Sorry." I was too embarrassed to look at him, so I settled for staring at the boat deck. "I'm beginning to think I'm not happy in the friend zone, either."

"Are you real right now?" Ge asked his face glowing with happiness.

I nodded. He grabbed me, lifted me off of the deck, and went in for a kiss. I enthusiastically returned the favor.

* * *

What? Well, that was a remarkably intrusive and vulgar question! Please keep in mind who it is that you are interviewing.

Apology accepted. Shall I continue?

* * *

We never cooked a proper meal. We snacked on the food stashed around the boat all night long. The next morning when I checked my phone, with it up and active all day long the reading was much more accurate. It claimed we had made 240 kilometers. I hadn't calculated last night, but it was now ten days until the vote, and it looked like we had less than 1,700 kilometers to go.

200

Since we had been up all night, it was easy to sleep during the day, even with everyone else up and moving around. I remembered to hand over the phone to AckTik and when we woke up late in the afternoon, it showed another 160 kilometers progress. So, nine days left and only 1,540 kilometers more or less to Novy Samara.

That's when my menses came back with a vengeance. Those cramps were as bad or worse than anything inflicted during childbirth, let me tell you. AckTik noticed my distress. I had explained menses, but I don't think anyone was prepared for the real deal. I scooped water from the river to rinse the blood out of the pads provided by the Grove seamstresses. Then, I would draw fresh water and wash them properly with soap and let them dry. A repulsive chore but unavoidable.

"Is it like this for your women all the time?" AckTik inquired anxiously.

"No," I explained. "This is especially bad because my implant suppressed my normal cycle for a long time. Normally, if I wanted to terminate birth control, I would be given transition treatments so that my body adjusts over the course of three months. But that's not available for me. My hormones are wildly imbalanced now. It's as if my body is compensating for last year's implant."

Ge corroborated, "Yeah. Moodiness, irritability, intensely painful muscle cramps, nausea, sleep disturbances, headaches, and bloating are all common. It passes in a few days. Best to leave her be to weather the storm. If the woman is distressed more than usual, there are treatments to alleviate the symptoms."

AckTik and I both stared at him.

"What?" he replied. "I'm a biologist. I have sisters. I'm just glad we're on the river, so the smell of blood doesn't attract predators."

When we beached that afternoon, after everyone had done their business, we scattered for the usual foraging. I spotted a paddle bush and called out to everyone.

Paddle bushes are head-high shrubs, with each 'paddle' rising from a stumpy central knob right at ground level. They shed their fronds seasonally and those dried fronds accumulate at the base of

201

the bush. The fallen fronds look exactly like the ace of spades with an exaggerated stem.

AckTik was closest and came over to see what I was so excited about. She was about to step closer, but I restrained her.

"It'll slice up your feet. But if we harvest the fallen ones, and slice off the sharp spiny edges, they make excellent paddles. Right now, only two of us can paddle together. With these, we'll all be able to paddle to help Ge out. Let's wrap our hands so we can harvest these."

We harvested enough fronds to equip ourselves with paddles. Ge got out his cutter and trimmed the edges and carved out handles at the base of the fronds. Then, he wrapped the carved bits with more of our rapidly dwindling supply of rope and welded the grips on with the cutter. In hindsight, we should have done all of that on the boat. But, oh well. We were loading the paddles and our foraged walnuts into the boat and preparing to board.

The dire wolf emerged from the trees. Dire wolves, for the off-worlders amongst you, are large low-slung beasts with virtually no resemblance to the Terran species for which they're named. They mass over 300 kilos, with the larger males weighing in at 400 kilos. They have wide faces with powerful short muzzles. The shoulders are enormous, tapering to smaller lithe hindquarters. They are equipped with razor sharp claws on their front paws. They sport mottled brown and black fur with a curly upright mane around their shoulders and running the length of the spine.

Thank God they're solitary hunters. They are now confined to natural preserves, but back in the day, they were the dominant apex predators of the temperate forests.

One would hope that such a large heavy animal would be slow. That would be a false hope. The evil things have lightning-fast reflexes and the lithe agility of cats. This dire wolf was one of the larger males.

KiKi screamed. The Acorans all immediately scrambled into the trees. Ge grabbed KiKi and tossed her to Kah, who was already on a low branch, "Catch!" Kah caught her and gently placed her in a high branch overhead.

Ge shouted to me, "Run!"

I ran. It whipped around its head to follow me. So, it was tracking my scent. Ge darted in and slashed at its neck with the cutter and danced back.

It whipped its head around to face this new annoyance.

Kah and AckTik swung into action with their slings and stones. Kah landed a hit with a large stone in the beast's right eye. It roared with pain and reared, thrashing out blindly.

It smashed Ge on the left forearm and Ge screamed.

I darted in on its right blind side. I still had a paddle in hand. I stabbed it as hard as I could between the ribs, jerked the paddle back out and ran away. It whipped its head around and snapped at me. It missed me by a few centimeters. I could feel its foul hot breath on my back as I ran.

AckTik and Kah continued to rain down high-velocity stones. I heard them thudding home. There was a sharp crack as one got him in the skull. I whipped out my stunner and blasted it in the head, being careful to miss Ge.

It shook off the effects of the stunner with a flick of its ears. The wounds we inflicted only enraged the beast. I stunned it again, and it lowered its head and shook his head hard, like a dog drying off after getting out of the water. But it wasn't showing any signs of slowing down or giving up.

Kah grabbed a smaller branch that hung over the riverbank with his hand-feet. The branch bent under his weight, and he retrieved two paddles from the boat with his true-hands and tossed one to AckTik.

Kah and AckTik hung from the branches stabbing the beast repeatedly along the back. It roared and sidled away from them. It turned its head to see what was harassing it.

In the bravest, most daring move I have ever heard of, Ge leapt *forward* and plunged the cutter up to the hilt into its remaining eye and swung the cutter back and forth before darting back. It collapsed, spasming, still dangerous in its death throes.

I ran to Ge. It was a compound fracture. The jagged ends of both the ulna and radius projected out, the rest of his wrist and hand dangling heavily.

AckTik and Kah dropped down beside us.

"Hold him. I'm going to set the bones," AckTik ordered. Kah and I each grabbed a shoulder. She pulled his lower arm back up and mated the bones as best she could. Ge screamed.

I was in tears. I turned to Kah. "Our medic kit, in Ge's pack."

AckTik grabbed a smooth river stone about the size of a fist and shoved it into Ge's armpit, pressing it hard. Relief washed over Ge's face.

Ge asked, "How are you numbing this?"

203

AckTik grimaced with effort. "Brachial nerve pinch. Thank the Mother yours are in the same place ours are!"

Kah arrived with the kit. I slapped the medi-bot on Ge's arm. It whirred into action, numbing, setting bone shards, delicately gluing blood vessels and muscles into place. It sprayed each reassembled layer with growth factors and antibiotics as it worked its way from the deepest part of the wound towards the skin. It closed the wound and applied a biofilm.

It was a tiny, outdated model with no voice. But the screen advised immobilization and rest for at least two weeks. AckTik released her death grip on the nerve pinch and applied the splint from Ge's kit. We retrieved the bloody paddles, rinsed them in the river, and got back in the boat. The Acorans navigated the boat and evaluated the new paddles. while KiKi manned the sculling oar as a rudder. Ge and I settled down in the tent.

"You. Are. Amazing," I said to Ge. "The weird thing is the only thing I thought about during the attack was you. I wasn't scared for myself so much as I was scared for you."

Ge grinned. "That's a clue."

I blushed and nodded.

"My feelings for you haven't changed, Li. If anything, I'm worse off now than ever. If you've changed your mind, let me know. If you still think not, I'll never harass you again. So, tell me, are you willing to get legal, add a hyphen to your last name, hang out with me 'till we're old and gray?"

I nodded. "Yes, Ge Oates. Becoming a tenure groupie for the Prometheus of xenoecology looks pretty good. I will get legal, hyphenate my last name, and hang out with you until we're old and gray."

* * *

"BanTik, would you please marry us?" I asked.

"I'm glad you finally decided, Li, but your families are not here." BanTik said.

"BanTik, I consider you - all of you - to be my family. AckTik, will please do me the honor of giving me away in marriage?" I asked.

"I would be honored," she replied.

"KiKi, will you adopt me into the Splendor Grove?" Ge asked.

KiKi enthusiastically agreed.

204

I turned to Kah. "Would you please be the official witness to our union?"

He grinned. "Happy to."

So, BanTik agreed to marry us. Since we can't properly hold foothands because of our deformed legs and feet, we faced each other and interlaced our legs as best we could. BanTik declared it good enough.

We made our promises. AckTik promised to accept Ge as my husband and recognize him as her own brother and kin. KiKi promised to adopt Ge into the family and give him away to the Bay Tree Grove. We were all weeping. Then I think we had one of the strangest honeymoon nights on record. No romance, no fancy vacation. Just navigating a boat downriver with the little assist motor, and only occasionally sculling. We talked and built dream castles of our future together.

KiKi cried herself to sleep that night, overwhelmed with longing for TikTik. We had only made 160 more kilometers, so only eight days to make it 1280 more kilometers.

30

THE FINAL PUSH

We started to see outlying isolated farms. Whenever Ge spotted an obstacle coming up, all the Acorans piled into the tent. At one farm, a couple of kids were fishing off the end of the dock and waved at us. We waved back and kept going. Between farms, we all got out and paddled so that Ge could rest. KiKi manned the sculling oar, using it as a rudder to keep us in the center of the river.

At one farm, they had ripe pears and apples. We beached, stole a keeping sack of each, and continued on our way. When we saw the farmhouse dock, we pulled up and hopped out. We started towards the farmhouse and were greeted by the farmer.

"Hi. We stole apples and pears from your trees." I held up the keeping sacks. "What do we owe you?"

I handed over one of the sacks to him, he judged the weight and named a ridiculously low price. I whipped out my phone and tapped it to his phone to make the payment. He quirked a smile and wished us luck with our honeymoon trip.

Ge asked, "That obvious, huh?"

The farmer winked and said, "Uh-huh."

We wished him farewell and took off again, with Ge sculling one-handed. As soon as we were out of sight of the farm, everybody got out and paddled.

"Well, with that transaction, we have just announced our presence and location to the CSO of Megacore. I'm counting on the proximity of witnesses to protect us from drone attacks. But be on the lookout, okay everybody?"

We alternated paddling and sculling, doing both at once didn't seem to work particularly well. Even though we were interrupted by small settlements and increasingly common farms. By nightfall, we still made over 200 kilometers that day. Paddling was working beautifully. After sunset, we weren't nearly so paranoid about being spotted and paddled well into the night.

Ge crashed while we paddled then I woke him up to take on one-handed sculling duties. We beached and all did our business. We decided to anchor there for the rest of the night. We still had seven days and less than 1,000 kilometers to go. The Acorans settled down in the tent. I checked my phone before settling down on the deck beside Ge.

* * *

#Forensic Investigation File:

AI: EMERGENCY ALERT – IMMEDIATE C-LEVEL AUTHORIZATION REQUIRED – EMERGENCY ALERT.

CSO: Now what?

AI: The collateral traveler of the eco-surveyor has resurfaced on the net. The login for a minor financial transaction was a clear and accurate match. The transaction originated less than 960 kilometers from Novy Samara. Potential result – CATASTROPHIC.

CSO: You useless piece of shit! Every damned thing you've done has only prolonged this ordeal. Deploy Roger.

AI: Roger is off-planet and will not be able to return for at least ten days planet time.

CSO: Of course, he is. Damnit! Everything I've worked for over twenty years, gone. Give me alternate suggestions.

AI: RECOMMENDATION: Immediate, discreet, permanent withdrawal. Activate a standby avatar so that travel arrangements can be made. Do you wish to authorize the activation of the Avatar B Identity? Do you wish to authorize the matching travel plan?

CSO: No. Not that. I meant suggestions for preventing her or them from arriving.

AI: I do not see any action that results in more than a 5% probability of success. My only suggestion is to activate the Avatar B identity and create the matching travel plan.

CSO: AUTHORIZE BOTH. Code: 564ft.8*DV. 35575umh. 407858.

AI: AUTHORIZATION VERIFIED. Avatar B being activated. Travel itinerary will be available within the minute.

* * *

The next day, we pulled up in Novy Bor, a town with some 30,000 inhabitants. I searched and found a marine supply house. We navigated to the Novy Bor Marine Supply dock and bought a used outboard motor. There were simply too many people on the river now. Even paddling at night would be risky as river traffic picked up. They installed it for us, and we were on our way in less than two hours.

"I'm going to go ahead and book us into the *Novy Ararat Imperskiy*. No need to worry about announcing our rate of travel along with our location at this point," I announced to Ge.

I arranged for one of their mid-sized suites. Misha assured me of the highest security protocols and directed me to the correct dock. With the motor purring away, we were flying down the river effortlessly. The sculling oar was only a rudder. When I checked after sundown, we had made over 260 kilometers. I also got decent location data, and realized we were only 720 kilometers from the hotel docks. We still had six days left. Even dodging heavy traffic and with some inevitable delays, we were only two or three days out.

That night we stopped at a rest station. I took KiKi and AckTik to the lady's room and explained how everything worked. Ge provided the same service for the guys. We pulled up and beached very early in the morning while it was still night. Everybody was pretty sick of being trapped in the tent, and the only time they could step out for some fresh air was in the dark. Even at night though, we had to keep a sharp lookout to avoid other river traffic.

We traveled that way for two more days. We still made excellent time even though we stopped frequently to hide every day.

We inevitably slowed as we came closer to the capital. The riverbanks were lined with businesses and river front residences, including high-tower apartments. The current was slower and the traffic heavier. We were still making good time, though. We passed the Novy Samara Air Terminal, and the sight of a large passenger grav sled lifting off amazed the Acorans. I was brought to tears, thinking how much TikTik would have loved to see it. They talked about it for hours. We put in once at a landscaped area and used the bushes. I felt pangs of guilt, and I hoped local dogs would be blamed.

Early the next morning, we found a little-used park, and we all used the facilities. I believe we escaped without being detected. Late that afternoon, we passed the Long Bridge, the most unimaginative name possible. It was the longest bridge in any of the settlements on Acora at that time, stretching well over a kilometer from bank to bank. This was another wonder to the Acorans. I texted Misha at the hotel to expect us within the hour.

Misha was waiting at the dock for me. Ge handed me out of our shabby little boat, which looked wretched compared to the sleek modern pleasure craft moored at the other docks. Misha greeted me with a huge smile.

"Misha, please meet my husband, Ge Oates," I said with pride.

"Pleasure, sir. You have crushed the dreams of thousands of men." Misha activated celebrity cloaking. "Welcome back from the dead, Mrs. Oates. We offer the very latest in cloaking technology. We are now in a reflective bubble that cannot be penetrated by the paparazzi or drone observation."

"Thanks, Misha." I turned to the tent. "You can come out now, guys."

Misha's jaw dropped open at his first sight of the Acorans. He stumbled back a couple of steps but quickly regained his professional composure.

"May I introduce the diplomatic mission from the indigenous peoples of New Philadelphia? Misha, this is BanTik, Regional Governor headquartered in Ifka'a Kifma'a, a major trade city and provincial capital with a population in excess of 820,000 individuals. He is the emissary assigned to contact humans."

BanTik smiled and stepped forward, offering to shake hands. "Delighted to meet you, Misha. I look forward to your facilities after our grueling journey."

Poor Misha shook hands, bemused and somewhat dazed.

"The rest of the introductions can wait. We have battled our way through 4,800 kilometers of raw wilderness. We need to rest and clean up. We'll place room service orders once we're settled in. Can you dig up a good gastroenterologist? We all came down with nasty intestinal parasites out in the wilderness and need to get checked."

"No problem, Miss." Then, he corrected himself. "Sorry. Mrs. Oates."

I grinned. "Oh, you flatter me. Honestly, all I care about is a decent shower!"

Taking the hint, Misha ushered us into a small, discreet doorway reserved for this use. We rode a private elevator, another wonder for the Acorans, and arrived at our suite in short order.

I ordered a fruit and veggie platter, several fish dishes and bread, which the Acorans had never eaten. Ge and I ordered steak dinners. I reassured Misha that I wouldn't shock his staff and Ge and I would accept all deliveries. I also asked him to pause housekeeping for two days, until our announcement went live.

We divvied up the rooms, and our packs arrived. I hopped in the shower. Ge signed for the food in the meantime and took a shower right after me. Swathed in a guest bathrobe, I set the table and called for a hairdresser.

There were three bathrooms in the suite. We were all groomed, although still somewhat damp, within minutes. The Acorans were fascinated by the clothes washer. We enjoyed a celebratory feast. I introduced them to croissants. They were declared delicious.

The Acorans hid while I had my hair done and put on a little makeup. I braced myself and called my parents on the suite's screen. Dad promptly burst into tears. I gave him our suite number and told him to ask for Misha at the desk. Then, Mom hopped on the line.

She gasped, "My God! You look terrible!"

"Hi, Mom. It's good to see you, too."

"I'm delighted to learn that you're still among the living, of course. But, my God, you're so brown!"

"I battled my way through 4,800 kilometers of raw wilderness. I conquered the Jutoma, the jungle, the New Himalayans, and evaded an attacking dire wolf. But the only thing you're worried about is my tan!? Jesus, Mom. Get a grip. Your living Barbie doll died in the wilderness."

Dad's voice floated through the connection. "Honey, we'll talk about it in the car on the way there. C'mon, let's get moving."

"We'll be there soon, sweetie." Mom signed off.

The gastro showed up, and after a brief flurry of shock, I introduced him to AckTik. Dr. Benson rose to the occasion quite well, I thought.

"I am so sorry," AckTik said. "While my Standard is pretty good, my medical vocabulary is poor, and I am completely unfamiliar with your medicine."

The gastro got out a medical 'bot and placed it over BanTik's stomach. AckTik was fascinated by the screen that showed BanTik's intestines. Dr. Benson fiddled with the controls and the remaining parasites stood out sharply in shocking orange. He fiddled with a few more controls. The 'bot began methodically killing each worm by targeting their heads, buried in BanTik's intestinal lining.

He explained to AckTik, "We use invisible beams of energy. One beam is very mild and passes right through tissue with no harm. Another beam a tiny bit separated is also harmless. When you have a ring of five beams, wherever they converge, the energy is deadly.

But only at the microscopic point of convergence, leaving all healthy tissues unharmed. The machine can focus on the parasite, specifically their sucker mouths. It never gets bored, or tired, and will eliminate any worms with no further intervention."

Dr. Benson turned to BanTik. "You will have very strange bowel movements for the next few days as your body expels the remnants of the worms. You may experience nausea, tenderness, or bloating until your body is clear of the parasites and their toxic residues."

"I brought another machine, who's next?" he asked, holding up the second 'bot. Ge and I got checked and the machine cleared the remaining parasites and parasite eggs in less than ten minutes. Then, it was AckTik's turn, then Kah.

I intervened for KiKi. "We need to use every precaution for KiKi. She didn't come down sick like the rest of us. She didn't eat the vine cabbage. But she's pregnant and rapidly approaching the first birth of her child."

Dr. Benson cocked an eyebrow. "First birth? As in primigravida?"

AckTik grinned. "No. As in, we are a marsupial species, and the baby is getting ready to migrate to mama's pouch. And also, preemeebraffuhda."

That seemed to knock Dr. Benson for a loop. I piped up, "Primigravida, AckTik. The salient point here, Dr. Benson, is that KiKi carries a baby in utero right now."

"Okay. I'll make the proper adjustments." He fiddled with the machine. AckTik stared at the screen fascinated.

AckTik exclaimed, "Oh, look! A boy, just like TikTik!"

We all had tears in our eyes. I explained to Dr. Benson. "TikTik was KiKi's husband, this is their child. We lost TikTik." I gulped. "TikTik fell to his death when we were crossing the mountains."

"I am so sorry for your loss," he replied and had the decency to sound sincere.

KiKi had picked up some parasites that were quickly dispatched. There were some worms still lurking behind the baby. After considerable fiddling around, with KiKi lying on her side, he got the 'bot to focus on the parasites and avoid the baby. KiKi took thirty minutes. BanTik's bot was still chugging away. Dr. Benson checked, and applied the second 'bot lower on BanTik's abdomen and both of them were zapping parasites. BanTik dozed off.

AckTik and Dr. Benson got into the weeds explaining how we picked up the parasites. KiKi had never eaten the contaminated vine cabbage but had been in close contact with BanTik and nursed him, so she must have picked it up from him.

"Yeah, they are nasty little buggers," I said. "They survived being washed *and* cooked!"

We discovered that the hardy cinnamon bark we had been dosing ourselves with is the origin of the Cinnalaquin he wanted to prescribe. So, we knew that the Cinnalaquin would be safe and effective for both species. He left a large bottle of tablets – extra for BanTik – to be consumed over the next three days to prevent any missed parasite eggs from hatching.

"That's the worst parasitic infection I've ever seen. BanTik will be tired and will likely sleep all day tomorrow. He should be okay after that," Dr. Benson said as he finally packed up his gear.

I had him thumbprint the non-disclosure agreement Misha had provided for us to use. I let him know it expired in two days, after our public announcement at the upcoming planetary charter vote. Then, he went fanboy on us. He tossed the professional façade aside and insisted on photographing us all with him. Selfies done, we thanked him and sent him on his way.

31

RESOLUTION

"Brace for impact, honey," I said to Ge.

"Huh?"

"Uh, I know meeting the parents is already fraught with peril, and I don't want to make this worse for you. But…"

He shrugged, "But?"

"Dad's gonna love you but Mom's gonna hate you, so brace for impact."

"Ah. Thanks for the warning." He grinned. "After the dire wolf, I think I can handle it." He turned the hotel's screen to me. "You've got to fill out your part of the form."

"What am I filling out?" I asked.

"Marriage license application," he answered.

"Lemme at it!" I filled out the form. Typical bureaucratic delay, it took 48 hours to actually issue. We would get a confirmation via mail to my phone address.

I contacted Huong Owusu. She gasped when she saw me.

"Hi, Huong," I started. "How would you like to have the interstellar exclusive on the biggest story to ever break? I mean, like even bigger than me coming back from the dead."

Her eyes narrowed. I could about see the cogs turning. "What do you have in mind?"

"I do not wish to discuss the details over an open unsecured comm line. I'm staying at the *Novy Ararat Imperskiy.*"

She glanced at the corner of her screen. "I can be there in less than an hour."

"Brilliant! Thanks, Huong. Ask for Misha at the front desk; I'll alert him that you're invited."

"Misha? Okay," she acknowledged, smiling. "See you soon."

I alerted Misha. My folks arrived less than five minutes later.

Mom hugged me briefly. Dad grabbed me next. He was in tears and cuddled me close, stroking my hair.

213

"God, I'm so glad. So glad." He finally stepped away and held my shoulders at arms' length and shook me. "Don't ever scare me like that again! Why the hell didn't you call?

"Couldn't call without alerting the bastard that sabotaged the grav sled."

"Let me get a look at you." I smiled, suddenly feeling shy. I did a full twirl for him. "You look great, baby."

"For future reference, mother, that is how to greet a prodigal daughter."

She sniffed with disapproval. "Why is it so hot in here?"

"Ah, some introductions are in order."

I went to the bedroom wing and called out, `"Time to introduce you to my parents."`

Everyone trooped out, still clad in practical coveralls, now clean. They were saving the formal robes for the Council appearance. Ge brought up the rear.

After the usual flurry of shock, I began. "Mom, Dad, I would like to introduce Ge Oates, my husband." Mom gasped. I continued without pause, "And the Acoran diplomatic emissaries to New Philadelphia, BanTik, KiKi, AckTik, and Ka'alka'eipeke." They each did a little bow. "BanTik officiated at our wedding."

Mom sighed with relief. "Oh. Well, that's easy to fix. Some primitive tribal ceremony with these creatures isn't even legal."

"Mother!" my voice cracked like a whip. "That is the most racist, ignorant, self-serving thing you have ever said. I am ashamed of you. The Acorans are not 'creatures'! They are the most intelligent, sophisticated, educated and courageous group of people it has ever been my privilege to know. Their sciences are more advanced than our own! Apologize."

Mom was offended and obviously felt betrayed and said, "You don't mean it."

I said, "I have never meant anything so passionately in my life. If you ever want to see your grandchildren, you will apologize."

Mom wasn't going to give up that easily. "For goodness' sake, Li. Why would you throw yourself away on a...on a nobody like him?"

"Ge is *not* a 'nobody!' He is the Prometheus of xenobiology and is about to land a Nobel prize. Besides, I'm of the age of consent, and your opinion is no longer relevant. I know you wanted me to hold out for a billionaire, but I held out for a hero. My adopted family," I gestured to the Acorans, "fought off a charging dire wolf to protect me. The wolf broke Ge's arm, and even with a compound fracture, he ran *towards* the beast and killed it for me. None of your precious playboys would have done that! Ge is not – and never was – a 'nobody.' Apologize!"

My mother's perfectly glossy lips formed an 'O' of astonishment.

Dad said, "Woah! Want to hear the full story on that!" Dad turned toward the Acorans, "A full-grown adult dire wolf?"

Kah shrugged modestly. "A large male."

Ge raised his wounded arm, "I even got the 'I forgot to duck bandage.'"

Dad said, "You have my undying gratitude, sir." He went over and shook everyone's hand enthusiastically.

Mom said, "Merle, you can't take this wild tale seriously. The 'marriage,'" she made air quotes, "is still not legal."

That was the instant my mother's voice in my head died. After being treated as an autonomous adult by everybody around me for over a year, I clearly saw my mother's attempts to control me for what they were: a desperate attempt by a profoundly insecure woman to prove herself to her stern and unloving father, now long gone. I felt relieved *and* angry at once. A split second later, I felt pity for her. But I would *never* fall for her lies again. It felt like I had unlocked a lot of extra space in my brain.

Dad sighed. "I hate to be the bearer of bad tidings, Chuchu, but you're making a complete ass of yourself, and embarrassing me."

Ge said, "Already applied for a marriage license, so we'll be registered as married under human as well as Acoran law."

Dad's face lit up, and he offered his hand to Ge. "Congratulations, son!"

"Thank you, sir." Ge grinned. "I'm the luckiest man in the 'verse."

Dad went in for a bro-hug. "Welcome to the family, Ge."

"For heaven's sake, Li," Mom protested. "What kind of a life can he offer you?"

"Ge and I have full ambassadorial credentials and authority to negotiate on the Acorans' behalf. We'll do fine," I answered

"What nonsense! Ambassador? *You?* You have no head for these things, Li," Mom snapped.

Everyone's quills snapped into "surprised" position. BanTik interrupted, his quills stiff, "With all due respect, Mrs. Carroll, I can assure you, Li has an *excellent* head for such things. I have the title of primary ambassador, but Li is *de facto* our Matriarch. Without her leadership, we would have foundered and failed."

215

BanTik dropped into the full squat respect posture. Everyone copied him.

BanTik said, "My Matriarch."

KiKi echoed him. "My Matriarch."

AckTik said, "My Matriarch."

Kah said, "Revered Grandmother."

Dad turned to Mom, shrugged in exasperation, put his arm around me and squeezed my shoulder affectionately. He said, "That's my girl all grown up."

He helped me out and handed me a tissue.

"I only did it for TikTik," I said between sniffles.

BanTik said, "We know," and added gently, "that's why you qualify as Matriarch. You may not be our Matriarch in body, but you most certainly are in mind, heart, and action. You are our Matriarch, Li."

No accolade or title I have ever been awarded meant as much to me as that brief salute in private in a hotel room. I exchanged enthusiastic hugs with them all. My mother stared at us, horrified.

"My daughter, Planetary Ambassador Li Carroll," Dad said, misty-eyed with pride.

"Uhm, that's Li Carroll-Oates, Dad," I corrected him.

Dad looked embarrassed. "Sorry, honey. It's a lot to take in."

Mom said, "We'll see about that."

Dad glared at her and said, "We'll talk about it in the car, Chu Hua."

She was startled and immediately subsided. Dad never called her by her full name unless he was absolutely furious with her, and she knew it.

"I noticed that you have not apologized to the Acorans, Mother," I said.

Dad glowered at Mom and said, "Don't force me to choose between you at your worst and Li and her found family at their best, Chu Hua."

That finally penetrated and Mom teared up. She took a deep breath, gulped and said stiffly, "I apologize if I have offended any of you in any way."

"Good choice, honey," Dad said to her.

I turned to Dad, "So, how's Mark?"

"Still laboring away in the lower ranks of a Big Twelve accounting firm. He's got another couple of years of grunt work gaining experience – and a couple more certificates to go – before he can set up his own practice," Dad answered.

216

Mom added pointedly, "Your brother is a licensed professional now, with a very bright future. He's decided to specialize in accounting for the non-profit sector."

"It's what you've always wanted for him," I said. "So, painting is just a hobby, now?"

Dad said, "Yeah. He does a lot of charcoal studies and pencil drawings now. He's not working in color very much anymore."

I said, "Understandable, given his current work environment. Also, Dad, I want to let you know, these guys," I gestured towards the Acorans, "create the most gorgeous tapestries and *objet* I have ever seen." I grinned. "You've already got an inside track. If you play your cards right, you might land contracts to supply not only your own galleries, but enough for export, too."

"Intriguing. I trust your judgment about the quality, but is there profit in it?"

"If you land a contract with SekBlik, the largest fabric house in Ifka'a Kifma'a, you'll make a fortune. I'll take you down there as soon as we have travel arranged."

The desk rang at that moment to let us know Huong was on her way up.

"I hate to do this to you, but we've got press on the way and a lot of interviews to get through. I'm doing a head-to-toe glow-up tomorrow," I said.

Mom interrupted me with, "Thank goodness!"

Irritated, I continued, "Can we get back together for dinner tomorrow night to share the whole story?"

"Sounds great, honey,' Dad said. "You want me to book us a table at Le Monde?"

"I would love to, but public appearances will have to wait until after the official announcement at the Planetary Charter Council meeting. I've been making everybody sign a non-disclosure statement. Are you okay with that? Unfortunately, it is a diplomatic necessity. We'll have to eat here in the suite."

"Of course, Li." He gave Mom The Look. "We're fine with that, right, Chu Hua?"

"Right. Of course," she said with a false smile planted on her lips, irritated because I had just deprived her of an evening at Le Monde on what she considered to be a silly pretext.

I hugged them both goodbye and we agreed to meet at six the following evening. I introduced them to Huong Owusu as she stepped off the lift.

Huong asked, "Why is it so hot?" before she caught sight of the Acorans.

Ge was prepared and caught her before she fainted. He set her gently in a chair. She took a couple of deep breaths.

I asked, "Who's the best videographer you know?"

Huong whipped out her phone, "Benny Graber. Just a sec."

He answered, "Hi, Huong, 'sup?"

"Ya gotta meet me at the Novy Ararat."

He snorted. "You can't afford me."

Huong replied, "Benny you fool!"

I snatched the phone from her and said, "Yeah, but *I* can afford you, Benny. And I'm not the story here. Get a look at the non-disclosure. Once you've signed it, I'll give you the exclusive."

The screen went to standby while the agreement displayed on his screen. Once the machine confirmed his thumbprint, his image came back on.

Benny came back on, obviously irritated. "What the hell? What could possibly require that kind of nondisclosure?'

"This." I panned the camera over the Acorans. Everybody waved.

BanTik said, "Hi, there, Mr. Graber. We all look forward to seeing your image capturing technology in action."

Benny's image disappeared from the screen. Apparently, he had fallen backwards because I saw him climbing back up from the floor.

He asked, "You said exclusive?"

"Yep," I confirmed.

"Novy Ararat?" I nodded. "I can be there in … half an hour," Benny said.

"Ask for Misha at the desk; he'll bring you up."

Then I alerted Misha and supplied Elspeth's entire 12,000-word report to Huong. I contacted Elspeth and arranged for her to be interviewed by Huong. Elspeth agreed, providing that she didn't have to give up her sources. Huong agreed and they hashed out a price. They set a meeting for the next day.

Benny showed up a little early. I'm amazed he didn't get a speeding ticket, but I could immediately see why Huong wanted him. Within ten minutes he had selected a location in the suite, arranged lights, set up chairs and plucked some set dressing from elsewhere in the suite. It was a very professional interview set. Benny tossed a handful of floating cams up, put on his main camera and was ready to go at lightning speed.

Benny dictated everyone's name and diplomatic credentials into his phone and got everybody to palm print the image release forms it created. He did the classic, "Five...four..." then switched to silent and held up fingers for 'three...two...one.'

Huong swung into action and Ge and I gave an extensive interview. We took a break, and it was BanTik's turn. BanTik changed into his ceremonial robes and was funny and wise and charming and won Huong's heart. Then they did brief 'pick-up' interviews with everyone else along with video and still photos of us individually and grouped in various ways.

Naturally, the one that went viral was the shot of KiKi giggling while sitting in Ge's hands. Even pregnant, she was only twenty five kilos, and Ge easily held her waist high. Huong arranged press passes along with celebrity non-disclosure security chips for the Acorans. Misha provided blacked-out limo service for us including Benny and Huong to get to the Planetary Charter Council meeting.

We wrapped up around midnight, all of us exhausted.

The next morning over breakfast, I announced, "You're promoted to General of the Barbie Liberation Army."

One of his eyebrows lifted. "Barbie?"

"That's what I was raised to be," I said. "Smile pretty, defer to men, never sweat, never ask for anything, and always – always – make sure Mother can brag about you. I spent years terrified of her opinion."

He made a low sound — half sympathy, half confirmation. "Now that I've met her, that seems completely appropriate."

I huffed a laugh. "I tailored myself to avoid detonating her disapproval."

"And now?" Ge asked.

"Now..." I looked at my reflection in the dining room mirror; older, bruised by life, but not small. "Now I think I have actually escaped Barbie-doll hell."

"And how does that feel?" he said.

"Unsettling," I admitted. "Like walking on legs I'm not sure are mine yet."

He waited.

"But," I added, "I think I can get used to this."

Ge smiled — not wide, but genuine, the kind that lands in the eyes. "Good. I would hate to liberate you only to have you defect."

"Relax, General," I said. "I'm not going back."

I got my glow on later that day. We gave the full story to Mom and Dad over an extended banquet. BanTik was visibly putting weight back on.

32

THE GIFT

The hotel corridor smelled like citrus cleaner and expensive wool carpet. I had just finished running BanTik's speechwriter's transitions in the mirror for the twentieth time when the chime sounded and the door panel glowed: DELIVERY.

"We didn't order anything," I said, half to myself.

Ge held up a finger. "I don't like the timing. The council hearing is tomorrow. A surprise *anything* tonight is an insult to probability."

I opened just the narrow safety gap. A courier stood there in a matte gray cap and a smile too eager for late evening. He lifted a wicker basket wrapped in translucent film and an oversized bow. Chocolates, fruits, a bottle neck glinting. A folded card gleamed white on top.

"For Ms. Carroll," he said. Accent neutral. Face forgettable. That was the problem.

"Who from?" I asked.

"A friend," he said.

Ge had been standing behind the door, out of sight. I felt the air change before I saw his face. He moved once—no wasted motion—and the door slid fully open. The courier's eyes flicked past me to Ge's chest and shoulders. In that fraction, something feral went cold in my gut.

"Set it down," Ge said. Calm. No smile. His gaze went to places normal people don't even know to look: the seams at the courier's wrist, the sole pattern on his boots, the way his right elbow held tight to his side like he didn't want it bumped.

"Company policy says hand-off only," the courier said lightly. "Congrats on the presentation—"

He took a half step forward. Ge stepped in front of me.

"Set it," Ge repeated.

The courier did a cheerful little shrug, dipped as if to comply, and then pivoted fast, rolling the basket toward the threshold.

Ge launched off the hallway runner—an impossible, clean leap—and hit the man shoulder-first.. The basket skidded, bumped the door jamb, and came to rest with the bottle clinking delicately against the cellophane. Ge and the courier slammed against the opposite wall, a hard, hollow sound that made my teeth ache.

"Li," Ge barked without looking, "call disposal."

My fingers were already moving. EMERGENCY. EOD SUSPECTED. UNSOLICITED PACKAGE. I slapped the universal hazard flag and the hotel's AI bleated the corridor siren—short, disciplined pulses. Doors up and down the hall slid shut and sealed.

Kah appeared at the door as if conjured, hair damp from the shower. He took in the tableau in a blink, then sprinted toward me. "On it."

The courier twisted like a fish, surprisingly strong. Ge had wrist and shoulder; the courier drove a palm for Ge's throat. Ge tucked his chin, took it on collarbone, and rolled the man into the carpet, pinning the elbow that had been kept so carefully close.

A knife winked between the courier's fingers—no, a micro-tool, printer-fabricated, the kind that cuts fiber as if it's seaweed. He slashed at Ge and missed. Kah arrived at speed and swept the man's forearm with a neat hook of his foot. The tool skittered. Kah kicked it farther. The courier hissed like a boiler.

"Who sent you?" Kah asked, not expecting an answer.

The man didn't give one. He jerked his head forward and cracked Ge on the brow. Ge's eyes watered but his grip didn't change. Blood slicked down his temple—a bright, clean ribbon.

"Get into the suite," Ge said to me, voice even.

Right. I closed the suite door behind me and set it for full view. I crouched down to examine the basket. The wrap was tight, factory work. The ribbon had no manufacturer markers, which told me more than a logo would have. The card lay atop a bed of figs and too-perfect strawberries. I crouched close enough to see past the cellophane glare.

There: under the bottle's nest, the faint squared edge that didn't belong in a foodie arrangement. The fruit arrays framed it like cushion. A small pressure plate? Or timed? No smell, no heat bloom, no obvious transmitter.

I swallowed into a dry throat. "I can see the bomb on the bottom, Ge."

"Uh-huh," he said.

The corridor lights strobed to amber. Two hotel security drones arrived first—quiet, beetle-black, each with a compact blinder mounted underneath. They bracketed the basket and projected a faint blue lattice over it, mapping density. The lattice fuzzed in the middle— non-organic, rectangular.

"Device confirmed," the hotel announced. "EOD team en route. All guests, remain sealed."

The courier heard that and made his move. He went deadweight, then whipcord, an eel's inversion. He wrenched his pinned arm at an angle that made me gag. Something popped, but he smiled through it. He slammed the back of his skull into the wall and smeared the panel sensor. The corridor lighting hiccupped. For a fractional second the drones hesitated, recalibrating.

He used that moment like a professional. He drove both knees up, hit Ge's ribs, and corkscrewed under his arm. Ge caught fabric; it tore. Kah lunged for him and missed by a centimeter. The courier shot down the corridor, one shoulder low, gait favoring the arm he'd half ruined himself. Not a courier. Not a minion.

"Grbić," I breathed.

He didn't look back, but I knew. You get to know an enemy by the silhouette of his choices.

"Kah, with me," Ge said. He didn't wait for agreement. He went off after him at that impossible, loping speed of a man built for heavier gravity. Kah poured it on and somehow matched his pace.

I stayed. I wanted to run; I wanted to help; I wanted to hurl the basket down the chute myself. But there was a weapon sitting in a nest of figs with my name on it, and if I moved wrong, we'd all be vapor and apologies.

The EOD team came like a storm in soft shoes—two human techs and a heavy crawler that folded itself out of a suitcase. The crawler's arm deployed like a praying mantis and began to pick at the bow. The techs murmured to one another in the sacred argot of people who think at wire speed. "Plate beneath the bottle cradle, Likely. See if he buried the trigger under the...yes. Copy."

One of them glanced at me. "Ms. Carroll, yes? Please step back."

"I'm good here," I said. "Tell me if you need my retinal on the door."

He blinked once at the tone and then accepted it. The crawler snipped the bow's anchor. The wrap loosened. The lattice sharpened. There it was: a composite brick thin as a music score, nested where the basket's floor should be. No timer visible. Relief fluttered up my spine and died when one tech said, very softly, "Smart trigger. Lid displacement plus mass threshold. If you lifted the bottle first..."

"Boom?" I asked.

"Boom," he said.

They neutralized it with a puff of gray foam and a hiss that smelled like almonds and a dentist's office. The brick's indicators – tiny, mean little green eyes – went flat to black. The tech exhaled hard through his nose, some bad day of his life slightly redeemed. "Safe."

"Thank you," I said. "Really."

He nodded once, professional, and then his gaze flicked to the corridor where Ge and Kah had gone. "Your man?"

"Yup. All mine," I said, too fast and with too much pride.

He didn't smile, but the corner of his mouth twitched.

The drones chirped that hotel security had eyes on the stairwell. I jogged, the adrenaline finally finding my legs.

We found Kah first, breath controlled, standing over a scuffed line of floor that showed where a body had slid. After a flurry of shock, I introduced Kah to the EOD techs. Beyond, a service door hung crooked on its hinge.

"He planned his exit route in advance. He had someone waiting to get him out." Kah said. He didn't waste words on the obvious: Grbić had planned to die with us or to vanish. Either outcome was a win in his head.

"Any blood?" I asked.

Kah gestured with his chin. There was a lot of nothing, and a thread of something bright on the hinge. Not much. He'd live.

Ge came up a moment later, chest heaving once and then settling. His brow was a red comma drying to brown. He wasn't angry. He was worse: focused.

"He'll have burned three identities by dawn," Ge said. "We won't catch him on foot."

"We won't have to," I said, almost calm now, a clarity that only comes after you realize you almost died. "We'll catch him by *name*."

"Elspeth," Ge said, understanding before I finished.

"Elspeth," I said. "I'll have her pull every archive, every early expedition log, every mirrored cache he forgot he made, every disavowed AI diary he thought was truly deleted. Make it sing. We'll turn everything over to the Interstellar Bureau of Investigations."

I made the EOD team sign a non-disclosure.

We didn't sleep much.

* * *

We arrived at the Council building the next morning all splendidly decked out in Acoran silk. We made it past all of the security checkpoints. Once we were inside, some poor intern struggled to direct us to the reserved press seats.

Ge laughed at her and said, "The press are here for *me*, doll, not the other way around."

I chimed in, "I'm Descendant of the Star Dancer and Sister of the First House, here to demand Right of First Speech."

Her mouth fell open with shock, but we marched right past her onto the speakers' dais and killed the celebrity cloak. Pandemonium ensued. As the bailiffs struggled to get everybody quieted down, I shouted into the mic, "I am Li Carroll-Oates, Descendant of the Star Dancer and Sister of the First House. I demand the Right of First Speech."

The Speaker of the House banged her gavel down and shouted out, "Granted!"

I launched into my little we-have-been-appointed-as-emissaries from the Central Republic and the Confederation of Northern Tribes speech. I concluded with, "I move that the vote for Planetary Charter Status be postponed until such time as diplomatic relations with the free indigenous peoples of this planet have been established, or one year from this date, whichever shall first occur."

I don't know who rose to the occasion, but a shout of, "Seconded!" came from the ranks of the minority party.

The Speaker said, "Motion entered and seconded."

"Madam Speaker," I continued, "I further move to call the question by immediate verbal vote."

The representative who seconded my first motion, promptly seconded that motion, too.

The Speaker said, "Motion to call the question by immediate verbal vote entered and seconded. All in favor of postponing the vote on Planetary Charter Status Initiative for a maximum of one calendar year while diplomatic relations with the free indigenous peoples of this planet are established, say 'aye.'"

There arose a massive chorus of 'aye' votes.

The Speaker asked, "Any abstaining representatives?"

She was greeted with silence.

"All those opposed to the motion say 'no.'"

Breathless silence descended on the room once again.

She slammed down her gavel, "Let the record show that the Motion to Postpone the Planetary Charter Initiative is hereby unanimously adopted."

Before anybody could say anything more, I spoke into the mic again, "May I please introduce Ambassador BanTik, primary emissary for this treaty?"

BanTik stepped up to the platform, which immediately telescoped down to accommodate his height. "Far be it from me to interfere with the workings of this august body, but could we all agree to change it from No Pheewoo..." he shook is quills comically and sighed, "New Fie weed alf..." he smoothed his quills theatrically, sighed again, and plaintively asked, "Could we all agree to call this good green planet Acora?"

His comedic timing was impeccable. He got a big laugh, and the leader of the majority party promptly moved to rename the planet and was seconded. The vote was overwhelmingly in favor.

I was the one to suggest that joke to him, you know. He could easily pronounce New Philadelphia. But we wanted to establish a positive mood, you know?

Well, you've all seen that history footage. You know – me in my white Acoran silk outfit. BanTik's brilliant oratory. Ignore the "recreations." I ten out of ten recommend Bennie's *The Universe Changed.* It gets you through the whole thing in about an hour seamlessly and without leaving out anything important.

33

HOME

We went back to Ifka'a Kifma'a only a week after that first vote to postpone. We went by grav sled, which was a real treat. KiKi's first birth happened in the comfort of the Splendor Tree Grove. I had to tell Matriarch that we lost TikTik. RinTik, Matriarch and I cried together while I cradled Matriarch in my lap. BanTik and Ge together planted TikTik's bay tree on the Philosophers' Tree.

Kah and AckTik were married once we got back. Matriarch blessed the wedding. Kah's family attended, and it was a double ceremony. They followed Northern Tribe traditions, then got married all over again, following Grove tradition. It was one of the most politically powerful actions that Matriarch ever took. The new river toll scheme was voted in and, although it will take generations for the wounds to heal, the border wars died out within a year. Matriarch ushered in a new era of peace.

The Matriarch had chosen a bench of woven limbs that looked grown for the purpose. The grove opened like a cathedral—trunks twisting up into a high green vault, light falling in long strokes. The air smelled like rain and sap and the clean sour of new fruit.

We told her the full story not just the bare fact of her loss. TikTik had loved this grove. He had told me once, shy, that the old trees made him believe in continuity. I wanted that belief inside my own lungs.

The Matriarch listened while I told the story all the way through, like it wanted to be told; in order, without exaggeration, with the weight of things left in. Her quills made a halo of attention. When I finished, she closed her eyes briefly and let the quiet stretch until the trees themselves seemed to breathe.

I looked at the green light in the air, at the trunks older than our arguments, at the place where TikTik had once stood with his hands clasped as if he were praying in a human chapel, and I understood that endings and beginnings wear the same mask when they first arrive.

"I have something to tell you," I said. The words rose without rehearsal, as right and inevitable as tide. "Matriarch, I'm with child."

The grove listened. Even the bugs seemed to pause their small, necessary work.

Her quills lifted—joy, pure and uncomplicated. "Then life answers your vow," she said.

Ge's breath hitched in the quiet. He turned to me with that unarmored look I've learned to accept; like I was the point of the whole expedition, not the liability. I let him look. I let myself be the thing he saw.

But for a few minutes more, I kept the world on mute and let the bay trees make their slow, cool shade around us, and I imagined a future that did not require anyone to be brave all the time.

I put Ge's palm on my belly, just there, as if blessing were a thing you could transmit by touch. He didn't say anything clever. He didn't need to.

We had almost been a basket of figs and a headline.

We were not.

* * *

The Interstellar Bureau of Investigations had Elspeth's packet within six hours: aliases, transfers, voiceprints in audio bed-noise, the private key he reused in 1.7% of his false identities because predators believe in their own luck. The rogue AI – a lean, hungry thing that had been shadowing Grbić's moves like a vulture for years – was located in a dropbox under an import firm two sectors over. IBI cracked the shell and took it cold. Megacore's board made brave faces until the warrant landed, and then they made legal ones. It didn't help. The Bureau suspended their planetary license pending review. The review took eight hours. The license died.

When we walked back through the grove, my comm was already filling with messages from attorneys who had sniffed Megacore's blood in the water. We would spearhead the class action. We would argue for damages not only in money but in access and care—set up a fund for worlds treated like ideas instead of places. We would do it in TikTik's name, because the vow meant something or it was noise.

As for Grbić—he was arrested three days later at a freight hub, trying to bribe his way onto a courier barge with a face borrowed from a man who'd been dead for nine months. He didn't resist arrest; men like him don't, once the odds reverse. The Bureau didn't call me. They didn't have to.

Megacore never opened another world. And somewhere, in a cell on Sister Moon, a man who believed in his own luck had finally run out of it. Grbić is serving a life sentence and gets to contemplate

227

the planet that was his downfall every waking moment. A fitting sentence, I think.

We lost Matriarch less than a year later. The whole nation mourned. I think losing TikTik killed her. I remember cradling her in my arms towards the end. She was so tiny! She weighed only twenty kilos. Matriarch will always be more my mother than my biological mother ever was. Her portrait was the first on the Bay Tree Grove's altar that was a photograph and not a painting. She would have liked that. She was honored with her own exhibit in TikTik's Philosophers' Tree.

They buried her next to her husband's tree at the Bay Tree Glade for the dead. We each dutifully threw a ceremonial seed into the grave. First Daughter and new Matriarch, RinTik's bay tree sprouted, as expected. By some miracle, so did Kah's silver-leaf tree, as well as my climbing rose. The trees intertwined and the rose encircled them. Each plant came from a different biome that couldn't possibly sprout in the tropical soil under the canopy, much less thrive, yet they all three grew and blossomed. I'm convinced that Ge fixed it on Matriarch's orders.

After that, it took eight years of wrangling, but we finally got a complete treaty between Humans and Acorans.

Now if you will excuse me, my grandkids are throwing me a birthday party.

I'm 100 years old tomorrow.

Oh. For the cameras?

I am Li Carroll-Oats. Honorary Matriarch of the Bay Tree Grove, Descendant of the Star Dancer, and Sister of the First House. Mother of five, grandmother of sixteen, great-grandmother of twelve. I am the first ever Licensed Xenoethnologist and with Ge, co-founder of the Xenological Studies Institute, the first inter-species university. I am Human Planetary Ambassador Emeritus for Acora. Ge and I shifted a paradigm, established a new social science, and transformed biology. We brought down Grbić, and Megacore along with him, and saved a civilization.

So, you see, we kept our promise. TikTik did not die in vain.

AFTERWORD

I certainly hope that you enjoyed "Native," and earnestly thank you for taking the time to read it.

I spent ten years reading about writing, taking writing courses, writing, editing, and re-editing. I joined writers' groups and trashed draft after draft. I think I wrote over a million words to finally winnow it down to the 70,000 or so in this book. I finally have a story that I like. It's not perfect. But I have learned that perfection is the enemy of completion. It is as good as I and my team of beta readers, editors, and proofreaders, are currently capable of producing.

This is my first time publishing a science fiction story and I crave reviews. As a novice author, you can be assured that I will read and consider every review. Your reviews give me the feedback I need to make my next story better and gives Amazon a hint to offer the book to more readers.

To put in your two cents, please visit: http://bit.ly/3HlVKts, and leave a review on Goodreads; or you can leave an Amazon review: http://www.amazon.com/review/create-review?&isbn=979-8-9905533-0-9.

ABOUT L.G. CONAWAY

Linda Conaway lives in Prescott, Arizona, high in the mountains to escape the heat. Once retired, she succumbed to the madness that compels otherwise normal people to write novels. A self-proclaimed nerd, bibliophile, and book cover snob, Lincoln is happy to embark on hours of research to make sure the titbits of science in her stories are accurate. Her garden is her happy place and often the site of inspiration.

Lincoln is busily writing another novel. To receive advance notice of her new releases, pre-release chapters, to become a beta-reader, or to obtain an Advance Copy of her next book, please provide your e-mail address at: **www.arborvalebooks.com**.

www.ingramcontent.com/pod-product-compliance
Lightning Source LLC
Chambersburg PA
CBHW051947220626
47052CB00004B/838